★ ★ ★ ★ ★ ★ ★ ★

THIS
SPECIAL
SIGNED EDITION
IS LIMITED TO
1000 NUMBERED COPIES.

THIS IS COPY ___531___ .

★ ★ ★ ★ ★ ★ ★

STEPHEN GALLAGHER

The
Authentic
William James

The
Authentic
William James

A Sebastian Becker Novel

...

Stephen Gallagher

SUBTERRANEAN PRESS 2016

Subterranean Press
PO Box 190106
Burton, MI 48519

subterraneanpress.com

Chancery lunatics were people of wealth or property whose fortunes were at risk from their madness. Those deemed unfit to manage their affairs had them taken over by lawyers of the Crown, known as the Masters of Lunacy. It was Sebastian's employer, the Lord Chancellor's Visitor, who would decide their fate. Though the office was intended to be a benevolent one, many saw him as an enemy to be out-witted or deceived, even to the extent of concealing criminal insanity.

It was for such cases that the Visitor had engaged Sebastian. His job was to seek out the cunning dissembler, the dangerous madman whose resources might otherwise make him untouchable. Rank and the social order gave such people protection. A former British police detective and one-time Pinkerton man, Sebastian had been engaged to work 'off the books' in exposing their misdeeds. His modest salary was paid out of the department's budget. He remained a shadowy figure, an investi-gator with no public profile.

—Out of Bedlam

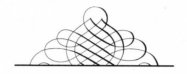

Boothstown, Pennsylvania
August 1913

1

It didn't take a detective to see that the man in the Capitol Hotel had been shot in the head, from behind, and at close range. He was seated at a writing-desk in his room, facing the wall. All the signs were that he'd had no warning. His reaction had propelled the chair back a few inches as he'd slammed face-down onto the blotter. Now his arms were hanging almost to the floor.

Taking care to touch nothing at first, Sebastian Becker inspected the body from every angle. He saw a man in his forties, clean-shaven, wearing a brown worsted suit with a waistcoat and necktie. The suit jacket was off, and slung over the back of the chair. Peering more closely, Sebastian observed matted red-brown hair marking the site of an entrance wound. Soot and unburned powder were scorched into the shirt collar below. On the wall above the desk there was a red sunburst of blood and darker matter, propelled with enough force to destroy wallpaper and plaster at its center.

There was one certain way to identify William James. Sebastian lifted one of the arms and, with care, drew back the shirt cuff to expose the hand. It only took him a moment to be satisfied, and then he restored everything as before.

A pen lay on the floor. He left it there. Whatever piece of writing the victim had been working on, his body was covering it. Sebastian would have to wait for the Sheriff or the County Physician to find out anything more.

Retreating to the door, he tested floorboards for creaks and noises.

A last look around the room. Shaving kit on the washstand, a carpet-bag stowed underneath it. William James was a practiced and lifelong traveller. A pair of brown shoes, nicely polished, was lined up at the foot of the bed. The corpse was in his stockinged feet.

Sebastian pulled the door closed on the scene, and went down to the Capitol's lobby.

The clerk looked up from his bookkeeping as Sebastian descended the stairway. The young man gave a pleasant smile and said, "Did you find him?"

"I did," Sebastian said. "Were you aware that he'd been shot?"

"Say again?"

"Your guest is dead."

It took a moment for the words to register, and a few more for their significance to follow. Without taking his eyes off Sebastian, uncertain as to whether the stranger's words might represent a prank or even a threat, the clerk reached for the house phone.

"Mister Quick?" he said into the receiver after a few moments. "Could you come to the front desk, please?"

And then he hung up the phone, still watching Sebastian, never blinking once.

"I didn't shoot him," Sebastian said, which seemed to offer the young man no reassurance.

Two well-heeled couples came in from the street and headed for seats in the lobby. They were too busy chatting to notice either of the men standing at the counter. The twenty-roomed Capitol was considered to be the finest hotel in this small Pennsylvania town, boasting the usual register of eminent one-time guests from Mark Twain to Theodore Roosevelt. The lobby was a dress-up affair, all brass and brocade with a moose head and a parlor grand, Victorian elegance from its hardwood floor to its hammered tin ceiling. A set of doors connected it to the hotel's saloon, which stood quiet at this early hour of the day.

Orville Quick, proprietor and manager, appeared within the minute. Something in the clerk's tone had alerted him.

"Is there a problem?" he said, while taking stock of the stranger before him. He was assessing Sebastian for attitude, gauging the likely extent of the trouble.

Mindful of the guests within earshot, Sebastian said, "I came here to see the man in room seven."

"And…?"

The clerk mouthed, *Dead*.

Quick was unfazed. "You're sure about this?"

"By another's hand," Sebastian said.

Quick glanced across the lobby. "Please don't say anything more," he said, and moved to the stairway.

"You should know," Sebastian said, "it's not a pleasant sight."

With a brief nod, the manager continued up the stairs.

"I'll be outside," Sebastian told the clerk.

He crossed the lobby and went out through the doors. The town had been ripping up the old wooden boardwalks and replacing them with cement, and this stretch of the main street had been among the first to be renewed. He walked a dozen yards and stood on the adjacent bridge, hands on the rail, looking out over the creek that ran beside the hotel.

There he took a breath, squared himself, and composed his mind. There would be questions that he'd have to answer as best he could. The tragic history of William James would have repercussions beyond his demise. Much would depend on the information that Sebastian was about to give.

At a sound, he turned and looked back. The prosperous-looking couples from the lobby had made their plans and were now leaving; the women deep in conversation and the men strolling behind them, all unaware of the unfolding situation on the upper floor of the hotel. They moved off down the sidewalk, one of the women popping a parasol against the August sunshine.

The stores all had their canvas awnings out, and the busy side of the street was lined with automobiles. Main Street itself was wide and, as yet, unpaved. Every feed barn in the nation might be turning to autolivery, but the car was not yet king; on his walk up from the train station Sebastian had been engulfed by the dust of one mule team after another. He wondered if the wheels, hooves and whipcracks could have made enough of a racket to cover the sound of a single gunshot inside a quiet hotel.

Now two men were heading this way on foot. They'd come from the courthouse, one block down. One was tall, the other shorter and struggling to keep up. Both wore brown suits and derby hats. They reached the hotel just as a truck pulled in and a rancher type alighted and joined them. Moments after they'd gone inside, a new-looking Ford Runabout—brass radiator, high running boards, whitewall tires—drew in behind the truck. The driver was inexperienced, and mistimed his declutch so the vehicle lurched forward a foot or two before he'd killed the engine. Then he jumped out, grabbed a doctor's bag, and followed the others in.

A man had died, and the forces of justice were gathering. Such as they were in this small Pennsylvania tank town, late in the summer of 1913.

Sebastian didn't wait to be called, but made his way back toward the Capitol's lobby.

2

Most of the newly-arrived had gone upstairs. Just one had remained in the lobby, and he was now leaning on the counter and talking to the clerk. It was the man who'd driven the truck, the one that Sebastian had mentally pegged as a rancher. His hat was on the counter and he was wearing a checked shirt, boots, and an outdoor jacket. Less formal than a banker, more swagger than a farmer.

"There he is," the clerk said, and the man turned to look at Sebastian.

He was around fifty, short and solid, his hair mostly gray, mustache still mostly dark. A friendly-looking bear with small, deep-set and calculating eyes.

He said, "You the one who found the body?"

"Sebastian Becker," Sebastian said, offering his hand. The other man took it and crushed it with a grip from which Sebastian reckoned it would take him around forty-eight hours to recover.

"Another Englishman," the man said.

"I'm working for His Majesty's government. I followed William James from England."

"His Majesty, eh?"

"Are you the Sheriff?"

"Under Sheriff. Sheriff's upstairs. With the County Physician and the Coroner and they're waiting on the County Attorney. Let's go sit in the saloon for a while and you can tell me all about His Majesty and..."

"William James," Sebastian said. "He's been travelling under a false name."

They moved through into the long saloon, away from the lobby where they might be disturbed or overheard. It had the same solid elegance of the other public areas, but few places could seem darker or gloomier than a saloon bar in the daytime. There were a couple of card tables at the end farthest from the street, and they made for those. Before they got seated, a voice from someone who'd followed them called out, "What's going on, Doc?"

"You can read all about it in the *Bulletin*," the Under Sheriff replied without turning. Sebastian looked back and saw a man standing in the doorway with the lobby behind him.

"I'll speak to the Sheriff," the man said.

"You do that, Frank."

The man headed back into the lobby, and they pulled out chairs and sat. Sebastian said, "Doc?"

"To my mother I'm Douglas. Doc to everyone else. Did you kill William James, Sebastian?"

"You know I didn't."

"I don't know anything about you."

"But you can talk to the guard on the train from New York. It got in at two-thirty and I came straight to the hotel. By then your man had been dead long enough for the blood to settle. You saw his fingertips? They were almost black."

"I do know you came out here to find him. So tell me. Who is William James?"

"He is—was—a showman. From a family of show people."

"Like the circus?"

"Fairgrounds and music halls. They have a Wild West show."

"A British cowboy? You've got to be kidding me."

"No kidding."

"How does that happen?"

"You can thank your own Colonel Cody. William James' father was a Lancashire publican until Buffalo Bill's Wild West came to Salford. He saw the show, loved the show, had some kind of an epiphany there and then. He got the whole family learning to rope and shoot and throw knives. Sold the pub and took their act on the road. William took over the business when his father passed on."

"Had you arranged to meet?"

"He didn't know I was coming. I've been tracking him. William James is a wanted man. Arson, manslaughter, possibly even murder. They say he burned down a theater with the audience inside."

"People died?"

"Around fifty of them. On a seaside pier. He admitted the crime but then escaped before his trial."

"So what are you, Mister Becker? A British policeman?"

"I've been many things. These days I'm the Special Investigator to the Lord Chancellor's Visitor in Lunacy."

"You hunt lunatics?"

"Just the bad ones."

Doc Sparks sat back in his chair. "Chasing madmen across the world for the Crown," he said. "I feel like I'm required to bow."

"It's not as grand as it sounds."

"I can see that by the coat you're wearing."

"The pay's not so grand either," Sebastian admitted. "I'll be looking for a cheaper hotel than this one."

"Try the Continental, on South Main. Tell them Doc Sparks sent you. Was anyone else on his trail?"

"I daresay he'll have no shortage of enemies. The body's lying on something. Looks like hotel writing paper. Is there any chance I might get to see it?"

"Speak to the Coroner about that. He'll want to talk to you anyway."

"I'll stay and see this through."

"Yes you will," Doc Sparks said, rising. "Make sure we can find you. And when you report back to your people, give my regards to His Majesty."

3

THE CONTINENTAL ON SOUTH MAIN WAS MORE ROOMING-HOUSE than hotel, a step down in quality that was reflected in the rates. While he was checking in, Sebastian mentioned Doc Sparks' name to no visible effect. After signing the register he asked for a telegraph form and wrote a short message to Sir James Crichton Browne, care of the Lord Chancellor's Office in London, with just the bare facts that he'd tracked William James to this Pennsylvania location and that more information would follow. He didn't state whether he'd actually found his man. Nor did he break the news that William James was dead.

The owner called for one of his daughters. The girl who appeared from the back of the house was no more than eight or nine years old, in a cotton sack print dress with her hair in bunches. He gave her the completed form and said, "Mister Becker needs an errand," then told her to run it to the telegraph office at the train station, and to collect Sebastian's Gladstone from the baggage room there.

Sebastian said to the owner, "Are you sure about this? The bag's heavy."

"Don't you worry 'bout that, Mister Pecker," the child said. "Daddy calls me the Flea. I'm little but I'm strong."

"I do call her that," the owner agreed.

And off she went, out into the street, running with his message held high where it fluttered like a flag of surrender.

"Sorry about the Pecker thing," the owner said.

"Don't worry about it," Sebastian said.

His message would be read in London within hours. Sir James Crichton Browne was a medical man, one of the most prominent in England, one of three Lord Chancellor's Visitors charged with assessing the psychology of anyone with a fortune or an income that might be put at risk by their erratic behavior. In extreme cases the Crown would take control of their affairs. Evasion was common, investigation often a necessity. Such men and women provided Sebastian's living.

Doc Sparks had mentioned *The Bulletin*. On his way over, Sebastian had spotted the newspaper's storefront office on South Main. When he left the rooming house, he crossed the dusty street to the two-story building with its painted cast iron façade. Gilt letters on the glass of the door spelled out *Frank E Lucas, Editor and Manager*.

The *Bulletin* was a hometown weekly, with a counter for taking in classifieds and a back room with a printing press. The door was fitted with a bell that danced on a spring as Sebastian stepped in. The response came from an old man in a printer's apron who leaned out of the back room and said, "If you're looking for Mister Lucas, he's up at the Capitol."

"I believe I may have seen him there. Can I look at some of your recent editions?"

"How recent?"

"Two, three weeks."

"Help yourself." With a wave of his inky fingers, the *Bulletin*'s resident typesetter indicated a stack of newsprint on the counter. There were at least two dozen back issues of the paper, all of them used and refolded so that the pile would never quite square up. "Anything in particular you're looking for?"

"Visitors, new arrivals in town, that sort of thing."

"Page two," the old man said, and left him to it.

Sebastian took the first copy from the pile and opened it on the countertop. Page two carried a few box ads and some legal notices but was mainly given over to a section titled *Local and Personal* with a subtitle of *Items of Interest Picked Up Around Town*. In narrow columns of tight print he read of the deeds and doings of the townsfolk—pretty well all of them, it seemed, with no detail too small to escape notice. Mrs C H Parmalee and the children came in from their summer cabin in the mountains on Wednesday. Chas. Fordyce of Lincoln, Nebr, is in town this week in the interests of the Teachers' Institute. John Newell left this morning for his mining claim on Kelly Creek.

And then—

Mr Reuben Jones came in from upstate Tuesday morning on a business trip, and was registered at the Capitol.

Reuben Jones. Careful study of the passenger manifest had revealed the false name used by William James for the sea crossing. His mistake had been to continue with it after landing.

Sebastian carried on scanning down the columns. P D Stockwell, of the forest service, came over from Richmond Saturday. Mr and Mrs Chas. Duffy arrived in town Sunday from Chicago. A G Chawning of Roanoke, Va arrived on Saturday to join his wife as guests of her mother, Mrs Jennie Anderson.

The bell danced again as the door behind him opened and a man said, "Mister Becker?"

Sebastian turned. It was a voice that he'd heard once, and only briefly, in the saloon about half an hour before. It belonged to a dark-haired man in his thirties, a man with a handlebar mustache and strip of beard in the French style. He wore a cream linen jacket with a floppy bow tie.

"I'm Frank E. Lucas," he said. "You're reading my paper."

"So I am," Sebastian said.

Lucas closed the door behind him. Out on the street, the child from the hotel staggered past the window with Sebastian's grip in her arms.

Lucas said, "I believe you're the man who found the body of the deceased. Was he a close personal friend of yours?"

"I can't say he was. We had business to discuss, that's all."

"And your line of business is…?"

"Nothing exciting. I'm a civil servant."

"From London."

"Yes."

"Well you're a long way from home, Mister Becker."

"And you're a very thorough journalist, Mister Lucas." Sebastian glanced down at the open newspaper and said, "Do you keep an army of spies or is this all your own work?"

"People in a small town like to share their news. It's never hard to fill the page. May I ask what you're looking for? I may be able to help."

Lucas was smiling, but his eyes were keen. In this young and growing country, it was the hometown newspaper that made communities and held them together. As well as keeping track of the town's gossip, he'd no doubt make regular checks of passenger lists and hotel registers.

Sebastian decided to take a chance.

He said, "Does the name Kit Strong mean anything to you? He may have shown up recently. He's said to have family hereabouts."

"Kit Strong?" Lucas gave it consideration. "I can't say it does."

Sebastian persisted. "A tall man with a young girl or a boy in his company? Of about fourteen or fifteen. I do know that he sometimes limps a little from an old injury, though he refuses a cane."

"And does this have any bearing on the murder of William James?"

"Just a personal enquiry."

And a calculated gamble. It was inevitable that Lucas would see something of the purpose behind the question. Sebastian could ask around town and cause a general stir, or ask the newspaperman directly and then deal with one man's professional curiosity. If Kit Strong was in the area or had passed through, alone or otherwise, Lucas would be the one to know it.

"A stranger comes into town, registers in the best hotel under a false name, and gets murdered," Lucas said, "Then you show up on his trail, and now this mystery man and a child. You're not just any civil servant, are you?"

"Ask your man Doc Sparks," Sebastian said. "If he's as sharp as he seems, he'll be wiring London to check me out."

• • •

SPARKS WAS, in fact, waiting for Sebastian at the rooming house. His truck was out front and Sparks was in the guest parlor, chatting to the Flea.

"Hey, Mister Pecker," the child said. "I put your bag in your room for you."

"You can call me Sebastian," he said, and tipped her a shiny Buffalo Nickel. "Seriously. I'll be grateful if you will." The girl skipped off to hand the nickel to her mother, and Sebastian turned to Doc Sparks.

"Were you looking for me?" he said.

"I was. Jonas Flynn wants to know what's to be done with the body after the inquest."

"Jonas Flynn?"

"Coroner and town undertaker. If no one lays claim then it's the Potter's Field for William James."

"I don't know about laying claim to a body," Sebastian said. "My job was just to find the man and bring him home for trial."

"Well, you can have Jonas box him up for the journey, but wouldn't you rather see him buried here?"

Suddenly Sebastian understood. "You're looking for someone to cover the cost."

"Won't be huge," Doc Sparks said. "It's just for a priest and a place in a communal grave. Unless you think he deserves more."

Sebastian considered his finances for a moment. Then he said, "I'll pay the funeral bill if I can get a picture of the body as proof."

"John does a good restoration," Sparks said. "But I hope your people won't expect too much."

"They've all seen worse." Sebastian reached inside his coat, and took out a postcard. It was a tinted portrait, a cabinet card with a theatrical photographer's imprint. They were ordered and issued by the dozen, by actors and performers of all stripes. This one was much-travelled and creased around the edges, but the image was intact. It showed a man of around forty years in knee-high leather boots and a buckskin jacket, wearing a broad-brimmed hat of impractical width. Both hands were clasped over a long rifle that stood upright before him, its wooden stock resting on studio grass. He was long-haired but clean-shaven, serious of expression, looking off into an imaginary distance.

A stage cowboy, in the kind of fantasy attire never seen on the range. Set in type in a white space at the bottom of the card were the words THE AUTHENTIC WILLIAM JAMES.

Sebastian held out the picture.

"You can give him this to work from," he said.

Sussex, The South Coast
May 1913

4

SEBASTIAN HAD PICKED UP THE CABINET CARD SOME FOUR months earlier, on the morning of his first meeting with William James. He'd needed something by which to recognize the man. It was inside his coat when he stood at the top of a hill in the gray light and salt wind of an English seaside town, newly arrived from London, looking down on the bay with its curving promenade and the smoking ruin of its pier.

The sight was both spectacular and tragic. The boardwalk out over the waves was mostly intact, its arcades and amusements abandoned in haste, its deck boards strewn with hoses and debris. The pagoda at its end was a twisted sculpture in blackened steel; a great People's Palace of the Arts reduced to an intricate skeleton of burnt sticks. At this distance Sebastian could appreciate the scale of the disaster—but remotely, as the gods might. Figures moved with caution around the edges of the wreckage, solitary firemen about their mysterious business, while a large and watchful crowd lined the rails along the shore.

After viewing the scene alone for a while, he began his descent. Less than a hundred years before, this fine resort had been a tiny fishing village of alleyways, steps, and donkey passages. It had grown, first with the sea bathing fad of the Regency gentry, then with the railways. Today a stunned and sickened silence lay over the entire town.

It seemed that almost everyone had gathered on the promenade before the avenue of great seafront hotels with their flagpoles and solariums. At the pier, he pushed through the muted crowd to reach a makeshift safety barrier. The barrier had been set between two undamaged tollhouses at the pier's landward end. There he stopped, his sense of the tragedy renewed.

"Good Lord," he said.

"A sight to make the angels weep," agreed the police sergeant manning the barrier. He was an older man, somewhat enormous, with a walrus mustache. His uniformed presence alone was enough to hold the curious at a distance.

He added, "Can I help you, sir?" in a tone that was definitely more of a challenge than an offer.

Sebastian reached for his travel warrant, the closest thing to a badge of authority that he carried. He said, "How many were inside?"

"Would you be one of those newspaper reporters, sir?"

"No. I'm on official business."

The sergeant took the warrant, held it at arm's length to bring it into focus, and then handed it back. "At least three dozen dead, is what they're saying. They're still pulling them out."

"I fear I need more detail," Sebastian said. "May I pass?"

"Do go carefully, sir," the sergeant said, moving the barrier to open Sebastian's way to the gates beyond. "The entire pier's unsafe."

The theater blaze had taken hold during the second house on the previous night, and it had continued to burn as the fire service fought until the early hours of the morning to bring it under control. Though they hadn't saved the pavilion, they'd prevented the spread of flames by turning their hoses onto the smaller buildings that lined the pier. By now the motorised fire engines and escape ladders had been withdrawn, but such had been the scale of the blaze that a number of older, hand-pumped appliances had been pulled back into service. Their compact size and lesser weight had made it possible to bring them the full length of the promenade deck, to the central bandstand and beyond, where they continued to serve on wherever small blazes erupted amongst the ashes.

Sebastian picked a path through, taking care not to get in anyone's way. The sea breeze did little to diminish the toxic aftermath of a major fire. It hung in the air like a stink in an outhouse. Sweating, sooty firemen in heavy wool coats were using poles and hooks to drag down whatever interior walls remained and could be reached in safety. When a wall or a ceiling fell, the men with the poles would quickly scatter, skipping over beams and rubble to avoid being crushed.

Sebastian found a group of desperately tired firemen taking a few minutes' break in one of the promenade shelters. Two of them raised their heads at his approach. The whites of their eyes were startling in their blackened faces, like those of coal miners newly emerged from the ground.

He asked to be directed to the man in command. One pointed out their captain.

The Firemaster in charge of rescue and recovery was a man in his fifties, blue-eyed and with sandy-colored hair cropped close to his skull. He asked Sebastian to wait, promising that he'd come over and speak when he could. Sebastian moved to a distance. As he waited, seagulls circled and dived on debris out on the water.

The Firemaster was as good as his word. He came and stood with Sebastian, while keeping his attention on the scene for which he was responsible.

He said, "Now, sir. What can I tell you?"

Sebastian knew only what he'd learned that morning. He said, "So the fire actually took hold during the performance? How was it started? Is there a witness?"

"As I understand it, the stage manager saw someone running from the backstage area," the Firemaster said. "Before he could challenge and see who it was, he saw a flame smoldering its way up a muslin curtain in the wings. He directed two carpenters to beat out the fire with stage poles. By the time the alarm was raised, it had spread up into the flies. The manager tried to drop the iron but the curtain stuck halfway down. The band played 'God Save the King' to calm the crowd, but all the canvas drops were alight by then and burning debris started to rain onto the stage. After that it was panic."

The 'iron' was the safety curtain, designed to impose a fireproof barrier between stage and auditorium and to limit the spread of any blaze. When it worked, it was the single most effective measure for saving lives in a theater fire. Not only by limiting the spread, but by preventing the entire building from becoming a single-chambered, draft-fed furnace.

Sebastian said, "How many were in the house?"

"There was seating for six hundred," the Firemaster said. "But we don't know how many souls were in the building because the fire took the box office. So close to Whitsun, the house was probably at capacity."

"I'm told there are bodies being washed up along the coast."

"We may never have a final number. Am I hearing right? Do the police have their man?"

"I've been sent to interview a suspect," Sebastian said. "That's all I know."

The Firemaster shook his head.

"A theater fire," he said. "It's a warden's worst nightmare."

Tearing himself away from the grim spectacle, feeling guilty at the fascination he felt at being so close to so much destruction, Sebastian made his way back along the pier. From the sergeant at the barrier, he obtained directions to the town's police lockup. While asking, he kept his voice low. The shore crowd was substantial in number, and the number showed no signs of diminishing. Some might have friends or family amongst the dead and injured. News of a suspect would surely turn their silent dismay into something more aggressive. Sebastian didn't wish to be overheard or followed.

His apprehension was well-founded. The lockup and police station were part of the resort's Town Hall, three streets back from the seafront. As Sebastian drew nearer he heard the rising sound of an angry gathering. When he turned the corner he discovered a crowd equal to the one on the shore, and far less subdued.

The street before the Town Hall was blocked by police motor vehicles at either end. Sebastian reached the front of the crowd with difficulty, and managed to get the attention of one of the officers.

"I'm here for William James," Sebastian said.

"They all are," the officer said. "If it was down to me I'd let them have him."

"I was sent by the Lord Chancellor's office."

"Another one?" the officer said. "Hang on."

Sebastian had to wait as one of the younger policemen was sent inside to verify his right to enter. When the man returned, he was nodded through. One moment Sebastian was surrounded by the pressure of the crowd, and in the next he was expelled like a pip into the empty street beyond the line. Sebastian walked across the open ground alone, self-conscious in the knowledge that half the mob had fallen silent and all were watching him.

The Town Hall presented a classical Georgian frontage that might easily have graced the better quarters of Brighton or Bath. Once through the portico the interior hallway was light, bright, and elegant, with a magnificent staircase leading to an upper gallery.

The police cells were a different matter. They were below ground at the back of the building, reached by a narrow stairway with white glazed tiles and an iron handrail like a Turkish Baths or an abattoir. Before he could descend Sebastian found his way blocked by an officer who might have been a close cousin of the man at the pier. An uglier, and less approachable cousin.

"Identify yourself," he said.

"Sebastian Becker. I'm the Visitor's Man."

"The what?"

"The Lord Chancellor's Visitor sent me to interview William James."

"What for?"

"In all honesty, I don't know," Sebastian said, his patience quickly approaching its limit. "But I have my orders and so do you. Take me to him, or to your superior. The choice is yours."

At that point, a voice came echoing up from the bottom of the stairs.

"Mister Becker?"

Sebastian leaned around the obstructing officer to see a uniformed Superintendent way below, looking up from the basement. "That's me," he said.

The Superintendent beckoned him down.

"Let's get this done," he said.

Sebastian descended and found himself with the Superintendent in an entry cage, looking through painted bars into a long, low corridor of connected archways. Each brick archway featured a cell door. On the other side of the bars was a plain wooden desk manned by a custody sergeant, who came forward with keys and set about the noisy business of unlocking the cage door to let them through.

As they moved into the secure area, Sebastian said, "How did you catch him?"

"He walked out of the burning building into the arms of the law. He was in with the other survivors until theater staff identified him. Earlier in the evening he'd been making threats against the management for breaking his contract."

"Has he confessed?"

"He's not making much sense. His daughter's one of the missing."

First, the sergeant relocked the cage door after them. Then they followed him down the corridor to one of the cells, where he fitted another key to another lock. Each time, the clatter of bolts and springs echoed down the tunnel. The cell door swung open, and for the first time Sebastian found himself facing William James.

Arsonist. Mass murderer. Madman.

The cell's only furniture was a wooden cot at its far end. A thin gray blanket covered it. William James sat on the edge of the cot, shackled at the ankles, elbows on his knees, head bowed. Both hands and forearms were so heavily bandaged that they more resembled blunted clubs than human limbs. He didn't look up or show any reaction as Sebastian entered. The cell door was slammed and relocked behind him.

Sebastian waited a moment. Then he said, "William James? My name is Sebastian Becker. Do you know where you are?"

Nothing.

Had he even heard? The prisoner was not in a good state. He had a waistcoat but no jacket, and his shirt collar was missing. The waistcoat was buttoned, his shirt sleeves ripped to the elbow.

"Do you know where you are?" Sebastian repeated.

Slowly, William James looked up.

The face was blank; not especially handsome, not memorable, nor unpleasant. The face of a clerk, a father, an average man. The eyes held on Sebastian with a dazed expression. Was he rational? The lack of any spark might be a temporary result of shock at the consequences of his deed. It could also be a sign of some deeper mental detachment.

Sebastian was about to repeat his question yet again when William James nodded, slowly.

"Say it," Sebastian insisted.

"I'm in a police station."

"Do you know why?"

But James seemed to gain some further measure of awareness, as if Sebastian had just now awakened him from a sleep and his memories were falling back into place.

He said, "Is my daughter safe?"

"I don't have any information on that. Someone will tell you when they know."

"When I ask," William James said, "they laugh and abuse me."

Sebastian was watching him closely. Though he worked for a psychiatrist, he made no pretence of being one. He was here to report evidence of madness, not to attempt to diagnose it. That was for others to determine, just as courts would decide the man's guilt.

Sebastian said, "They believe you set the fire in the theater. Are they right? Did you?"

William James met his gaze. "I don't know," he said.

"Can't you remember?"

It seemed not. "If you say I did it, perhaps I did."

"That's not how this works. I have to assess your state of mind."

"Are you a doctor?"

"No."

William James held up his bandaged hands. The strips of linen were soiled and stained. Not with blood, but with the clear fluid of weeping burns. The attention they'd received was rudimentary, and he'd been imprisoned like this for hours. Sebastian winced inwardly at the thought of the skin underneath.

"My hands hurt," James said.

"You should be in a hospital. They couldn't risk taking you through the crowds. Do you understand why?"

"They want to kill me."

"Quite possibly."

William James looked up at him again.

"You should let them," he said.

At that moment there was a crash and a clatter as the cell door was unlocked and opened. The Superintendent stood in the doorway and said, "Finish your business, please, Mister Becker, I need to move him out."

"I'm not done yet."

"I'm afraid you are. The mob are lifting cobbles. Some of them are getting bold and threatening to stone the building. I don't have the officers to deal with a siege."

"Then call in more!"

"I don't have any more to call. He's going to London. Right now. And don't imagine I'm happy about it."

Two men pushed past Sebastian into the cell. They set about unshackling William James, readying him for the move. Sebastian saw the futility in protesting, and stepped out with the Superintendent into the passageway.

As they waited outside the door, the Superintendent lowered his voice and said, "Be straight with me. What am I not being told?"

"I wish I could say," Sebastian said, "but I know less than you."

"Special Branch men were here before the dawn. The fire was still burning and they were searching the dead."

"They were?"

This was news.

"My men took them for thieves and received a rebuke when they tried to interfere. Why the Special Branch? Tell me. Are Fenians behind this? Is it one of their Irish outrages?"

"I swear to you, I know nothing of it."

The Superintendent clearly didn't believe him, but gave up on pressing the point. Then as William James was being brought out of his cell, there was a distant sound of breaking glass from somewhere up above. Either the crowd had broken through the cordon, or there was an unusually strong throwing arm amongst their number.

Both men moved back to let prisoner and escorts pass. The officers were grim in their duty, a stony efficiency that masked their anxiety at the prospect of the situation outside. They'd draped the gray blanket over James' shoulders, and his bandaged arms were concealed by its folds. He offered no resistance as they walked him down the passageway, through the cage, and up the narrow stairway to the ground floor.

Sebastian followed last. Outside, the cordon was holding. The shot had been a lucky one, with a stone taking out a window on the front of the building. Sebastian had briefly considered asking to accompany James in the wagon, but knew better than to complicate a dangerous operation.

The crowd knew that something was about to happen; they could see that a transport vehicle had been brought to the door and that extra officers had joined the line. At a signal the officers linked arms against an expected surge as William James was brought out of the entrance, four constables now shielding and crowding him. The group moved as one, hustling him across the pavement and into the back of the waiting Black Maria, while behind the cordon the mass of onlookers responded with a rising cacophony of boos and yelling.

Once William James was secured the constables hopped onto the running boards, two to a side with truncheons at the ready. One shouted to the driver, and the wagon set off with them hanging on.

The human chain of constables split, and their two lines opened up to force a corridor through the mob. The mob surged as the wagon went through, and on one side the police line broke. Men and women threw themselves at the vehicle. The two running-board constables laid about them with their truncheons, cracking heads and smacking limbs with no regard for grief or gender. In less than a minute it was over, reduced to the rear view of a disappearing vehicle with a handful of stragglers running in its wake.

And that, for Sebastian, was that.

The point of his mission was now gone, its subject taken out of play, leaving Sebastian feeling no wiser nor any better-informed. With stern encouragement from the remaining police, the crowd now dispersed. No one would own up to breaking the window, or give up the culprit.

Special Branch? Arriving incognito and searching the dead?

• • •

SEBASTIAN RETURNED to the shore for a final look at the scene. Those antique pump appliances were now being taken back to storage, and a team of carpenters had arrived to board up the entrance to the pier. Down on the shingle beach, a group stood around a sheeted form as a handcart was maneuvered toward it. Another dead body, burned or drowned and brought in on the tide. The cart moved with difficulty, its wheels sinking down into the fine stones like quicksand.

Judging by the shape under the sheet, this body was small. It must have washed up within the past hour. Some victims had leapt into the sea to avoid the flames, others would have fallen through when the floor collapsed.

By asking around in the shops and businesses close to the pier, Sebastian learned that most of the dead had been taken directly to a group of long sheds at the edge of town where local fishermen laid out their nets for repair.

Two local doctors had set up a triage station in a Penny Arcade to deal with the survivors. The most lightly injured were given immediate first aid, keeping hospital capacity open for the more severely hurt. Throughout the night until the dawn, a regular traffic of ambulances and private carriages had shuttled back and forth with stretcher cases. A third group had been diverted to the quiet of an empty restaurant next door, where priests and ministers attended to their final moments.

He even found some witnesses, and through conversations in a public house pieced together a few more details of the night's events. The name of William James came up without prompting. No one in the town was in doubt of his guilt.

In a brick alleyway by the public house, on a wall thick with posted bills and paste, Sebastian made a poignant discovery. It was that week's playbill for the Pavilion Theater, already partly covered by a notice for a womens' suffrage meeting and an advertisement for a miracle linctus. There it was: twopence for the pit, fourpence for the stalls, a shilling for a seat in the Grand Circle. A headliner direct from London's Palace Theater, a Trio of Novel and Entertaining comedy gymnasts, a Bioscope film titled *Mabel's Lovers*. There were a dozen speciality acts in all and in the middle of them, legible despite an attempt to deface it, THE AUTHENTIC WILLIAM JAMES and his troupe of MONTANA MAIDS and BRONCO BOYS featuring KIT STRONG, late of BUFFALO BILL'S WILD WEST.

Kit Strong. The name meant nothing to Sebastian then.

But that would change.

5

As the day reached its end, Sebastian was stepping down from the train at Waterloo Junction. From a seaside tragedy to a darkening city of heads-down homebound workers of every trade and level of society, it was as if a two-hour journey brought him from one world back to another. It was too late to stop by his office, a poky basement room in Bethlem asylum that he avoided whenever possible. He preferred to pick up his messages from the cabmen's outdoor refreshment stand under the railway on Southwark Bridge Road, where he had an arrangement that suited him better. The stand was open at all hours, and the cabbies' informal network was the equal of any Post Office.

One message awaited him today, a scrawled note in the handwriting of Sir James Crichton Browne.

Your concerns are understood, it read. *All will become clear tonight.*

Sebastian read it, and then read it over again. He rarely had cause to question his instructions, but he'd wondered at the Chancery interest in a police investigation. And tonight? No one ever contacted him at home. So what more could Sir James expect him to learn tonight?

"Something there to puzzle you, Mister Becker?"

All the cabbies were out and Joe Glass, cook and pieman and co-owner of the pie stand, had time to lean on his high counter and look down on Sebastian. Joe had the broad shoulders and wide neck of a circus strongman.

He stewed his tea and cut his sandwiches to a thickness that it took a strong man to handle.

"There's always something around to puzzle me, Joe," Sebastian said. "It's been the story of my life." Everything would no doubt become clear in time. He folded the note and stowed it in the pocket with the cabinet card.

"Cuppa tea before you go, Mister Becker?"

"No, thanks, Joe," Sebastian said. "It's been a long day and I'm bushed."

"Ay, don't keep the little woman waiting," Joe said.

Sebastian smiled and said nothing, but raised his hand in thanks and farewell as he moved north toward Southwark Street and home.

There was no 'little woman' in his life. When alive, Elisabeth would have bristled at the term. Their time together had ended the year before, the consequence of a blood infection. Elisabeth had been clerk to the Receiving Officer at the Evelina charity hospital, where a drunken father with a dirty knife had been just one daily hazard among many.

Which was not to say that Sebastian was entirely alone. He saw his son, Robert, every week. And then there was Elisabeth's sister Frances. She'd lived with them since her teens. She had family over in Philadelphia and Sebastian had expected her to go home, but she'd chosen to stay on in London and serve as his housekeeper.

Things ticked along. His apartments were in a side street across from Borough Market, above a wardrobe-maker and piano shop. Between the two shops stood an anonymous door with a stairway behind it, leading up to their four rooms and an attic. He'd considered advertising for a lodger to help with the rent. There was a room to spare since Robert had moved out, but he baulked at the thought of a stranger in his home.

Frances stepped out of the kitchen as he was hanging up his coat.

"Sebastian," she said. "Robert's had his laundry bill. It's nineteen shillings."

"Doesn't his landlady take care of the laundry?"

"She does it," Frances said, "but she charges extra. I'd bring it here to save the money but it's just too far."

"Get it from my desk," Sebastian said. "You don't have to account for every penny."

"I keep a record in the housekeeping book, Sebastian," she said. "For my own satisfaction, if not for yours."

"And do our books balance?"

"We survive. Though a few more lunatics wouldn't go amiss."

"As long as God keeps making the British aristocracy," Sebastian said, "we'll have food on the table."

Frances returned to the kitchen, and Sebastian went to wash his hands before supper. Robert had given them much cause for worry as he'd grown, but his phenomenal memory and urge to classify had found him a niche in the Natural History Museum's department of geology. He shared digs in South Kensington with four other junior assistants, in a house run by a Scottish woman unfazed by their various eccentricities. She was a stern mother to them all, and all adored her.

There was rabbit on the table tonight. Frances knew a man on the market who often cut his prices near the end of the day, and always timed her shopping accordingly. As she brought the dish to the table, she said to Sebastian, "I starched you a shirt."

Sebastian was blank. "Do I need one?"

"For the museum. Tonight."

The museum. Now he remembered. Some event for which Robert had sent them tickets. Now it all made sense.

"You'd forgotten," she said.

"As if I would," he said.

"Your shirt's on a hanger in your bedroom."

He said, "On the evidence, I'm guessing Sir James is attending. I had another of his mysterious messages on my way home."

"From the pie stand." She made it sound like a reproof.

"If you could see my Bedlam office, you'd understand why I stay clear of it. Are you joining me tonight?"

"I wouldn't miss the sight of Robert in his place of work," Frances said. "Mrs Jankowski let me borrow a dress."

"You deserve something more than a borrowed dress, Frances."

She dismissed the idea with a wave of the serving tongs. "Not for one night," she said. "It would be a waste of money."

Though she'd been a part of their family for years, Sebastian realized that he was only now beginning to know Frances. She'd always been the shy younger sister, a helping hand through Robert's troubled childhood.

He didn't know whether she'd grown in confidence over this past year, or if he was seeing her qualities for the first time. Now, in addition to keeping house for Sebastian, she brought in some extra money by working as a part-time clerk and bookkeeper in the piano shop below. At quiet times Mr Jankowski, the owner, allowed her to sit and play the instruments—encouraged her, even. She took any opportunity, and to Sebastian's ear she played well, but she'd falter if anyone stopped to listen. As a young girl in Philadelphia she'd taken lessons, but over the years there had been few opportunities for her to practice.

As they settled to eat, Frances raised the subject of the pavilion fire.

"The news is all over London now," she said. "It's so terrible. So many people dead."

"I barely had two words out of William James," Sebastian said. "The man was in a daze. And his hands were badly burned. He must have been in terrible pain."

"Are they right about him? Do you think he's guilty?"

"That's a matter for the police and the courts, not the Lord Chancellor's office."

"So why send you down there?"

"I don't know," Sebastian said. "As far as I can see, I achieved nothing of use. We barely exchanged two words before they carried him off in a Black Maria and I had to put the story together from what I could learn."

He told her what he knew of events that had preceded the fire, much of it learned in the saloon bar of the resort's Jerusalem Hotel. The first-house performance of the Wild West act had been a fiasco. The troupe's stage act involved sharpshooting, trick roping and bullwhip work, all choreographed to the house band playing *At That Bully Wooly Wild West Show*. One of the routines had gone wrong and an audience member had been hurt. The management had cancelled the troupe's second-house appearance and the company was dismissed. An argument over money followed, and threats were made. William James returned to the pier head during the second house and his daughter followed, hoping to dissuade him from confrontation. She was fourteen and played an Indian squaw in the show, shooting clay pipes out of her aunt's fist. A witness saw her backstage, searching for her father, a short time before the fire began. She was later numbered among the missing.

"On the face of it, her loss is a bitter irony arising from the ill-judged actions of an angry man," Sebastian concluded.

"Of what interest is this to the Lord Chancellor's office? Why did they send you?"

"I really don't know. Nothing I could see suggests a Chancery case—nothing so obvious as a rich lunatic, anyway. I know some showmen can be well-off, but I doubt that William James was one of them. I saw the poster. His Wild West act was a long way down the bill."

"Then perhaps sending you was a mistake."

"Perhaps. The Superintendent told me something curious. And it was confirmed by one of the shopkeepers."

"What was that?"

Sebastian hesitated. Then he said, "Just don't repeat it."

He told her of the Superintendent's concern over the presence of Special Branch men. And how, according to a tinker with a dog in the Jerusalem Hotel, the restaurant's owner had been telling of armed men turning up and taking one of the bodies away, only to deny his own story an hour or so later.

"He'd been told to keep his mouth shut," Sebastian said.

"A conspiracy?" Frances said.

"I'd dismiss it," Sebastian said, "if I hadn't heard more or less the same story from another source. Now I don't know what to make of it."

"Perhaps you'll find out."

"Perhaps I will."

Frances started to rise. "I'll clear these away," she said. "Then I need to change for the evening."

"Don't forget the money for Robert's laundry," Sebastian said.

"I took it from your desk this morning," she said. "It's all in the book."

6

London's Museum of Natural History, planned by founder Richard Owen to be the nation's 'cathedral of nature', was a long terracotta palace of serious architectural beauty on South Kensington's Crompton Road. Night had fallen and the streetlamps were lit. For the occasion, they'd taken a cab. The mix of motor cars and horse carriages before the museum made for a uniquely modern scene.

They stood in the entranceway, Frances on his arm. More carriages were arriving, more people were ascending the steps behind them.

"That's a relief," Sebastian said, surveying the gathering before them in the Great Hall.

"What is?" Frances said.

"It isn't black tie," Sebastian explained.

"You never said it might be!"

"Only just occurred to me," Sebastian said, and wondered why her fingers dug into his arm so.

They moved forward through a Romanesque arch, past the bronze effigy of Owen and into the main part of the hall. Starched shirt or not, Sebastian felt distinctly out of his social league. The evening's event was a fundraiser to help clear the debts of Captain Scott's Terra Nova Expedition, an Antarctic adventure whose title was forever to be preceded by the words 'ill-fated'.

Had the expedition been a success, its costs would have been covered by the revenue from lecture tours, exhibitions, medals, memorabilia—any means of wringing cash from the glory. As it was, the expedition had failed in its aim to be first to the South Pole. All those involved in the final push had perished on the return journey.

While looking out for his employer, Sebastian found himself casting a professional eye over the assembly. Most of tonight's guests could probably boast land, money, a title, or all three. He reckoned that a significant part of his income could depend on the inbreeding of three or four dozen of these blue-blooded dynasties.

"There's Robert!" Frances said.

Sebastian's boy was coming over, taller than his father now, scrubbed and spruced and with his hair slicked down. The junior assistants had been 'volunteered' as ushers for the evening.

"May I take your coats?" he said.

"You look very handsome tonight, Robert," Frances said.

"I know!" Robert said delightedly. He added their coats to the growing pile on his arm, and rather than ferry them to the cloakroom, went off hunting for more.

Frances watched him go.

"We'll never see those again," she said.

Robert had stopped, and was now all but wrenching the stole off a Duchess' shoulders.

Someone was calling for silence. That had no effect until other, louder voices joined in. It took more than a minute for awareness to spread throughout the great hall and for conversation to abate to a point where the tiny, bald-headed, bearded Chairman could be heard.

It was unclear of what he was Chairman, but from a podium before the great staircase at the hall's end he introduced the widows, Lady Scott and Mrs Wilson (to applause, polite and uncertain, for how does one really applaud widowhood) and then handed over to Lord Curzon, former Viceroy and Governor-General of India, President of the Royal Geographical Society and a leading member of the Scott Memorial Committee.

Lord Curzon took his place at the podium. He was smooth of face, domed of forehead, a straight-backed man in his fifties with a military manner and, large on his lapel, the Star of Something or Other. His voice carried well in the great chamber, and he seemed to enjoy the sound of it. He thanked all for coming, congratulated the museum on its acquisition of Captain Scott's diaries, and was proud to announce that the memorial fund now stood at eighteen thousand pounds (more applause).

The speech went on. Medals were presented to the widows. Sebastian could sense Frances shifting her weight from one foot to the other.

The memorial was proving to be a much greater success than the expedition. Scott's failure was seen as heroic, with the successful Norwegian somehow becoming the villain of the piece. Getting there first—it was just the kind of unsporting move you'd expect from a foreigner. Why celebrate planning, when you could celebrate pluck?

Finally it was over. There was more polite applause.

"Is he done?" Frances whispered.

"I think he is," Sebastian said.

Frances went off to look for Robert, leaving Sebastian to seek out his employer.

As he scanned the crowd, he recognised expedition photographer Herbert Ponting. He was by the stuffed African elephant, speaking earnestly to a group of ladies. He'd survived because Scott had excluded him from the final push to the Pole, citing his age as the deciding factor.

Suddenly there was a hard grip on Sebastian's shoulder.

"Walk with me, Sebastian," a voice said in his ear.

He found himself being propelled and steered away like a schoolboy by Sir James Crichton Browne, the Lord Chancellor's Visitor in Lunacy.

"Did you hear the speech?" Crichton Browne said.

"I did."

"Poor George. But he put a brave face on it."

And Sebastian said, "George who?"

Crichton Browne—balding, cravat with a tiepin, a spreading white mustache that merged into muttonchop whiskers—found them a quiet spot between glass cases devoted to the display of vertebrate morphology. Amidst shelves of small creatures all stripped to their bones, he said. "Curzon had himself convinced that the expedition diary was going to the Royal Geographic. But Kathleen chose the museum instead."

Sebastian said, "Are we going to talk about Sussex?"

"Sussex."

"The pier fire. Why did you send me there?"

Crichton Browne kept his voice low. "I had my reasons. Did you meet William James?"

"Yes."

"And you got a good look at him?"

"Barely. There was a riot outside and they couldn't get him away quickly enough."

"How did he strike you?"

Before Sebastian could answer, they were interrupted.

"Is this your man?"

It was Lord Curzon, all forehead and medals. Curzon didn't wait for an opportunity to enter the conversation, nor did he introduce himself. He cut right in, looking closely at Sebastian.

"Yes, George," Crichton Browne said. "May I present Sebastian Becker. My Special Investigator. What do you think?"

Curzon looked Sebastian up and down, as he might a horse. Sebastian was half-expecting the man to grab his head and check his teeth.

Curzon said, "I suppose he'll do. Does he know what's at stake?"

"We're discussing that now."

Now Curzon addressed Sebastian directly for the first time. He spoke slowly, as if to a dull and unresponsive child.

"Now you listen here," he said. "You breathe a word of this affair to anyone, and I'll see you swing alongside that cold-blooded cowboy circus clown."

By 'cold blooded cowboy circus clown', Sebastian guessed that he meant William James.

He said nothing.

"He's discreet, George," Crichton Browne assured him. "He's the best."

"National security. Do you understand me, Becker? That's what's at stake, here. National security." He gave Sebastian the force of his stare a moment longer, to be sure he understood.

Then gave a nod to Crichton Browne, and walked off. An inrushing air of relief filled the space that he left behind.

"He exaggerates," Crichton Browne said. "A little."

Sebastian looked around. Right now he could have used a glass of port swiped from the tray of a timely passing waiter, but the event was a dry one, and he was disappointed.

He said, "You hardly need an investigator to prove William James mad, if that's your purpose. He's in custody. Use doctors."

"You're not to prove him mad. You're to see if you can prove him sane."

"What?"

"You heard me. And keep your voice down."

"And where do Special Branch come into this?"

Crichton Browne plainly heard him, but kept his face blank.

"Oh, come on, Sir James. Their presence was an open secret. They were searching all the bodies and spiriting one away."

At that the Lord Chancellor's Visitor glanced around, and shook his head. "You're far too good a detective," he said.

"If listening to pub gossip makes me a good detective, then the nation's tap rooms are full of such," Sebastian said. "I don't understand. It's a theater fire on a seaside pier. Where does national security enter into it?"

Crichton Browne breathed in deeply, then let it out with a sound of quietly exasperated resignation. He seemed unhappy at the position he was being obliged to take.

He said, "Have you heard of Prince Max of Erbach-Schonburg?"

"I can say with some confidence, no."

"Minor German royalty, twenty-two years old, related as closely to our own King as to the Kaiser. This is indelicate, Becker, and it goes no further. Do you understand me?"

"I hope to."

"The boy was sent to Paris and London to sow his wild oats. He posed as a visiting student and the Palace assigned a couple of guardsmen his own age for protection and to show him around. They rather threw themselves into their work. At the Lewisham Hippodrome he developed an unnatural passion for a muscular young acrobat and began following him from venue to venue. You might say the young man led him a dance."

"I take it the prince was in the audience on the night of the fire."

"Incognito in the stalls, and not among the survivors. One of the guardsmen died with him and the other's in the hospital. Do you see where I'm going with this?"

Sebastian did not wish to appear a fool. Especially after Lord Curzon making him feel like one. But...no.

Crichton Browne said, "The boy was a favorite of the Empress. He was under British care. Relations with Germany have never been more fragile. They're building up their navy and, if you believe the Daily Mail, there's a German spy on every street corner."

Sebastian began to understand. "We kill their prince, they sharpen swords," he said.

"We can't conjure a young man back to life. But we can close this down before either side's warmongers catch on."

"With the sacrifice of William James."

"There seems no doubt as to his guilt. And it'll be hard to keep the outrage going once justice has been done."

"Then why call on me?"

"His defence will claim insanity. Do you remember Sapido?"

"Who?"

"The Belgian who took shots at the Prince of Wales on Brussels station. He was found insane. Detained for just a few years and then they let him out. We can't have that."

"Blood calls for blood."

"If it's doctor against doctor it'll end in a shambles. We'll need facts and background to prove the case."

"And if the case is one for compassion?"

Crichton Browne spoke slowly, and with careful emphasis.

"What must be must be," he said. "But be very sure before you put me in that position."

A bell rang. Oh joy. The evening was to continue with a lantern slide lecture from Herbert Ponting, in the gallery behind the great staircase.

So the job was to prove a man sane. So they could hang him, and hang him quickly. And so move the whole story into the past tense, and head off the likelihood of a diplomatic incident over a dead German prince with an eye for a chap in a leotard.

Now Sebastian understood.

• • •

THEY LEFT early to avoid the lecture, retrieving their coats from a massive unsorted pile in the butterfly gallery. Passing all the private carriages that waited outside, they crossed Exhibition Road to reach the cab stand at Thurloe Place. Alone, Sebastian would have ridden a tram. But Frances had worn her borrowed dress without envy or complaint, and deserved better.

There was a line of taxicabs down the middle of the wide road, sturdy French-built motor vehicles with shelter for their passengers and none for their chauffeurs. The first two drivers stood by their machines, as the law required, while the rest had crammed into the steamed-up wooden refreshment hut at the end of the line.

The first driver baulked at crossing the river at this late hour but then the second, who knew Sebastian, set him straight.

As they settled in, Frances said, "You seem unhappy. What is it, Sebastian?"

"It's nothing," he assured her.

"Did you find Sir James?"

"He found me."

The cab's route took them by the high walls of the Palace and down the long straight of Birdcage Walk to Westminster, a very different version of the capital to the one they saw daily. No tenements, no tanneries, no smokestacks or trains. Electric street lamps lit the way to Westminster Bridge. Above the dark bulk of the Houses of Parliament, the dial on the clock tower of Big Ben shone like a second moon.

Rather than press him, Frances waited until Sebastian could contain himself no longer.

"The message was unstated," he said, keeping his voice low even though the driver was the other side of a glass window and unlikely to hear. "Satisfy your conscience, but be sure to reach the necessary conclusion."

"I don't understand."

He explained their conversation, and Curzon's intervention. How the political need for a scapegoat was impressed upon him, in the confidence that it would be hard to keep an argument alive over a dead assassin.

"What will you do?"

"I don't know. This isn't what I'm employed for."

"I don't like to see you in distress, Sebastian. Can you not look else-where? There must be other jobs."

"Not many in my line, for a man with my history. We have to live. And it'll be some time before Robert draws enough of a wage to support himself."

"Mister Jankowski says I could give lessons, if I'd a mind to."

"We can press on a little longer," Sebastian said.

• • •

HE PAID off the cabbie at the end of Stoney Street, where market delivery wagons with the next morning's produce were already beginning to dam up the thoroughfare. It would be easier for them to walk the rest of the way.

Sebastian said, "This irks me, Frances. I wish I were a better provider."

"Elisabeth never complained," Frances said. "And nor do I."

He shook his head. "So much would have been different if she'd never married me."

"Yet here we are," Frances said, and linked his arm with her own.

"Forgive my mood," Sebastian said.

"I don't imagine we'd ever have been Philadelphia society girls. When the money ran out we'd have been shipped west to live with aunts and cousins."

"That doesn't sound so bad."

"You never met my aunts and cousins."

Frances was avoiding mention of the more likely possibility, which was that both sisters would have found well-born husbands from Philadelphia families. As young girls, they'd been raised in a privileged household. In their early teens, their father's investments had failed. Social shame had ensued. Yet somehow the loss of Raymond Callowhill's fortune hadn't exactly led him to destitution, just to a smaller mansion with fewer servants, from where he might one day brag of his familiarity with hardship.

Callowhill had disapproved of Sebastian, and had threatened to cut all ties with his daughter if she went ahead with the wedding. Had he known that Elisabeth was pregnant with Robert at the time, Sebastian could only imagine what his reaction might have been. Frances had acted as conciliator and go-between for a while, until pressed to choose where her loyalties lay.

Suddenly she said, "I forgot to tell you. I had the strangest encounter."

"Where?"

"At the museum. A newspaperman heard my accent and took me for Mrs Ponting. Asked me how I felt about having a husband so long absent from home. I'm afraid I teased him a little."

To a British journalist, one American accent probably sounded much like any other. Ponting's wife was known to be a high-society Californian, if one could imagine such a thing.

Sebastian said, "What did you tell him?"

"That after so long an absence I must have forgotten I had a husband. But then I couldn't be so cruel, so I explained his error. Then we both laughed."

Sebastian smiled at this, but felt awkward. Frances had never expressed it in words, but he sometimes wondered how she might feel. That she'd seen her youth slip away in the quiet service of others? That, despite changing attitudes over the first decade of a new century, the marriage season of a young woman's life had passed her by?

If so, much of the blame must lie at his door. But what could he do? What could he say?

He was still searching for suitable words as they made the turn into a brick passageway that gave them a shortcut to their street.

Whereupon she unlinked his arm and moved to a proper distance, lest the neighbors see.

7

AFTER HIS TRANSFER FROM THE COAST, WILLIAM JAMES HAD MADE a brief appearance before a magistrate's court. He'd been held in police cells overnight and then transferred to Brixton, the grim citadel south of the river that served as the remand prison for all of London. Sebastian received these details in a message via the usual channels and took a number fifty-four tram to Jebb Avenue, so named for Colonel Jebb, the Surveyor General of Prisons at the time of the gaol's construction. Brixton was a half-hour journey from Lambeth.

That morning, it rained.

The bad weather was keeping the numbers down but there was still a small crowd maintaining an angry vigil outside the prison gates, kept in order by one unhappy-looking police constable in a rain cape. A second, smaller group stood apart from the first. These were the representatives of the national press, huddled together and swapping stories while keeping a curious eye on everyone who came and went.

Sebastian presented himself to the caped policeman.

"I'm here to see William James," he said.

"Name?"

"Sebastian Becker."

"You're expected," the officer said, and without turning around he gave two raps of his truncheon on the timbers behind him. There was a sound of keys and of bolts sliding, and then a smaller wicket door opened within the gate.

Sebastian stepped through, and waited as a warder refastened the locks after him.

He was led forward to an inner courtyard. Ahead of him stood a hexagonal block of unusual design, dark yellow brick in a Regency style with three tall chimneys and a white clock tower. This was the old Governor's House, once his residence, now used for storage and administration. Its appearance was somewhere between a lighthouse and a fairytale castle, though it was a structure of more menace than charm. The prison's great cell blocks loomed behind it.

Once inside the Governor's House he identified himself and showed his official letter to another, senior warder.

"Wait here," the second warder told him. "We'll have him brought over."

The place of waiting was a bare room by the superintendent's office, one floor up. It contained a plain table and three chairs—one for the prisoner, one for the visitor, and the other by the door for a member of staff. Sebastian considered draping his wet overcoat on the iron radiator, but decided against it. This was hardly the place to be making oneself at home.

He seated himself on the far side of the table, facing the door. It was fifteen minutes or more before the rattling of shackles announced the approach of a prisoner, slowly making his way up the stairs.

The door swung open, and William James was brought in.

He was chained hand and foot, with manacles fastened over his bandages. Though a remand prisoner, he was in in a broad-arrow canvas jacket and trousers, his head shaved under a prison cap like a third-class, hard-labor man. He seemed considerably more alert than on the occasion of their first meeting. His face was drawn and his eyes sharp, as if fear had shown up, settled, and made a permanent home there.

The escorting guard pulled out the second chair so that William James could seat himself at the table, and then withdrew to his own place by the door. The prisoner sat slowly. With equal care, he lifted his chains and then, with a moment's tension followed by a slight gasp of relief, rested his arms on the table.

Sebastian said, "Do you remember me?"

William James took a moment to study his face.

"No," he said.

"My name is Sebastian Becker."

"Still no."

"I came to see you the morning after the fire. We were interrupted then. It will go better for you if you answer my questions now."

"Really?" William James said. "In what way? I know I'll hang. Barely an hour goes by without someone telling me how the gallows is too good for me."

"That one time we met, you asked about your daughter. I take it she was there on the night of the fire."

Suddenly Sebastian had the prisoner's full and intense attention. He said, "Melody?"

"You remember me now?" Sebastian said.

"You have news of my daughter?"

"I looked for her in the list of injured and survivors. It's incomplete, of course. So many fled the scene."

In fact, the records were a shambles. Relatives had besieged the hospitals and forced their way into temporary mortuaries, desperate to look for loved ones, hoping at least to establish that they were not amongst the dead. Some were to be disappointed. Many of the bodies had been taken away by those same relatives before they could be documented.

William James said, "Did you find her? Did she escape the fire?"

"She appears on no hospital list," Sebastian said. "Of the dead, four bodies are still unclaimed. They're too badly burned to identify. One is a man, two are women. The other is a child of around eight years old."

"A girl?"

"They believe so. They've been unable to say for sure. Might it be her?"

James lowered his head. After a few moments, he began to shake it slowly. Sebastian was looking at his bandaged hands. The linen was fresh, but not clean; the skin beneath continued to weep through it. Even if they weren't screwed down tight, those heavy manacles could only be compounding the agony.

Sebastian said, "The child was found under debris backstage. I don't know what else to tell you."

William James looked up. The color had drained from his face but his eyes were red.

"Eight years old?" he said.

"Eight or thereabouts," Sebastian said.

William James said, "If my Melody's gone then I've nothing left to lose. Be straight with me and I'll be level with you. Exactly what am I to you and you to me, Mister Becker?"

"I am the Special Investigator to the Lord Chancellor's Visitor in Lunacy."

"Lunacy, you say? Are you here to prove me mad? Tell me the truth. As for the consequences, I really do not care."

"I don't make the judgments," Sebastian said. If only the man knew of the pressures and the influences being brought to bear, all to ensure that he be served up dead. Sebastian said, "I gather information. It's for others to decide what the information means."

"What do you want me to say to you?"

"Explain to me why you did what you did. What reason drove you."

"Or lack of it?"

"Indeed."

"I'll tell you. But I set one condition."

"I can't agree to conditions," Sebastian said.

"At least hear what it is. You know what I'm accused of. No defence will save me. If I'm to die then I need to make peace with my mother. Her name is Elspeth James. My father's gone, my sisters have families of their own. It's for her sake more than mine. Is that so much to ask?"

"You should discuss the matter with the Governor."

"I've tried. I get no quarter from anyone here. Your conversation is the first reasonable discourse I've known since they laid hands on me."

It would have been easy to lie. Some would have shown little hesitation in making an empty promise to a condemned man, thinking it a sin without consequence, and therefore no sin at all. But Sebastian was not among them.

All he could say was, "I suppose I can raise the question."

"All right, then," William James said.

Sebastian waited.

After a few moments of silence on both sides he said, "And?"

"I'll speak again when you've raised it."

Over by the door, the attending warder was smiling and looking at his feet, pretending not to listen, not trying too hard in the pretence. Sebastian had been, as the expression had it, snookered. He was about to protest, but saw the resolve on the prisoner's face.

William James added, "Make the arrangement, Mister Becker. I promise you, my story will be worth the wait."

"And why should that be?"

Chains clinked as William James leaned forward and lowered his voice.

"If you want my confession, you can have it," he said. "But my crime was not to set the fire."

"Then why not say so?"

"My crime was to open up my family to the devil. The disaster and all the suffering spring from there. Does that make me responsible? I'll accept all blame. But Kit Strong is the reason I came to this, and it's thanks to him I will hang. I would go to the scaffold with the lightest of hearts if only it were for the ending of his life."

Upon that, William James sat back. He winced as the chains moved and chafed against his wrappings.

"Who's Kit Strong?" Sebastian said. "Is that a real name?"

"It's real. *He* is real. A demon who walks the Earth with no disguise. He even warned me of this day. That's how the Devil works, Mister Becker; he lets us choose our fate and steer toward it of our own free will. And Mister Becker, you will forgive me, but that is all I'm willing to say for now. I have nothing to bargain with but my soul and my story. It seems that one of those is already forfeit, and you're the first person to show any interest in the other. So…into your hands."

The interview was over.

William James got to his feet, and the procedure for his return to the men's block began. As he the prisoner was led out, the remaining warder said to Sebastian, "Wait here, please," and stood with him as William James made his slow progress down the stairs.

Sebastian said, "I understand the leg irons. But you can see the state of his hands. Why the manacles?"

"Instructions from above," the warder said.

"And why crop his hair like a hard-labor man?"

"Headlice," the warder said. "We take no chances with theatricals."

8

HAD HE KNOWN THAT HIS REQUEST TO SPEAK TO THE SUPERIN-
tendent, and to have the prison chaplain present, would result in a wait of
more than two hours, Sebastian might have reconsidered his strategy. As
it was, he had plenty of time to observe the rain falling on every part of
the prison from what had once been the Governor's drawing-room window.
Here the purpose of the building's hexagonal design became clear. From its
position at the heart of the site, the entirety of the gaol was visible from one
window or another. The converse being, of course, that every aspect of the
Governor's life was visible to those he governed. So it was no surprise that for
some years now, the men in charge had elected to live elsewhere.

At the end of the wait Sebastian was escorted across the gravelled yard,
past laundry and cookhouse, to reach the chapel. It was sandwiched between
the wards, a building in the Victorian Gothic style with high arched windows and a roof of carved oak beams.

They met in the panelled vestry, where the chaplain's clerk was sorting
the prisoners' mail. The superintendent was a square-built man with thin-
ning hair and a grip like a bricklayer. The chaplain was ex-navy. Sebastian
had met the chaplain once before, over the transfer of a prisoner from Brixton
to Bethlem, and had found him both compassionate and outspoken over the
welfare of his charges. This had never kept inmates from referring to him
privately as 'Creeping Jesus'.

Sebastian put his case to the two of them. The superintendent revealed that he'd already received letters from the family of William James, petitioning for a visit, and that he'd been minded to refuse.

He said, "You should know that I'm under orders to keep prisoner James under the closest supervision."

Sebastian said, "Are you going to let some higher authority dictate how you run your own prison?"

"I don't have much choice," the superintendent said. "I believe that's what the phrase 'higher authority' implies."

Sebastian turned to the other man. "Chaplain?"

"The higher authority I serve is not the one we're talking about, Mister Becker," the chaplain said with a raised eyebrow, "and well you know it."

"I thought you might have an opinion."

"I may be Brixton's voice of Christian charity, but I also have to work here."

"Here's what I fear," Sebastian said. "That William James has been judged already and there's a temptation to withhold basic human decency because everyone thinks he deserves nothing better. Whatever his crimes, he's a man like other men. He's grieving for his daughter and he needs medical attention."

"He's getting the same care we'd give to any prisoner in his state."

"And broad-arrow clothes on a remand prisoner?"

"His own were beyond saving. Don't presume to instruct me in my duties, Mister Becker. He's being treated exactly as the law requires."

"Then allow him a visit," Sebastian said.

"You're showing an uncommon interest in his welfare, even for a Visitor's man. What's in this for you?"

"His confession," Sebastian said.

"And what's to be gained by confession? Begging your pardon, Chaplain," he added in a hasty aside. "But a conviction's hardly in doubt."

"That may be so," Sebastian said. "But he's implicating others."

"He's playing with you."

"I'll know that for sure when I verify his story."

"Look," the superintendent said, "I'm not an unreasonable man. And despite what you seem to think, I *am* the authority here. So here's what I'll agree to. His mother alone. The shackles stay on. And one of my officers present throughout the visit."

"One could ask no more," Sebastian said. And then; "May I see the letters?"

"Which letters?"

"The ones from his family. Petitioning to see him."

"To what purpose?"

"To determine an address? I'd like to speak to them."

"There's no return address," the supervisor said. "They're itinerants. His solicitor says he'll take any messages."

• • •

THE RAIN had ceased by the time Sebastian reached home. But the streets of the Borough were slick and shiny, the day was fading through pewter toward darkness, and the lights in every window above every workshop and business glowed with the pale warmth of a hundred private havens. He felt a surge of gratitude that in this challenging, often wearying world he had somewhere—someone—to come home to.

Frances was there as he stepped through the door.

"Sebastian," she said. "Your coat is soaked through."

"Believe me," he said, with her pulling it from his shoulders as fast as he could unbutton it. "I know."

"Go and change," she said. "You'll catch a chill."

"I've survived worse," he said. But he did as he'd been told.

When he came down from his room Frances had spread his coat on a folding wooden rack by the stove. Sebastian topped up the coals on the drawing-room fire and sat close to the hearth, to warm his bones. He could hear Frances rattling jars and bottles in the kitchen. Then she brought him a generous tot in a glass.

"I thought I'd finished all the brandy," he said.

"That's what I let you think," Frances said.

The windows gradually steamed up as Sebastian relaxed and his overcoat dried out, and the rooms grew pleasantly muggy.

Frances settled across from him.

"Supper won't be long," she said.

He stared into the fire. She waited.

He said, "I'm being drawn into something, Frances, and I don't like the feeling. I like to know where I'm going."

He told her of the day's events at the prison and she said, "I thought this was all about a German prince."

"The German prince is not the story."

"No?"

"He's the reason my employers need a hasty scapegoat for the disaster. Questioning the scapegoat's guilt is no part of their plan."

"But he's admitted his guilt to you. Hasn't he?"

"Therein lies the intrigue," Sebastian said. "He claims he's responsible for the tragedy, but stops short of owning to the fire. He seems all but ready to hang. But for some different reason."

"Kit Strong?"

"A name on a playbill," Sebastian said. "Some kind of star attraction in the Wild West act, and so far that's all I know. Something passed between them and disaster followed."

He downed the rest of the brandy.

"Once William James has made peace with his mother," he said, "I hope to learn more."

9

HE MADE A REQUEST FOR SIGHT OF THE FAMILY'S CORRESPON-
dence through the Lord Chancellor's office. Copies reached Sebastian's desk
almost a week later, during which time he attended to other business, tracking down a lunatic hidden in squalor by his dependents, and then destroying
the campaign of a set of grasping relatives bent on gaining control of the
fortune of a perfectly sane widow. By then the Brixton visit of Mrs James
had been approved and arranged through the family's solicitor. Sebastian
read pale copies of the letters by electric light in his basement room at the
Bethlem. They'd been taken on damp tissue in a letterpress, censor's marks
and all. All were in the semi-literate hand of one Florence James. A carbon of
William James' one letter out, dictated and typed, was included.

As he was reading, Sebastian heard an ominous approaching rumble
from the passageway outside. It rose in volume, reached a peak, and stopped.

There was a knock at the door.

"Yes?"

Thomas Fogg, one of the Men's Ward assistants, stuck his head around
the door. "Mister Becker, sir," he said.

"I'm on a flying visit, Fogg," Sebastian said. "I don't intend to stay
around. What is it?"

"Doctor Crichton Browne is in the building, sir."

Sebastian laid down the letter. "Does he need me to go to him?"

"No, sir…when he's done with his patient, I believe he intends to come down and see you."

Though it would never quite shed the name or reputation, Lambeth's Bethlem Royal Hospital was a very different beast to the Bedlam of old. The criminally insane now went to Broadmoor. Though Bethlem had its incurables' ward, most of its patients led decent lives under a modern regime of treatment. A handful were Chancery lunatics, their affairs taken under the control of the Masters of Lunacy at the Visitor's discretion. Each received a yearly interview with Sir James Crichton Brown, where he would check on their welfare and reassess their condition.

Sebastian said, "I'll need a second chair."

"Right here, Mister Becker," Fogg said, and bumped the door wide open to reveal the source of the rumbling; it was a rather nice leather-upholstered swivel chair on castors, that he now rolled into the room.

"Can I keep it?" Sebastian said.

"I'm afraid not, sir. It's Doctor Stoddart's favorite."

Sir James Crichton Browne arrived a half-hour later. He didn't knock; but then he hardly needed to, preceded as he was by the noise of his hard-soled shoes and walking cane. The man was over seventy, but that fast striding gait could belong to no one else. He closed the door behind him.

"Have you been speaking to anyone?" he said, taking a seat on the borrowed chair. "Anyone at all?"

"Are we talking about William James?"

"It's leaking out. Some people are starting to ask some very pointed questions. If the papers get hold of the German connection they'll create their own conspiracies. Northcliffe's rags especially. We must keep it in the family."

"I've discussed it with no one," Sebastian said with a clear conscience. There was Frances. But Frances was family.

"What have you found?"

"William James is grieving but rational," Sebastian said. "I can't speak to his guilt, but he denies nothing."

"Grieving, you say?"

"It would appear that his own daughter died in the fire. No one would give him any information, but that allowed me to make some progress in gaining his confidence. I arranged a visit from his mother. In return he's sworn to open up and tell me his story."

"Excellent," Crichton Browne said. "Use the mother. Even the lowest thug caves in before his mother."

Sebastian started to frame a question, hesitated, and then framed it again. He said, "Is this right?"

His employer didn't understand. "Right? Is what right?"

"I'm neither his doctor, his defence, nor his confessor. And with the purpose I've been assigned to, I can't in all conscience present myself as his friend."

"Do what you need to, Sebastian. Let me and the lawyers worry about the morality of it."

"Tell me, Sir James," he persisted. "Am I an instrument of justice, here, or one of revenge?"

Crichton Browne rose to leave. "Consider yourself an instrument of diplomacy," he said. "And save your doubts, Sebastian, since you haven't even heard his story yet."

He turned toward the door, stopped, looked back at Sebastian.

"Do you believe me to be without integrity?" he said.

"No, sir."

"Then trust me to do my job. And I'll trust you to do yours."

With that, he left.

10

Sᴇʙᴀsᴛɪᴀɴ ᴀʀʀɪᴠᴇᴅ ᴀᴛ Bʀɪxᴛᴏɴ's ɢᴀᴛᴇs ᴀʀᴏᴜɴᴅ ᴛᴇɴ ɪɴ ᴛʜᴇ morning. He was intent on taking full advantage of any gratitude that William James might feel driven to express. The crowd had thinned over the days and was now gone completely, journalists included. Outrage never burned for very long in those hangers-on who were not directly entitled to it.

Sebastian was there in time to see the prisoner's mother leaving, escorted to the gate under well-rehearsed security procedures. A small woman of advanced years, her distress was self-evident. Sebastian's own guard waited until her group was clear before allowing him forward.

"Your timing's good," his warder said. "He's still in the interviewing room."

The interviewing room was locked, and the key could not be found. Even then, suspicions were not yet aroused. A duplicate was sent for, and took five minutes to arrive. Consternation only began to grow when knocking brought no response from the other side, nothing beyond an ominous silence.

When the room was opened—no William James. Just a prison employee in woollen combination underwear, gagged and secured to a chair with the prisoner's own chains. Sebastian took a moment to recognise the senior warder from his earlier visit.

They freed up the gag, and the humiliated warder spat it out with a force that peppered Sebastian's shirtfront with spittle and blood.

"Prisoner on the loose!" he gasped. "Raise the alarm!"

Outside the Governor's House, the alarm was already being raised. Whistles were shrieking, wooden rattles spinning a noisy racket. As they unscrewed the manacles to set the senior warder free, here is how the man told it:

"They bring the old woman in. I'm left with the pair of them. There she is, all weeping and wailing about his poor burned hands. She takes them in her own and the next thing I know, the shackles are off and the two of them are upon me. There's a sock in my mouth and I'm pinned to the floor. I'm twenty years in the job and I thought I'd seen everything, but I don't know how it happened. Then off came the hat and the dress and it's a little man, bald and strong as a monkey with a sailor's tattoos. I fought them, be assured of that. But these circus types, they're hard as nails. You can punch 'em and nothing happens. The two of them switched clothes and the monkey-man took my uniform."

William James had then walked out in the dress and veil, crouching within the skirts to disguise his height, with gloves drawn over his bandages and a handkerchief to weep into. The other man had donned the warder's uniform and posed as his escort. They'd locked the room behind them and taken the keys. The deception had lasted as far as the gate, where it had been spotted and the two men challenged.

There the escapee and his confederate had resorted to swift violence, overpowering the gateman even as he was summoning help. The gate was opened and the confederate fought on while William James hitched up his skirts and ran. A motor truck was waiting in Jebb Avenue with its engine idling. Those in the lane saw hands reach out and drag one racing old lady into the cab.

Back in the yard, it was almost as if the monkey-man had chosen to sacrifice his freedom to ensure that of the prisoner. Three prison officers got a grip on him and threw him into the gatehouse, where they secured him in the one-man holding cell under lock and key. Others ran into the street, too late. The truck had reached the end of the lane and turned onto Brixton Hill—no one could even say in which direction. Word was sent out to watch the bridges, with little hope of success. There was no further sign of William James.

By now the entire prison was locked down, the yards cleared, men and women in their separate wings hustled back to their cells without explanation or warning, all internal gates and doors secured against further disruption, the police alerted. The prison superintendent came down to the gatehouse, tight-lipped and narrow-eyed and looking for blood. Somebody's blood. Anyone's blood.

He demanded to see the captured confederate. What he found at the gatehouse was an empty cell, all bars intact, all locks still secured. The occupant had removed himself with an escapologist's speed and apparent ease.

The superintendent turned on all gathered there.

"How could this happen?" he said.

He saw Sebastian.

"You!" he said.

Sebastian said nothing.

At the moment, it seemed like the wisest course of action.

11

WILLIAM JAMES' MOTHER HAD DIED THREE YEARS BEFORE. THE family would have read his request for a visit as a call to conspiracy. These were show folk, a race apart. It was suspected that somehow, despite the scrutiny of the prison censor, they'd exchanged hidden messages in the language of their correspondence. The censor had struck out certain words of unclear meaning, most of them some kind of circus or carnival patois, but the phrase 'look to cousin Jimmy' was now considered to have been of likely significance.

Sebastian attempted to contact his employer. Sir James was out of town, he was told. When pressed, his office revealed that he'd journeyed down to Broadstairs to confer with the ailing Lord Avebury on private business. On hearing this, Sebastian was minded to step back and let someone else break the news. Sir John Lubbock, Baron Avebury, chaired a high level Anglo-German friendship committee founded to counter the dangerous mix of jealousy, alarm, and anxiety that drove the warmongers of both nations. Avebury's heart was failing, and he was too ill to leave Kingsgate Castle. With its clifftop location and thirty-nine steps to the sea, Kingsgate made the perfect location for an unofficial peace conference. The place would be filled with the great and the powerful, along with their staff. Given Sebastian's role in the William James escape, this wasn't the time to go seeking their attention.

When he reached home late that morning, it was to find Frances in a distracted state. There was a letter in her hand. It had arrived in the second delivery and Mrs Jankowski's boy had brought it up from the piano shop.

"Bad news?" Sebastian said.

"No," Frances said, "it's nothing." But her manner suggested otherwise. Sebastian went into his room and changed his spittle-hit shirt, thinking that he could get one more use out of the collar. When he emerged, it was to find Frances still on the same spot, re-reading her note.

"What is it?" he said.

She was about to fob him off again, but then seemed to change her mind.

"It's from the man I met at the museum," she said.

"Which man is that?"

"The one who mistook me."

Sebastian struggled for a moment and then recalled her story of the man who'd taken her for the expedition photographer's American wife.

He said, "And he feels compelled to apologize by letter?"

"He's asking me to meet him for afternoon tea."

"Oh," Sebastian said.

"Yes, oh. What should I do?"

He wasn't sure what to say. A man that Sebastian didn't know had asked his sister-in-law to meet socially. And for some reason this was a matter on which he now had to express an opinion.

He said, "Do you want to go?"

"Why's he asking me such a thing? What does he want?"

"I imagine he wants to know you better."

"Yes, but to what purpose? Look at me. I'm no spring flower. This doesn't happen."

"It's only afternoon tea," Sebastian suggested.

"Of course it isn't just afternoon tea," Frances said. She didn't seem at all flattered. If anything, she seemed angry. Whatever he might say risked making it worse.

She said, "We spoke for two minutes. I gave him no address. But on whatever scant information he drew from our conversation, he tracked me down."

"From the guest list, perhaps? Not a major feat of detection."

"I don't need this, Sebastian," she said. "I have…things I have to do."

He stopped her there. He'd begun to sense what she needed from him, and it wasn't to hear that her problem was a matter of no great consequence.

He said, "Frances Callowhill. You're a kind, generous and loving person. Who wouldn't want your friendship?"

She waved the words away. But he sensed that he'd said the right thing.

"I mean it," he said.

She said, "You're telling me to go."

"May I see the note?"

She gave it up. Sebastian glanced over it with a professional eye. Sometimes handwriting could betray an unreliable personality. This was a normal-looking hand. Signed *Yours Most Sincerely, F. R. Warren*, a name he didn't know.

He said, "I suppose I am telling you to go. I see nothing sinister here. But if you'd care to put him off for a day or two I can look into his circumstances."

"Like one of your lunatics? I don't think so, Sebastian."

"Then go. What harm can it do?"

Frances was about to speak. But then she hesitated, and seemed to change her mind about what she'd intended to say. She took the note back.

"I'll think about it," she said.

"Would you like me to be there?" he asked.

"Good Lord no," she said.

• • •

HE WAS relieved that Frances hadn't taken him up on the offer. Sebastian had enough on his mind, and on his plate. That afternoon, he sought out a detective based at the Kennington Road station. The man was an old-style thief-taker much given to grousing about the deficiencies of modern methods and the follies of his superiors. From him Sebastian learned what was now known to the police; that the evening before the escape, the James family's sideshow wagon and caravans had been removed from a storage yard in Bethnal Green. Not even their solicitor, who handled the affairs of many Romany and show families and was familiar with their ways, had any idea of where they might be.

Or so he claimed.

Sebastian stopped by the pie stand late in the day. He was anticipating some word from his employer, but was surprised to find a message from Frances. *Come as soon as you read this*, it said, giving a location close to Covent Garden market. He sought out the cabbie who'd brought it, and asked, "How old is the note?"

"I couldn't tell you for sure," the cabbie said. "It fell into my hands not half an hour ago."

Come to me as soon as you read this.

It could be interpreted in so many ways, every one of them with an element of urgency.

Within half an hour he'd reached Covent Garden. Sebastian crossed the empty flower market, its debris cleared and its gutters awash after the day's earlier trade. He'd travelled to meet Frances with a sense of foreboding, concerned for her welfare. Was she hurt? Helpless? Had something gone wrong? There was nothing in her note to offer him any further clue.

He found her at the appointed spot on Tavistock Street, behind the Floral Hall. She was on the corner by the offices of The Era magazine.

She stood alone, waiting for him. She wore her best dress and bonnet and seemed well-composed.

"Frances?" he said. "Is everything all right?"

"Come with me," she said.

She was collected, determined, purposeful. She led him down through Covent Garden's back streets toward the busy Strand, where she drew him into a shop doorway. Across the Strand was the forecourt of Charing Cross station. From here they could observe without being seen.

"There."

An omnibus went past, blocking his view for a moment. Then beyond the traffic he saw a man of around thirty-five years old, wearing a loud suit, loitering before the portico of the Station Hotel. He was clearly waiting for someone, checking the passersby.

Frances said, "His name is Frederick Warren."

"Why are we doing this?"

"He thinks I'm bringing you to meet him."

"I don't understand."

"Afternoon tea was a ruse," Frances said. "He set out to charm me. But only in order to get to you."

"So at the museum…"

"That mistake was genuine enough. He knew that the photographer took a bride in California. So when he heard me speak, he jumped to a conclusion. He was very easy to talk to. He questions people for a living. I can see how I told him far more than I should."

Across the street by the hotel, Frederick Warren pulled out a pocket watch and checked the time. His patience was clearly wearing thin.

"A newspaperman," Sebastian said.

"He's willing to pay for information. He's interested in one of the bodies pulled from the seaside fire."

"Is he, by God. Just one?"

"He knows, Sebastian. He's picked up some backstage gossip about the Royal infatuation and he's desperate to confirm any German connection."

"What did you tell him?"

"Nothing. But I got him to tell me plenty, by promising him an introduction to you."

Sebastian looked at Frances. So the invitation had been insincere. Frederick Warren's only interest on her had been as a conduit to the Visitor's Man. She would say that it didn't matter, that she'd attached no importance to his proposal, and that disappointment didn't enter into it. Sebastian would go along with all that. But he felt a rising anger for her. Frances deserved better.

Her eyes were still on the deceiver in the loud suit, but there was a grim satisfaction in her expression. The player had been played.

Sebastian said, "What did he tell you?"

"I know where the family is," Frances said. "After tomorrow's early edition, so will the police and everyone else."

Over there by the hotel, Frederick Warren's patience ran out. She'd kept him on the hook for more than two hours. Warren seemed to decide that his mark had let him down, and to call it quits.

"We've disappointed him," Sebastian said.

"Good," Frances said.

When the newspaperman had disappeared in the direction of Trafalgar Square, they moved out of the doorway.

Sebastian said, "It annoys me that he's trifled with you."

If Frances was downcast, she wasn't letting it show. "He was wasting his time," she said. "I have not wasted mine. We have to get ourselves to the White City before it's too late."

12

Deep under Oxford Street, travelling westbound with Frances on the Central London Railway, Sebastian took a moment to appreciate his sister-in-law's handling of a delicate situation. There would be no end of opportunity for national mischief if certain newspapers learned details of the German prince's squalid demise. They would seize upon the measures being taken to appease the Imperial family. Why were we bending the British knee to the Kaiser? The proprietor of the Harmsworth Press believed in a rich man's right to exert political influence in proportion to his wealth, and on a visit to Germany wrote that "every one of the new factory chimneys here is a gun pointed at England." Now his readers were sighting phantom Zeppelins over the Yorkshire moors.

The darkness hurtled by. Their carriage shook and there was a screech of rim against rail as the tunnel took the slightest of bends. Sebastian glanced at Frances. She was looking down, absorbed in her own thoughts.

Sebastian was angry to think of her being exploited so, to be courted and disappointed in a matter of hours. But he knew that Frances would never show the depth of her feelings. His wife had been the pretty sister, the outgoing one, the one who never sought attention but drew it anyway. Frances was the quieter, younger sibling. In looks she and Elisabeth were not so different, but in manner, worlds apart. When Frances played piano, she never sang; it was as if she was one of life's accompanists, seeking no audience of her own.

He found himself watching her. The young Frances had served as peace-maker and go-between for Elisabeth and their disapproving father. As the years had gone by her life had shaded into theirs, caring for Robert and helping with the household in return for her keep. To Sebastian's eyes she'd changed little over those years, if at all. She must have. But he couldn't see it.

As their train passed somewhere under Marble Arch, she suddenly looked up and said, "I had one useful piece of information out of Mister Warren."

"Really?" Sebastian said. "What was that?"

"William James had a life before the Wild West show. He took on the management of it when his father died. After I left Warren at the Station Hotel I went to the offices of The Era. He thought I'd gone to fetch you. I let him go on thinking so while I went through the obituaries in their back numbers."

The Era was a theatrical weekly, known by many as The Actors' Bible. It covered all of the entertainment world, from the legitimate stage to the saloon and music hall. Frances had met him outside the magazine's building.

Sebastian said, "The obituaries? Why the obituaries?"

"For the father's notice," she said. "As my starting point for information on the rest of the family."

She went on to explain.

Cedric James had been a publican. The James family lived above the large hotel that he managed for the brewery on Salford's Langworthy Road. He'd become besotted with Buffalo Bill's Wild West during its five-month season at Manchester racecourse, but young William's enthusiasm had begun to wane after the tenth compulsory visit. As a dutiful son he'd tagged along with his father to Howard Street, where Colonel Cody had his lodgings. Cedric lifted him up to knock on the door to present their compliments. There William had suffered the embarrassment of a mortifying rebuff from the landlady that had affected his father not at all.

In the brick yard behind the pub Cedric taught himself to spin a lariat, and there he set the girls to practising tricks with their skipping ropes. Every Sunday on Barton Moss he worked on his trick shooting, using raw eggs in place of glass balls for target practice. Before the year was out he'd sold on his license and plowed all of his savings into costumes, props, and a second-hand booth that he repainted himself.

Now known as The One and Only Bronco Billy James, Cedric took the family on the road. His wife Elspeth sat in the cash box, and the children were all brought into the act. It was scrappy at first, but they improved. Cedric's patter was good and audiences were uncritical. They played fairgrounds and carnivals in the summer, graduating to theaters and Music Halls in the winter. Young William was not a natural performer but his sisters, Florence and Lottie, proved to be adept with their .22 rifles. They were joined mid-season by Cedric's brother and his stepson Jack, who showed some talent as an impalement artist. But only some. Jack's knife throwing was best restricted to balloons and playing cards, no human targets. Cedric's brother would leave the life, but Jack and Lottie would later marry.

At the age of twenty, to his father's disappointment and dismay, William dropped out of the act. He'd met a nice girl who wanted no part of a life on the road. They were wed, and he took an office job with a Liverpool shipping firm.

All went well for a while, but after the birth of their daughter his young wife grew depressed and spent some months in a sanatorium. She began refusing his visits. Later she took up with a group of artists, posed naked for various paintings that only avoided scandal by being so avant-garde that they were unrecognisable as nudes, and moved out to live among her new friends on a communal farm in Derbyshire.

"Wait a minute," Sebastian said. "This all sounds a little racy, even for the *Era*."

"You won't find the best parts in the paper," Frances said. "I engaged with some of the theatricals who hang around the front office, waiting for the classifieds to come out. Theirs is a fascinating world, Sebastian. Everyone knows everyone, and they all gossip."

"I can imagine."

"With the least encouragement."

"Don't underestimate the power of your charm."

"You don't need charm. They're actors. Start them off, and you can hardly get a word in."

So the nice girl that William James married had found a new calling as a model and a muse. She was, some might have said, a free spirit. Frances seemed not entirely to disapprove.

William was left alone with a young daughter, Melody. Their life was not easy. His income barely kept them and there was no family on hand for support. All his close relatives were out on the road. He put about that he was a widower, to cover the truth and to deflect curiosity.

When Cedric first fell ill in the winter of 1907, the sisters contacted William. There was a reconciliation in Bolton. Rejoining the travelling show seemed like an answer to William's own difficulties. He was still no great shakes as a performer, but he now had bookkeeping and management skills to help with the business. And instead of a cold rented room with shared bath and a daily commute, here was an extended family where everyone looked out for everyone else, everyone had a part to play, and the care of children was never an issue. So his daughter grew up amongst sideshow and circus folk, while he took pains to ensure that she got at least the rudiments of a formal education.

Shortly after Melody's twelfth birthday her grandfather, The One and Only Bronco Billy James, patriarch and owner of the sideshow, died. William James found himself with no choice but to step up and take over the management of the troupe. Obliged also to take over his father's role in the act; he grew side-whiskers and learned to fire a pistol without blinking. Loading his pistols with birdshot meant that he could break a glass ball in the air without too much need for accuracy. Melody joined the show as a parader, fitted with one of Lottie's cut-down costumes. Over time she would also prove to be a natural sharpshooter.

Sebastian said, "So…that would make Melody James around fourteen years old now?"

"It would seem so."

"Not eight?"

"I'm only going by what I was told. What's so funny?"

"I'm not laughing. When I told William James that one of the unclaimed was an eight-year-old girl, he let me think I'd brought him bad news. When in fact I was telling him that Melody most likely survived. I not only provided the man with the means to escape. I also gave him the will."

They were arriving at Wood Lane station, for the White City.

13

Wood Lane was a one-track, open-air station. As arrivals disembarked the train on one side, returning passengers waited to climb in the other. The Central Line extension had been built to serve the Franco-British Exposition of 1908, when in under two years more than a hundred acres of scrubland had been cleared for a showground of twenty white palaces, each a fairytale structure in plaster and steel surrounded by lagoons, bridges, bandstands, pavilions, galleries, exhibition halls, and the world's largest Olympic stadium. All resembled some magnificent sacred city of the Far East. All was meant to be temporary, including the station. But like the Great White City itself, the line continued in use.

Few people alighted from the train with Sebastian and Frances, and even fewer climbed on board. This was outside the exhibition season and the showgrounds were deserted, save for the workforce tearing down last summer's Latin expo and rebuilding for the Anglo-American next year.

The big gates were closed. However their destination was not the park itself, but a service area that was screened from public view behind the pleasure gardens. It was on this land that the showground's transient workers were allowed to pitch their tents and caravans for the term of their engagement.

In high season the entire plot would be teeming like a bazaar. For now only a corner of the hidden site was occupied. Those few travellers in residence had crammed their vans and vehicles together, as if to make a village. There were several horses tethered and grazing on the common land outside its boundary.

All was quiet. No one challenged them as they made their way through. Sebastian noted that the site was not particularly well-cared for. Trash blew around, and the most-used thoroughfare had been trampled into mud. Frances raised her skirts a few inches and made no complaint.

Between two wagons Sebastian spied a man working on a light motor lorry, a Darracq truck that had seen some hard use. The man was standing with a bucket in his hand, painting over a design on the side of the truck's canvas canopy. As they approached, Sebastian caught a whiff of the glue-size that scene painters used. This painter's coverage was hasty and uneven. Some of the old design was still showing through.

Sebastian hailed him. The man looked back over his shoulder, without any expression of welcome.

"I'm looking for the James family," Sebastian said.

"No one of that name here." He spoke with an unusual accent, and turned back to his work to end the conversation.

"Are you sure?" Sebastian said. "Because I'd swear that's the name you're in the process of painting out."

The man sloshed on more paint, and pretended not to hear. He was small, compact, powerful, and bald. Much like the description of the man who had switched clothes with William James and subsequently disappeared from inside a locked prison cell.

Sebastian said, "I'm not your enemy. I arranged for William James' mother to visit the prison. Imagine how popular that's made me."

"Bad mistake," the man said without turning around.

"Does it not even buy me a hearing?"

"Can't help you."

Sebastian noted the man's sailor tattoos. "Let me guess," he said. "Escapology?"

The man set down his paint bucket and laid his brush across the rim. Without taking his eyes off Sebastian, he calmly rolled down his sleeves.

"What's your business?" he said.

"It concerns Melody James."

Sebastian was aware of the glance he was getting from Frances, but he kept eyes on his man.

He went on, "The news of her survival drove him to escape. I know there's more to the night of the fire than William was prepared to say. I'm not the police, but you can be sure they won't be far behind me. Is he here?"

Silence.

Frances said, "Please tell us. Is he here?"

Her voice, added to Sebastian's appeal, had an effect. After several long seconds, the man gave the slightest shake of his head. It was more convincing than any verbose denial.

Sebastian said. "You show folk, you keep it all amongst yourselves. When they catch him—and they will—that kind of silence will hang him. All very well, if he deserves it. But does he? He promised me the truth in exchange for my help. He got my help, and a bargain's a bargain. Or does that mean nothing in your world?"

No response.

Sebastian said, "He told me that he didn't cause the fire. If that's the case, I need to know."

The man considered for a moment. Then he picked up a rag to wipe off his hands, and cocked his head for them to follow. He led the way into the maze of tents and wagons. Sebastian and Frances exchanged a glance, and went after.

They ducked under washing lines, in and out of drying sheets. At a plain-sided wooden van, also newly repainted, the man stopped and knocked.

"Lottie?" he called.

The door was opened. It was no Lottie, but a man of around thirty who stood there in shirtsleeves and braces. He had strong brows, a weak chin. He looked down from the van, deeply suspicious of these strangers in the camp.

"Who's this?" he said.

"This one says he has news of Melody," the bald man said.

Without taking his eyes from Sebastian and Frances, the shirtsleeved man called back over his shoulder.

"Lottie!"

He came down the wooden steps from the van. After him, two women emerged—one dark, one fair. The fair one was a striking beauty, by fairground standards. Sisters with no more than a year or two between them, was Sebastian's guess.

"He's talking about Melody," the shirtsleeved man said.

"Our Melody's gone," the dark one said. "Leave us be."

The bald man was backing away. "You call me if you need me, Lottie," he said.

"We're all right," the dark one said. "Jack's here."

If the dark one was Lottie, then the fair one must be Florence. And the shirtsleeves would be Jack, Lottie's husband.

Florence spoke up.

"If you're from the newspapers," she said, "leave while you can. We ran off the last one."

Frances chipped in again. "He's not a reporter," she said.

"My name's Sebastian Becker, and this is Miss Callowhill. I'm neither a reporter nor the police. I work for the Lord Chancellor's office and I'm looking for a way to resolve this without anyone else being hurt. William James is your uncle?"

"You're wasting your time," Lottie said. "We haven't seen him."

"I suspect you've seen him, but I'm ready to believe he isn't here now. Not with the police on his tail and a missing daughter to find."

"Our Melody's dead," Florence said.

"We all know that's not true. Yet he's willing to let the authorities believe it, and to shoulder the blame for all those others. Why would a man do that? He named Kit Strong. Is that who's to blame? And if he is, why not say so?"

At the mention of Kit Strong, Florence spat. He heard a sharp intake of breath from Frances. Without looking down, he reached for her hand and squeezed it.

"A popular company member," Sebastian said, and glanced at the side of the wagon. "I see you took extra care to paint his name out. Two coats."

"Throw them off the yard, Jack," Lottie said.

"Not necessary," Sebastian said as he gave a nod to Frances for them to back away.

The three were beginning to argue as Sebastian and Frances departed. He couldn't pick up their words but they spoke in low and passionate tones that sounded almost vicious in their intensity. With Sebastian leading the way he and Frances followed the same route out, through the hanging laundry and past the battered Darracq.

The escapologist had picked up his brush again, and was completing the show truck's new anonymity.

Sebastian said, "Neat trick with the manacles, by the way."

"I wouldn't know what you mean."

Frances broke away from Sebastian and pushed her way in between painter and canvas, so close that he had to draw his arm back or risk catching her with the brush.

She said, "I know you people like to settle your own scores. But this is beyond reason. We could have just turned you all in to the police. Hasn't Mister Becker shown you where his sympathy lies?"

He looked down, she was looking up. He was trapped and awkward and suddenly his position seemed just a little ridiculous.

The man looked back at Sebastian.

He said, "What's Kit Strong to you?"

"Apparently he's the devil incarnate," Sebastian said. "Or so William James seemed to think. If he played a part in the fire, and he's somehow using Melody to force your boss to accept the blame, you'll appreciate my curiosity."

The man looked pointedly at Frances until she stepped out of the way.

Then as he dipped his brush in the paint he said, "I'll be taking my supper in the snug at the Royal Hotel."

Sebastian could see that Frances was about to reply, and gave her a warning look. She understood immediately, and said nothing. This was a breakthrough, of a kind. There was nothing more to be achieved right now, and everything to lose.

They'd passed the Royal Hotel on their way from the station. It was a big old corner public house, yellow brick and white cornerstones, the kind they built by the hundred in Nelson's day.

As they walked out across the open green, through the grazing horses and away from the camp, Sebastian said, "I expect we'll be paying for his supper."

"Then let's hope he can sing," Frances said.

14

He came in. He sat.

"You are clever people," he said.

They faced each other across the table. The seats were old leather, the walls lined with English oak. Though the electric fixtures were modern, oxblood panelling and a century of candle smoke sucked in their light to create a gloom that was permanent and deep.

Frances said, "We don't know your name."

"My name is Jencsik, so they call me Jimmy." He looked at Sebastian. "You guessed well. Escapes and magic. My speciality was the rope tie escape, until these hands..." He held them up, as if showing invisible shackles. They were strong hands, but bent out of shape, the knuckles enlarged with arthritis.

"But you can still pick a lock and escape from a cell."

Jencsik shrugged, as if such feats were nothing special. He said, "The first Mister James took me on when I could no longer perform. I would never betray Cedric's kindness. I would never betray this family."

"I'm not asking you to," Sebastian said.

"Then what *are* you asking?"

"I want to hear about Kit Strong. Who he is. How he features in this tale. And what there is between him and William James."

"What William is doing...I can't say it's wise. But he has his reasons. I'll tell you nothing that would hinder him."

"That's fair."

And so Stefan Jencsik, the Hungarian-born former street magician and escapologist known to the family as Cousin Jimmy, began his tale with the death of Cedric James.

Cedric had been unwell, on and off, for at least a couple of years, but he was such a towering and exuberant figure that no one could imagine him coming to any permanent grief. He'd refused to see doctors, considering them quacks and a waste of money. Through episodes of illness he medicated himself with brandy and cigars, in what he considered to be true Old West style. It hastened his end just as surely as it killed those old cowboys. The cause of his death was recorded as congestive heart failure. Though it might have been foreseen it was relatively sudden, and it left the family on the road with dates to fulfil.

Cedric was buried in Weaste Cemetery, close to the old family home on Langworthy Road. Notice of the funeral was placed in the World's Fair newspaper, and over two hundred people attended. The Showmen's Guild ran a collection that paid for the stone, which featured crossed pistols and a Stetson hat.

Cedric had been a natural showman, an instinctive manager, a lover of crowds who related easily to total strangers. His confidence had been enormous. He wanted to be a cowboy, so he became one. A Salford cowboy, whose wide Missouri was the River Irwell, and whose accent owed more to the cotton mill than to the cotton fields.

His eldest child, though now in charge, was different in almost every way. William was meticulous, analytical, a worrier. In place of Cedric's confidence, he struggled with a tormenting sense of responsibility. He took the troupe back onto the road to fulfil its engagements, but the act was now a man short. To William's analytical mind the show was no longer balanced.

With no instinct to follow, he took to studying other Wild West acts. It seemed to him that all the other shows had some unique feature to offer.

"He thought about adding horses and riders," Jencsik said. "He'd seen Johnny Swallow's new act in Wolverhampton and thought an arena show might be the way to go. Imagine that. How spectacular! But how expensive, and impractical. Good for a circus, but no good for a sideshow or the music hall. For the James family it was always the sideshows in summer, halls and theaters in the winter. That was the business he knew. But how to stand out? His father was a big man with a big personality. William was something else. He was raised in the life, but he left it as soon as he could. He was much happier as a clerk than as a cowboy. But now he had to make it work or see the family broken up."

William tried several strategies, none of which succeeded. He persuaded Jack to grow his hair and stain his skin to become an Indian Chief, and dug deep into their operating capital to order a buckskin suit and feather headdress from a costumier in Edinburgh. The effect was impressive, but the war bonnet and regalia raised expectations that could never be met by Jack's limited knife throwing skills. Also, Jack had a temper and was too easily provoked by hecklers into giving the game away. After a month of Jack parading as The Son of Geronimo, popping his balloons and then arguing in a broad Lancashire accent with every beer-fuelled lout who found it funny, William sold on the costume and looked for something else.

For a while they were joined by a Sheffield-born veteran who went by the name of Wes Riding. He'd toured with Wild Harry from Walsall and he'd strummed a guitar in Prairie Bob's Band, but again, he was not the answer. He'd lost the knack, he'd lost his edge, and worse than that he'd lost an eye, which made him lethal with a bullwhip.

Then William got to hear of Kit Strong.

It had to be borne in mind that every Wild West show in the British Isles claimed a connection with Buffalo Bill. Colonel Bill Cody had captivated the nation with three major tours of *Buffalo Bill's Wild West* in a period that spanned a quarter of a century, drawing crowds of anywhere up to 5,000 a day and creating a legacy of British-born imitators, impersonators, and emulators, from the North Country dynasty of Texas Bill Shufflebottom down to the smallest carnival dog and pony show. Cody was their validation. They'd all ridden with Buffalo Bill, or they'd come over on the boat with Buffalo Bill, and some of them even claimed to *be* Buffalo Bill.

But here in Kit Strong, by all accounts, was the real thing. A genuine American roper, rider and sharpshooter, over six feet tall, who'd arrived with William Cody's 1903 tour. He'd been left behind when the company sailed for home, after a serious riding accident that had taken him out of the show before the tour ended. His injuries had been severe, his recovery lengthy.

Scarred and with one leg shorter than the other, he was currently making a living as a wrestler. Over the years he'd worked with a few Western shows, but had stayed with none of them for long.

That might not be a good sign. A bitter man could be hard to deal with. But William's thinking was that if he could set the right conditions, and if Kit Strong could straighten himself out, he'd be a valuable novelty and a considerable attraction. And there was always a saving to be made when buying damaged goods.

At the time, Strong had a two-weeks' engagement at the Holborn Empire. William James went down to see him.

"I drove William down in the truck," Jencsik said. "I was there when they first met. I saw it all."

Jencsik explained that he himself had boxed a little in his early days, mostly in the booths and once in a sporting club, but he'd never wrestled. Professional wrestling was then, as ever, athletic showmanship in the guise of a sport. Any contest of pure technique tended to be brief and dull, drawing cries from the audience of "Fake!" or a sung chorus of "Dear Old Pals" as two well-matched fighters waltzed around the ring in a Graeco-Roman hold that each struggled endlessly to break. A good exhibition wrestler knew that he was there to entertain, and would outdraw a sportsman any day of the week.

Even better, a cheating bad boy—as Kit Strong would prove to be— could stir the paying public with all manner of broken holds, head-spins, and devious monkey tricks performed on the referee's blind side. People loved their heroes, but they loved their villains even more.

In Holborn, William James bought tickets for the evening's event. He and Jimmy took supper in a local pub and then joined the crowd heading in for the opening bout.

It was Music Hall, pure Music Hall. The featured grapplers at the Empire were almost all foreigners—Poles, Italians, Germans, Turks—with Kit Strong the sole American on the bill. His was the second bout. Strong had a hard, lean physique, in contrast to his heavily-muscled opponent. The style was catch-as-catch-can. The Turks were notorious for covering their skin with a greasy substance that only became slippery as they warmed up. Strong countered with the ruse of dragging his opponent around the canvas, flipping him over and dragging some more until the dust and grit had scoured the grease off. The crowd booed him, but more to express their enthusiasm than any serious disapproval.

At one point, he threw the referee into the orchestra. The referee climbed back into the ring, and for the rest of the round Kit Strong fought with both men at once until the bout ended in glorious chaos.

While the contests continued, William James sent a note to the stage door. He and Jencsik were admitted to the dressing rooms a few minutes later.

Jencsik paused here.

"I try to remember my first impression," he said.

Strong looked much older close-to, he recalled. His hair was long and thin, secured by a headband for the ring. His face was drawn, his eyes narrow and hard to read. But that might have been exhaustion; the sustained play of brutality had clearly taken all that he had. Reclining on the dressing room's threadbare sofa in an equally threadbare robe, he was a somewhat intimidating figure. Very slow-speaking, very knowing, and with the air of a man who had perhaps travelled a little too far and seen a few bad sights too many.

He listened to William James' proposal.

"Is there money?" he interrupted to ask.

William James confirmed that there was money.

"I am not averse to money," was all he would say to that. "Carry on."

William James would later say that he believed he had the advantage in negotiation; that Strong must surely see the deal that he was being offered as a welcome escape from the life he was leading. Strong was no longer a young man, and he lived with old injuries. Even if the rough-housing in the ring was exaggerated for effect, it was still brutal.

Watching in silence from the back of the dressing room, Jencsik saw it differently.

Strong was courteous and sober. He presented himself well and seemed interested and intelligent. William James seemed anxious and eager, as if he'd glimpsed in Strong their salvation and was blind to everything else.

Kit Strong let his visitor describe the act and lay out his plans for the family's future, and then said a strange thing.

Jencsik claimed to remember it word for word.

He said, "William James. If we do this, there's something you have to understand. It's only fair to warn you that I'll change my nature for no man.

I seem to challenge people without even thinking about it, and I expect I'll challenge you. Keeping me in line is your job, not mine, and I'll rely on you for that. Don't let me down. Because if things go bad and I'm out of control, you'll probably have to shoot me to stop me. And I don't think either of us wants that."

William nodded in agreement, but Jencsik could see that he didn't really know what to make of this. Then they talked money. Kit Strong named a figure that was higher than William James felt able to pay. He justified it by saying he had expenses relating to the injuries he'd sustained in the riding accident that had—in his own words—left him washed-up and abandoned in England.

Jencsik said, "They didn't make a deal there and then, but shook hands and William said he'd have to consider. Kit Strong said, 'You think it over,' and there was a look in his eyes…it wasn't a friendly look, though his manner was friendly enough. He seemed amused, as if he'd read his man with too much ease. Now he could see all the way to a future that William was failing to imagine.

"I know that William had some reservations. When you bring a new member into a family troupe, it's important that they fit in. But I don't think his reservations went far enough. Kit Strong didn't seem to me like a man who would fit in anywhere."

After the interview they drove back north. A bad week in Doncaster followed. Their losses left William James minded to meet Kit Strong's terms. He cabled Strong a week later. Strong joined them at the end of the month, and so it began.

Jencsik said, "Look. The family has my love and my loyalty, but I'm not a James. They took me in and though I've travelled with them for ten years or more, when it comes to family secrets I'm on the outside. But this I know. Kit Strong went on to corrupt Melody James in plain sight of all and suspected by none, until William James faced him down on the night of the fire. If the child lives, she's with Kit Strong; and wherever they are, William James won't be far behind."

Somewhere deep in the hotel, a clock was chiming the hour. Jencsik abruptly rose to his feet.

Sebastian said, "Do you know how the fire was started?"

"I do not."

Frances said, "Can you tell us what happened between them?"

"I have to go," Jencsik said.

In an instant his manner had switched from one of candour to evasion. Sebastian had caught his momentary reaction to the clock chime, and believed that he knew why.

"Thank you for your time," Sebastian said.

Jencsik gave a bow of his head, first to Sebastian and then to Frances.

"I have enjoyed our conversation," he said. "Good evening to you."

He stepped out of the snug and then, through the bar counter, could be seen quickly crossing the saloon and leaving the hotel.

When he'd gone, Frances said, "He didn't get his supper."

"He didn't come here to eat," Sebastian said.

"But—"

"He came here to keep us occupied for an hour. That's all it takes for practised travellers to get themselves on the road. If we call in the police now, there'll be nothing to find. They're gone, and that's it."

15

HE WASN'T WRONG. WHERE THE TRUCK AND THE WAGONS HAD stood only a short time before, there was now bare ground.

As they waited for their train back into town, Frances said, "What will you do now, Sebastian?"

"I don't know," he admitted. "The closer I look, the harder it is to say. It's gone from an open-and-shut case to an unwelcome tangle of intrigue. If Kit Strong's the guilty party, why not say so?"

"An American villain. Even better."

"You know what I mean."

"Trust me, I'm serious. If there's one thing the British can hate more than a murderer, it's a foreigner."

"Point the finger at an American to keep the Kaiser happy. Offend an ally to appease an enemy. I can't see my masters embracing that."

"They're not your masters, Sebastian. They're your employers. It's not as if they own your soul."

As their train arrived Sebastian refrained from pointing out that those employers were keeping both of their souls fed and clothed. This was no time to be critical of Frances. Today she'd risen above personal disappointment to display a resourcefulness and speed of thought that would have put a Scotland Yard man to shame.

The train arrived almost empty, and they had a carriage to themselves. It was well into the evening now. Sebastian was thinking that they'd stop at the George on Borough High Street for some supper, when Frances suddenly said, "I can imagine a reason for his silence."

"Whose?"

"William James. There'll be a reason why he'd rather run from justice than see the truth about Kit Strong made public, whatever that truth may be."

"And that would be?"

"She's his daughter, Sebastian. We don't know what she did, or what was done to her. A father might want to keep it that way."

16

Sebastian stood on the pavement before the mansion block on Devonshire Street, a letter of introduction in his hand. This was Doctor country. Harley Street was just around the corner, and it was brass plates and consulting-rooms all the way from here to Regents' Park. This block was residential, with residents who were eminent, well-heeled, and mostly retired.

The porter sized him up before directing him to the apartments he was seeking. The lift was in use, so he took the stairs.

Some days had passed, and the refusal of those on high to concern themselves with detail meant that Sebastian managed to evade any significant share of the blame for the escape of William James. He might eventually be called to account, but in the meantime more obvious heads would roll. Though he rarely felt it so, there was sometimes an advantage to working 'off the books'.

Meanwhile the fugitive had been spotted in Glasgow, trying to get a passage on a ship. Or so it was reported. Some doubted the information, but no one was inclined to take any chances. With the cooperation of the Allan Line Steamship Company the police set a trap, but William James didn't show up. Now they'd increased the watch on all the ports and put a price on his head.

Reaching the landing at the top of the stairs, Sebastian was remembering words of warning from Sir James Crichton Browne.

Forbes Winslow, the Alienist? Step carefully, Sebastian. He has a reputa-tion for upsetting justice with his interpretations of the lunacy laws. Remember Sapido? The Belgian? Pot-shots at the Prince of Wales? It was Winslow's advice that got him off.

He knocked, a woman answered. A minute later Sebastian was shown into the presence of a florid, heavily-built man of around seventy years. He sported wide, white whiskers and round wire eyeglasses. He was seated at a broad desk in a buttoned leather swivel chair, which he turned around to face Sebastian. He did not rise.

"Doctor Winslow," Sebastian said, offering his letter. "My credentials."

Winslow took an opener from his desk, slit open the envelope, and extracted the paper. As he was reading, he compressed his lips together and breathed heavily through his nose. When he'd done, he refolded the paper with delicate moves of his hands.

"Doctor Crichton Browne," he said. "My greatest respects to that gentle-man. How can I help you?"

"Do you recall the name of Kit Strong?"

"I think I may."

"In November 1903 he took part in an endurance race. Two of Buffalo Bill's horsemen against two motor cycles. It was at an indoor venue, the Agricultural Hall in Islington. The event was covered by *The Illustrated London News*. You were a visitor on the fourth day?"

"If I seem circumspect in my replies, Mister Becker, it's because I'm waiting to see where this is going."

"There was an accident. Kit Strong was badly injured. He didn't finish the race."

"That is so."

"The *News* gives only the barest details. Can you tell me what happened?"

"Can you tell me why I should?"

"Our paths may cross and I've heard it claimed that he's a dangerous man," Sebastian said. "But that's all I know of him."

"And after ten years you think I may be able to give you some special insight into his character?"

"I'm not asking for insight, just trying to piece the facts together. The article said you gave medical help at the scene."

Winslow reached back and rang a small bell on his desk. Sebastian thought that he was about to be ejected, but when the woman appeared Winslow asked her to bring them some tea. Then he took off his spectacles, rubbed at his eyes, and replaced the spectacles before going on.

"The race was an attempt to repeat a popular stunt from an earlier tour," Winslow said. "Back in 1887, Broncho Charlie Miller and Marve Beardsley had ridden eight hours a day, six days straight, against two champion bicyclists. They rode in half-hour relays with frequent changes of horse. It was a marathon intended to prove the endurance of the riders, not to exhaust their mounts. An estimated fifteen thousand spectators showed up to the Agricultural Hall over the week to cheer them on. At that time I was one of them.

"In 1903 the Matchless Motorcycle Company hosted a new version of the challenge with Kit Strong as one of the horsemen. The motorcycles were to race on a sloping board track, with the horses running on dirt alongside.

"I wasn't there on the first day, but I'm told that on this occasion nothing went smoothly. Mechanical problems delayed the start, and then the sudden noise of the motorcycle engines spooked the Western ponies. After one of the mustangs bucked and almost threw its rider into the crowd, there was talk of abandoning the event. But it went ahead, and the air of danger meant a daily increase in the number of those who came to watch. Rising to the occasion, the riders grew more daring.

"More than fifty horses were used. Two died. Then, around halfway through day four, a dog got through the enclosure and onto the outer dirt track during one of Kit Strong's stints in the saddle. It ran ahead of the galloping pony, tongue out, ears flapping, causing the jet black mare to swerve and leap the barrier onto the wooden track. Motorcycle and animal collided. All went down with an almighty crash, and Kit Strong was crushed under his horse."

Sebastian said, "You came to his aid."

"I may be a psychiatrist by profession, but I'm still a doctor by training."

"Can you tell me anything further? I don't mean about the accident. I'm interested in his recovery and any later dealings you had with him."

"I fear not. Given that he was my patient."

"Come, Doctor Winslow. You stepped out of a crowd and gave him first aid. I don't think it's quite the same thing."

"Now now, Mister Becker. My feelings of respect for Sir James don't overcome my reservations about the nature of his office."

"No one is seeking to take over anyone's fortune, if that's what you're thinking," Sebastian said. "If I tell you that there's no profit in question, and that a man's liberty and possibly his life are at risk…"

"Kit Strong's?"

"Another's."

"Has he done someone harm?"

"That would be of no surprise to you?"

Winslow considered for a few moments. Clearly the notion of Kit Strong as a danger to others did not strike him as unlikely. Sebastian waited.

"Strong's injuries were quite severe," Winslow said. "His pelvis was crushed under the horse. He also had a depressed rib fracture with lung herniation. I did what I could for him at the scene, but I tell you the truth. I never expected him to survive the journey to the hospital."

He went on to explain that the other rider had completed the day's competition alone; a hundred miles, by the judges' count. But the challenge was then abandoned, to the secret relief of all involved.

Forbes Winslow had handed Kit Strong over to the care of others, but had kept an interest in his progress.

"His recovery took months. He was in constant pain. You're correct, he was never my patient, but out of a sense of professional duty I paid him a visit. At the time he was in a bitter depression because the Wild West show had returned to America without him. Though what else he expected to happen when he was too ill to travel, I don't know. Colonel Cody had left money toward his treatment, but that was quickly used up. Strong was living as a charity case on the cripples' ward because he had no funds and nowhere else to go."

"Yet he made a full recovery."

"You may call it a recovery."

"Enough to make a living in the wrestling ring."

"By dint of morphine and force of will."

"Morphine?" Sebastian said.

"Morphine," Forbes Winslow confirmed. "Administered in emergency, and continued out of necessity. However much they gave him, I believe he obtained more. He dulled his pain and treated his injured body like a beast to be whipped into service and driven to its limits.

"You should have heard him. 'See,' he said, and swung his feet off his bed. He wouldn't let me help him stand. He said, 'They forbid me to rise, yet here I am. They tell me patience before I can walk, and yet I move.' He stood there with his arms outspread. A damaged creature with no Doctor Frankenstein to raise him, nothing to hold him up other than the power of his own will."

Winslow leaned forward, looking Sebastian straight in the eyes. The light caught and reflected from his spectacles, concealing his own.

He said, "You may call it a full recovery. I would call it a defiance of nature. Defy nature, and you will always pay a price."

"I take it he became an addict."

Winslow sat back. "I expect so. As an alternative to constant, destructive pain. Like stopping your ears to the scream of a broken engine as you push it to the extreme."

"When did you see him last?"

"That was my one and only visit. What I saw was a morphine-driven monster with a grudge against the world in general, and Colonel Cody in particular. I never saw him again after that."

"I appreciate your help."

"It was a long time ago. I can imagine him capable of something terrible. What has he done?"

"That's exactly what I'm trying to establish."

17

Sebastian recalled the time when Robert was a boy, and they'd played host to former prize fighter Tom Sayers in their Philadelphia home. Robert's obsession then had been with dime novels, and Sebastian was struck by the wonder in his eyes when Sayers had told him that he was now shaking the hand that once shook the hand of Buffalo Bill. Frances had been little more than a girl herself. Sebastian remembered how she'd blushed and become flustered around Sayers, that figure of bruised and hulking masculinity.

After their arrival in England, Robert had switched his interest to British story papers and magazines. The Buffalo Bill stories that he found in London were either reprints or locally-written versions of the adventures, all of which he considered inauthentic and unworthy of collection. Conan Doyle and Rider Haggard absorbed him for a while, then Wodehouse, Kipling, and Austin Philips, until his interest suddenly switched again, this time to South American Beetles.

But while it lasted, Robert had become well known to newsstand owners and magazine sellers of the area. It was, ironically, through the W H Smiths lady on Waterloo Station—albeit indirectly—that Sebastian learned of William James' departure from 'these shores'.

"Sebastian," Frances said. "You should see this."

She handed him a copy of *The Era*, open at one of the pages of classified advertisements.

"Hardly your usual reading," he said.

"I'm acquiring a taste for it," she said. "Actually I was looking for any mention of Kit Strong, since he has to make a living and he has no reason to hide. The Smiths lady saved this one for me. Read where I marked."

Sebastian read *Pavilion Theatre, Renfield Street, Glasgow. By Kind Permission of the Management. Twice nightly from Tuesday to Saturday, the ABSOLUTELY FINAL APPEARANCE on these shores of KIT STRONG the COWBOY WONDER, late of BUFFALO BILL'S WILD WEST, with KID BILLY the BOY APPRENTICE in a living exhibition of trick roping, sharpshooting, knife throwing & gunplay. Last chance to see the famous TOMAHAWKS OF DEATH, prior to the Pennsylvania native's departure to join V. C. Seavers YOUNG BUFFALO troupe on its tour of the Eastern states. Kid Billy will demonstrate unrivalled rifle skills with the impossible and spectacular POKER HAND SPLIT.*

Frances said, "The boy apprentice. Could that be Melody?"

It was not an unreasonable guess. Melody James was young enough to pass as a boy. And Sebastian had learned that her speciality, developed in the act, was for Strong to fan a poker hand of five cards which she'd then split edge-on with a single rifle shot. The escapologist Jencsik had claimed that Strong corrupted her, but he had not detailed how. This seemed to confirm that Melody was most likely alive, and that she was travelling with the American. Sebastian began to understand something of the torment that must be felt by William James.

"When was this?" Sebastian said. He turned the magazine back and forth, looking for a date.

"It's three weeks old," Frances said. "They'll have sailed by now."

Sebastian read the item again, and as he was reading, Frances added, "It was a left-over copy. She gave it to me for nothing."

"He was seen in Glasgow," Sebastian said.

"Who?"

"William James." The Glasgow sighting made sense now. "He'll have missed them in Glasgow, so he was trying to book a passage to America. I dismissed the sighting because I couldn't imagine he'd flee the country and leave his daughter in Kit Strong's hands. But he wasn't trying to flee the country. He was trying to follow them."

"It says here that Kit Strong had an engagement waiting."

"Which no doubt paid for their passage. If he really is joining the Seavers troupe, then a determined man will only need a tour schedule to find him."

Pennsylvania (2)
August 1913

18

"Hey, Mister Pecker. Jonas Flynn says there's a body all ready for you to look at. You want me to show you where?"

"I know where to go," Sebastian said. "Thank you."

If The Flea had another name, no one seemed to use it. And everyone in town seemed to know her. She'd spring into your presence and keep talking until someone, usually her father, intervened and told her to leave. Then she'd skip off, undaunted, completely happy.

"You like my new dress?"

"It's very pretty."

"Momma made it from a feed sack. You'd never think it, would you?"

"I would not."

"*Flea!*" came her father's voice from the lobby downstairs.

"I have to go now," she said, and went.

Sebastian stepped back into his room, and straightened his few possessions before leaving for the funeral parlor.

He'd been attempting to write a letter home to Frances, and finding it an unexpected struggle. What kind of tone would be appropriate? Not the one he used in reports to his employer, for sure. He was painfully aware that his sister-in-law's education was superior to his own, and that nothing undermined respect for a person more surely than ignorance betrayed through the written word.

He'd deal with it later. Now he needed to walk up South Main, which was growing more familiar to him every day.

Flynn & Jones operated a storefront business. They had no chapel, as such, with viewings and funerals mostly being conducted in the homes of the deceased. Though they offered the only mortuary services in town, the town was a small one and some kind of a sideline was essential to making a steady living. While Jonas Flynn combined the duties of undertaker and coroner, the funeral parlor also served as a furniture showroom. The hearse doubled as an ambulance. When not making coffins, the workshop could frame your diploma. Jean Flynn taught music, daughters Ruby and Janie sang in church, and for recreation the entire family was involved in local amateur dramatics.

The undertaking rooms were behind the showroom where rockers and recliners were available for visiting mourners to try and, if so inclined, buy. Sebastian waited for as long as it took for Jonas Flynn to remove his frock coat and put on an embalming apron, and then was led behind the scenes.

"You need to see the body before I get the photographer in," Flynn said. "I want to be sure I got the features right for you."

The undertaking room was light and cool, with walls of plain tile like the buttery in a dairy. Its windows were set high, and of frosted glass.

The body lay on a long table, sheeted to the chest. The head was slightly raised on a block, and the cabinet card photograph had been propped alongside it for comparison.

Flynn had repaired the exit wound with wax. The face had then been painted and powdered over to blend in the new work. The forehead was too smooth, with a slight bump showing. The eyes were closed, the jaw drawn up with a suture.

"Yes?" Jonas Flynn said.

Sebastian realised that he'd fallen into silent contemplation, and for a few moments he'd lost track of time.

Jonas Flynn added, "If you're happy, I'll dress him in the clean shirt from his luggage. I'll have to use the same suit. There's no other."

Sebastian looked from corpse to card, from card to corpse.

"Is the face maybe a little too gaunt?" he said.

"I can pack his cheeks and make it more like the picture."

"The people we're doing it for, the picture's all they'll know," Sebastian said. "Just don't spend any more money."

"I can deal with that."

"All right," Sebastian said. "Make the adjustment and then call the photographer. I won't need to see him again."

Jonas Flynn reached for his tray of tools. He said, "After I've dressed him, I'll send over his things. Will you speak at the funeral?"

"Me?"

"Since you're paying for it."

Sebastian hadn't anticipated this, but could see the reasoning behind the suggestion. William James might not have a single friend in the American continent but Sebastian had, at least, known and spoken to the man, and it qualified him more than any other.

"Just as long as no one expects too much," he said.

He left the undertaker to his work, and walked the short distance back to his hotel.

Sheriff Frank Smith was pursuing the theory that William James might have been gambling in the Capitol's saloon on the evening before the murder. One report told of a stranger on a winning streak, who claimed to feel unwell and retired from the game when his luck began to turn. Though such a move would make eminent sense to any normal person, to a diehard gambler it would be an ungentlemanly action, denying others the chance to win their money back.

Smith wondered if William James had been followed upstairs by a card player with a grievance. Though the room had shown no sign of being ransacked, no money had been found there either.

Sebastian had another theory, which for reasons of his own he had chosen not to share.

Back at the Continental, he again set out pen and paper. He then spent the next quarter-hour attempting to achieve the frame of mind necessary to begin writing. He was sitting at the table with his back to the door. It occurred to him that he was all but recreating the murder scene in his own room, which did little to help.

He cleaned his shoes. He arranged his toilet kit. He paced.

William James had been a shipping clerk, once. The evidence suggested that after failing to intercept Kit Strong on the steamer out of Glasgow, he'd used contacts in the trade to arrange a stealthy passage out of Liverpool. No ticketing, no documentation, a false name on the manifest. The murderer Crippen had been caught at sea by Marconi's radio, but the technology was yet to be developed that could run down a ghost.

Eventually, Sebastian once more pulled out the chair and sat.

He wrote:

> *Dear Frances.*
>
> *I am writing from a small town in Penn. where there have been developments that I don't want to get into right now. When I finally get to explain, I know you will understand why. I should tell you that when I landed in New York I sent a note to your father requesting an interview. When I am done here I intend to go to Philadelphia where the Pinkerton office has some back-pay for me from my coalfields work, being danger money that I did not know was owed. Once there I hope to have a reply from your father waiting. I dont expect him to think any more of me than he ever did but I want to look him in the eye and tell him how Elisabeth lived and died and how proud he should be of his grandson. If there is anything you want me to say to him, write to me care of The Keystone Hotel or at Pinkertons National Detective Agency, No 45 South Third Street, and I should no doubt pick it up when I get there. I wrote to him last year of our family tragedy and he never replied then, but Im hoping that a face to face visit will be harder for him to refuse.*
>
> *I am,*
> *Your ever loving,*
> *Sebastian.*

Having written those last lines, he was seized by doubt. Ever loving? Was that appropriate? Or too intimate? Yet to scratch it out and write something else would only make it worse.

He took another sheet and wrote the entire letter over again, this time ending it with the valediction *affectionately yours*. But was that any better? Then he noticed that this time he'd misspelled *tragedy*.

So he crumpled up the second version and quickly folded and sealed the first, before he could change his mind.

He took the letter downstairs, looking to give it to The Flea as an errand, but there found Doc Sparks coming into the hotel from the street.

"Something for you," the Under Sheriff said, and held out a sheaf of typewriter paper bound up with a ribbon like a lawyer's bundle.

Sebastian took it, and looked at the first page. With a surge of excitement he realised that it was a typed transcript of a document from the hand of William James. The very document retrieved from under the body at the murder scene.

"Sorry it's so faint," Doc Sparks said. "That's a second carbon."

"And the original?"

"That's evidence. The sheriff wants you to read the copy and then he wants it back. You see anything in there that could have bearing on his murder, he'll need to know. As far as we can make out, it's all about things that happened back home."

Sebastian had already seen the opening line.

To Mr Sebastian Becker, it read. *A promise kept.*

The Testament of William James (1)

19

LET ME FIRST SAY HOW MUCH I REGRET DECEIVING YOU. OUT OF all who dealt with me, your behavior was the closest to any form of kindness. My actions have been a poor form of repayment but when you have read the words that I am about to set down, I believe you will understand what lay behind them.

I care nothing for what happens to me. My sole concern is for the fate of my daughter Melody James. Though Kit Strong has managed to extinguish in her any love or loyalty she may have felt for her father, mine for her remains undimmed. Such, I suppose, is the instinct of the human animal.

This is much harder than I imagined it would be.

Where did it really begin? When I took her out of Liverpool, I imagine. I removed her from friends and the only home she knew for a life on the road, an only child among adults. But my father was dead and his legacy was there, demanding that I take it up. I had little enough to show for my own efforts; no wife, no savings, and a few possessions in two rented rooms on Parliament Street. There was also the livelihood of my bereaved mother and my sisters to consider. I looked into the possibility of selling the show and dividing the spoils, but the paper value of the assets was negligible. If I knew one thing well, it was bookkeeping. Our family's fortune lay in costumes, weapons, wagons, some practised skills, and a book of dates. All of these added up to this one great intangible, a thing of value but with no material substance—the Act.

I began by writing to the managers at all our bookings, assuring them that dates would be kept and obligations met. Florence set about altering my father's wardrobe to fit me, and I began to practice those skills I'd tried hard to forget. My father's patter was fixed in my memory still; I would rely on it, having little talent for improvisation of my own.

Then there was the matter of the name. I could have continued as The One and Only Bronco Billy James. But after giving up everything else to be drawn back in, I was unwilling to disappear completely into my father's shadow. I sized up the lettering on the wagons and the banner and settled upon The Authentic William James, a change that would incur the least expense with the sign painter.

Melody took to the life, in a way that both relieved and depressed me. Relief of course, for who does not want their children to be happy. But the rapport she found with her aunts and with the vague, extended and ever-fluid family of show folk was something that I envied. She and I had never been as close. She got on well with Lottie and Jack, and Florence had a breezy charmer of a husband at that time, a ride operator on the steam yachts. His name was Frank Leatherbarrow. Melody would help on the ride and he'd let her pick up the change that fell from customers' pockets.

It was Florence who persuaded me to let Melody dress as an Indian Squaw and join the act as a parader, and it was Florence who began teaching her how to use a rifle.

"I don't know, Florence," I said. "She wasn't born to this."

"None of us was, William," Florence said to me, "but we took to it when we had to. She'll not thank you for denying her a part."

The husband didn't last but the rifle lessons did, and we adapted the act to give Melody a spot where she'd shoot out a balloon that we'd filled with confetti. It was a good effect, and a cheap one to achieve. Florence said, "She's got a good eye and a steady nerve. She's one of us, all right."

It was not enough. On the fairgrounds we got by, but on theatrical dates our weaknesses were exposed. Other Western acts offered more, from a horse thief lynching to complete two-act dramas with scenery. Jack set out to write us a sketch but managed no more than two pages, which was two pages more than the playwright who took my money and produced nothing.

When a captive audience grows restless, there's no mistaking it. One manager's words stung me when paying us off at the end of the engagement; "Not so wild, this Wild West of yours, is it now?" he said.

He was right. For a bunch of cowboys, we were not very dangerous. All the whooping and hollering couldn't disguise the fact that the heart had gone out of the act. My father could split a playing card in your hand with a bullwhip, shoot a pipe out of your mouth while looking over his shoulder in a mirror, outline a human target with his giant knives. What could I do? I could repeat his patter. I could draw fast and spin guns in both hands. I could even shatter a glass ball in mid-air, with a little bit of cheating. But Jack couldn't be trusted with a human target, and I could not enthral the public as my father once had. That's a gift, and I don't have it. Florence was our major talent now, but she could not carry us all.

My aim in business was to get us onto the books of one of the major variety circuits. At this rate, it wasn't going to happen. After my failure in securing a play I tried various other strategies, but it was only when I heard of Kit Strong that I believed I might have found our missing element.

I interviewed Strong at the Holborn Empire and came away with mixed feelings. At the time he was making his living in the wrestling ring, a fighter in tights and a headband, but if he possessed half of the skills that he claimed I could see him being a valuable asset to our company. Given his circumstances, I'd hoped to get him cheap. In that I was disappointed.

He joined us a few weeks later, and we set about reshaping the act. Because of a leg shortened in an accident, he couldn't handle some of the rope tricks that had once been part of his repertoire. His accuracy with a pistol had never left him—he brought his own guns, a pair of well-used and workmanlike Colts—but he was no longer able to spin a rope and step in and out of it with the grace he once had. He could pull the arm bounces and rolls, the thrown loops and catches. But the Texas skip and the crow step, the spoke jump and the butterfly—all were off the menu.

He said to me, "You seem disappointed. You wanted more roping?" It was a Saturday morning and we were running through some routines away from the public's gaze, in the yard of a pub in Islington.

I said, "That was the hope I had. Until I knew the extent of your problem with the leg."

"Problems are there to be beaten," Kit Strong said. "Can you fetch your daughter?"

"For what?"

"A demonstration. An experiment. Whatever you want to call it."

I sent for her. Kit Strong was coiling the rope in his hands as she came over.

He said, "Hello, Melody." I don't believe they'd ever addressed each other directly before this.

"Mr Strong," she said.

"Did you ever play jump rope, Melody? I'm guessing that you have. I never knew a little girl who didn't."

Melody looked to me, confused.

"He means have you ever played with a skipping rope," I said.

Melody said, "I have, sir."

Strong held up the coil for her to see. "The *vaqueros* call this a lariat," he said. "The rubes call it a lasso. I just call it a rope. See this metal runner? That gives is a little weight to the spin so I can do this."

He took a step back from her to give himself some room, and began to spin the line. In his hands looked easy, almost effortless, as if the rope itself had taken life and was doing the actual work.

As he worked it he kept up a commentary, saying, "You've seen me do this. The flat loop. This here's the merry-go-round. And this one's called the wedding ring. Okay, Melody. Come and stand close. Face me now."

She did as instructed. I could sense rest of the family gathering behind me to watch.

The loop was spinning over their heads, describing a perfect circle in the air. Strong said, "I'm going to bring the loop almost down to the ground between us. When I say now, you skip over it."

He kept his roping arm high above his head, and the loop descended around Strong, encircling him. This was the move that he'd called the wedding ring. As he accelerated the spin, the loop grew larger.

"Now," he said.

Melody was short enough to skip inside the loop without fouling it. Now they were both inside the ring. They were only inches apart and Florence and Lottie clapped for encouragement.

Then Melody tried to skip out on his cue, but her feet tangled with the rope and it all went wrong.

"I don't think so," I began, but Melody said, "Let me try again."

Kit Strong said, "Why don't you leave us be for a while. I'll call you when there's something to see."

That was where it really began.

They perfected the wedding ring, and went on to add a vertical loop with a version of the Texas skip with Melody hopping in and out, side to side at increasing speed. I admit that it became breathtaking to watch, and when added to the act it always ended to cheers and applause. Florence modified Melody's squaw costume so that she could move more freely. Other new elements in those first weeks included Strong's bullwhip work, and reinstatement of the knife throwing with Lottie as target girl.

My instinct had not been wrong. Kit Strong made an enormous difference to us. He brought the authenticity and sense of danger that our presentation so needed. Under Florence's teaching, Melody's rifle skills increased to the point where she joined us as a second trick shooter.

We now had two versions of the act, one for the sideshow and one for the stage. For sideshow music we had our old Calliope but for theaters I had new band parts copied, as I felt this was where our future lay. I was confident that before too long, we'd have our chance with one of the circuits.

When business took me away, Jack would step into my boots with no great loss to our presentation. During a winter engagement at Northampton's Palace Vaudeville I'd planned to take a day in Leicester, where I'd commissioned a lithograph poster from Wilson's. We'd left the wagons in Eastbourne and travelled up to Northampton by train. In our digs that morning, Florence came to tell me that Lottie was indisposed.

I said, "What's the matter with her?"

"Nothing to concern yourself with, William," Florence said.

"Is she ill?"

"I said she's indisposed." Florence's sharp tone was warning me to press it no further.

"Well," I said, "you'll have to stand in for the flying knives."

"Kit wants Melody."

"Does he," I said.

I went to find Kit Strong. He'd found himself a quiet corner and made it his own, as was his habit. All he ever needed was his old Indian blanket, a pouch of tobacco, and a cheap edition of something to read. I don't think he drank. When it came to the act, he was always professional.

He looked up from his novel and I said to him, "Florence is the target girl tonight."

His face betrayed nothing.

Then he simply said, "You're the boss," and returned to his book.

Florence was not the target girl that night. Melody was, in defiance of my instructions, and the first I knew of it was when she walked onstage. Florence gave me some unlikely explanation about a last-minute emergency. I did not hide my anger. But it was late, and I would deal with the situation in the morning.

I hardly slept. I have never seen a family business that did not carry at least one idiot. I did not wish to be perceived as ours.

What happened in the morning only made it worse.

I came down to breakfast to find several copies of the *Echo* around the table. The paperboy had made his daily delivery, and Jack had been sent out for more. The *Echo*'s critic had attended the previous night's show and had singled out the James family act as the highlight of the turns, and Melody as our *'exquisite little Girl of the Golden West, a shot to rival Annie Oakley, an English Rose as brave in the face of bladed danger as any moving picture heroine'*.

Who can complain in the face of success? But a leader whose decisions aren't respected is no leader at all, and here was fuel for further disrespect. I said my piece about trust and authority, and the company pretended acquiescence. The extra newspapers were shredded for cuttings and that evening saw a crowd at the Palace box office, all of whom had turned out to see our exquisite little Girl of the Golden West. With Lottie still indisposed, I had to concede and let Melody continue. Receipts for the week were up, and when the engagement ended the management gave us a modest bonus.

Nonetheless, at the end of the week I said, "Enough's enough. As soon as Lottie's well again, she goes back in the act."

To which Melody said, "I want to do it."

"It's Lottie's job," I said. "You don't take another performer's job."

"Since when?"

"Melody. Don't argue with me."

But you can imagine my disquiet. My word had been disregarded and no disaster had occurred. The opposite had happened. The real problem would arise the next time I made a leadership choice that someone in the company didn't care for.

I couldn't say for sure who'd undermined me; Florence had been the spokesman and Melody the most disappointed, but the disturbance had been started by Kit Strong, who'd then stayed silent throughout.

Melody knew better than to argue. But as surely as I'd been damaged as a leader, I'd been challenged as a parent. I could only hope that she wouldn't develop a will and a temper to match her mother's.

I did my best not to be unreasonable. As a sharpshooter Melody was becoming the equal of Florence, and would soon surpass her in accuracy and speed. I gave her more gunplay to go with the rope tricks, and the act flourished. It took some persuasion to get Jack to fan the cards and hold them for the Poker Hand Split, but with each flawless shot his discomfort was diminished. Melody never missed. With Lottie back on the target, Strong added a blindfold and a second row of knives for an even bigger finale.

Lottie said to me, "It's a mistake to keep me up there, William. After the build-up with Melody I'm not the one they want to see."

Dear Lottie, she had none of a performer's jealousy. Or perhaps she just wanted someone else to face a blindfolded impalement artist every night. Whatever the case, I held out.

When there was some money in the kitty I took us all down to the studio at Beagles' where we posed in full costume for a set of cabinet cards. I ordered up a batch of the postcards with the intention that we'd sell them after each performance. I learned that Kit Strong was making himself some extra cash by appearing with his bullwhip at the stage door, where he'd tell a few tall tales and then split your card for a souvenir while you held it at arm's length.

As the warmer weather came, we went back on the road. Melody was already smitten with Strong, I think. Florence and Lottie were resistant to his doubtful brand of charm, but pragmatic about his importance to the troupe. Women in the audience were less reserved. I suppose they were moths at a safer distance from his flame. They saw a glamorous and world-weary figure who had seen sights and been to places that they would only read of in magazines or the novels of Elinor Glyn. No matter that he was a practised fabulist, and could be a consummate liar. During the roping tricks they no doubt imagined themselves in Melody's place.

I hardly dare think what they'd be imagining as the knives flew.

Things were going well. Most people still considered us more of a side-show than a theatrical act, but that had begun to change. I should have been happy, but I was not. I might say that I was glad that Strong chose to spend so much of his time alone, as I was never easy in his company. And I'd often remember the strange warning that he'd given to me at our first meeting.

We had a gaff hand name of Jancsek. My father had taken him on and he travelled with us everywhere, as anything from driver to baggage master. One night at Hull Fair he came to me and said, "William, something's bothering me."

I said, "What would that be, Jimmy?"

"You know how Strong likes to open his tent to the audience after a show?"

I did. He sold his cards from the tent when we were on the road. Some he'd split with the bullwhip, some he'd just sign.

Jimmy said, "I looked in just now and the tent's full of children with Strong sitting there as naked as the day he was born."

"What?"

"Pointing out his scars," Jimmy said.

I rushed over. The tent flaps were down and any crowd was now gone. I found Strong alone and pulling on his jacket, getting ready to head into town. I repeated what Jimmy had told me and Kit Strong said, "He's mistaken."

"That's a hard mistake to make," I said.

"You'd better take that up with him," Strong said. "I have nothing to explain."

"No?" I said. "Consider this a warning, and I'm making a rule. No more of these private audiences after the show. Especially children. Or your impressionable young women."

"Especially?"

"We don't need rumors."

"Can I still sell my cards?"

"Sign them out front. It's better publicity."

"You're the boss."

"Am I? Sometimes I wonder."

"Don't wonder, William," he said. "Be clear. Your God-given job is to hold this show together. You brought me in. You're in control. If you ever let me walk away thinking I got the upper hand, then someday we'll both have reason to be sorry. And when the day comes, just remember how I warned you."

With that, he pushed his way past me and out of the tent.

• • •

AND WITH that, Sebastian lowered the pages and massaged his aching eyes. He'd lost track of the time. The daylight was all gone and the room's sole electric bulb made a poor substitute. For some time now the copy had been crying out for a fresh sheet of carbon paper, and the typist hadn't used one. There was more to read, but he'd reached the point where his mind was struggling to take it in.

Reluctantly, he laid the pages down.

He'd resume in the morning. First light.

20

Léo Delibes was her composer of choice. At six years old Frances had been taken, along with Elisabeth, to an afternoon performance of *Coppélia* at the Academy of Music. They were in the charge of their governess, and the trip had been Elisabeth's treat; but it was Frances who sat entranced, Frances who went on to have nightmares about clockwork ballerinas, Frances who tried to pick out the Waltz on their drawing-room Bechstein and who now, almost twenty-five years later, played it easily, inaccurately, but with a deep sense of connection on one of Mr Jankowski's jangly piano store uprights. Though she'd since learned to read music, it was this arrangement of her own devising that came naturally. She didn't have to think about it. Some trusted part of her took over, and released her imagination from this world.

Jankowski dealt in second-hand instruments at the cheaper end of the market. This was an age where any household of modest means aspired to a parlor piano, whether or not there was a musician in the family. They were important furniture. Those with nice veneers or intricate inlays sold quickly, regardless of how they played or sounded. Though their frames were cheaply made, and hard to keep in tune, they were the most in demand. Even Jankowski called them 'bangers', but only when there were no customers around to hear.

He'd gone out for an hour. His wife was at her sister's and he'd asked Frances to look after the shop. He asked her often, and she always obliged.

This was no West End showroom. It was just a poky store in a narrow Southwark street, three rooms crammed with as many bangers as could be fitted in, a creaking floor over a damp cellar stacked with piano stools and old sheet music. Of those that could be reached and played, this one was her favorite. It was nothing to look at—boxy, painted, with no brass or fancy fittings—but it had the lightest touch and the sweetest tone of anything here and so, of course, it hadn't sold.

She played it whenever she could. When the shop was empty and there was no one upstairs she'd sometimes make use of the loud pedal, and on the low notes she'd feel all the other pianos reverberate in sympathy, like a memory stirring in a roomful of old Generals.

That governess they'd had, long ago, in another life. The one who'd taken them to the ballet. Mademoiselle Mauricette. She'd taught them French, music, and drawing. It was said she'd once posed for Rodin.

At the sound of the shop door, Frances stopped playing.

"Please," a man's voice said. "I didn't mean to interrupt."

The voice was familiar. She turned.

There he stood.

"Mister Warren," she said.

"I hope you'll take note that my hat is in my hands," the newspaperman said. "I believe it's the recognized mark of a man's contrition." He wore a different suit today, just as loud as the last. He closed the shop door behind him. "There was a telegraph lad knocking at your door. I told him I knew where to find you."

He held out an envelope. The small, flimsy kind that contained a printed cable. Frances had no choice but to rise and move to take it. Telegraph lads were supposed to wait for any reply. Warren must have tipped this one to get rid of him.

She said, "I suppose you read it before you came in?"

"See for yourself."

She turned the envelope over. It was still sealed. From Sebastian, she imagined. She had no intention of opening it while Frederick Warren was around.

He said, "Are you keeping well?"

"Well enough," Frances said. "What are you doing here, Mister Warren?"

"I apologize for tracking you down a second time," he said. "But I've been thinking about you. Ever since I tipped the police about the James family being in White City, and the Detectives found they'd already flown."

"Perhaps you shouldn't have waited so long to tell them."

"It was only a matter of hours, and I'd a story to protect. Had to see the edition to press first. Now they're gone and no one can find them."

"What has this to do with me?"

"The fact is, Miss Callowhill, when we met that afternoon I think I lowered my guard in your company a little more than I should have."

"On the contrary, Mister Warren, you worked very hard to disguise your purpose."

"That may be so. And the slightly forbidding man with a fetching young woman who showed up and spoke to the family that same afternoon, I suppose they were unconnected to the James family's disappearing act?"

To that, she said nothing.

He said, "Look. It's water under the bridge. By now everybody in Fleet Street knows about the German Prince and his Continental ways, and we've all had our orders not to print. I've a source in the Pinkertons confirms that Becker's been sent after William James, so that's not why I'm here either."

She waited.

He said, "You're not making this easy for me."

"I have no idea what you're trying to say."

"I won't deny that I approached our meeting as business. I saw your disappointment when you sensed that was the case. But I was disappointed too, when you left me and didn't return."

"Oh, Mister Warren."

"You've no reason to trust me, I know. So if I were to ask if we could disregard what happened and begin again, I wouldn't expect the answer to be yes."

"Not in that suit."

"Is that a perhaps?"

"It's a no. Forgive me, Mister Warren. We've little in common and nothing to discuss. Our friendship was brief and if you feel that I made unfair use of it, then let's say that we're even."

"I can be persistent."

"Please don't persist."

Though he seemed disappointed, he was hardly destroyed. He said, "Then will you play me something before I leave?"

Frances said, "I play only for my own pleasure."

"That's a shame. I hope you get over that." He placed his hat on his head, then tweaked its brim to fix the angle. "I listened for a while from the street before I came in. When it comes to music, what I lack in erudition I make up for in ignorance. But a talent like yours should be shared, or it's wasted. Life is too brief, Miss Callowhill. Good day to you."

"Mister Warren."

He left the store, taking the two steps down to the street. She saw his hat go past the window. He didn't look back.

Fetching? Young?

Though she'd been composed throughout their conversation, it left her upset and distracted. She'd almost forgotten the telegraph envelope in her hand. She tore it open, wondering what Sebastian might have to say, wondering what would become of the James family now. Would they disappear into the community of show folk? Or make a return to a more everyday existence, passing undetected with a change of name?

Frances was staring at the printed cable for a few moments, failing to take in the message, before its significance registered.

It was an international wire, from the United States, as she'd expected. She'd assumed it must be from Sebastian.

It was not.

It was from her father.

21

SOMETIME IN THE EARLY HOURS, SEBASTIAN WAS AWAKENED BY a knock at the door of his room. A rude awakening. There was light around the edges of the window shutters, but not much. He swung his legs out of his bed and sat on the edge of it for a moment, trying to order his thoughts enough to speak. He meant to call out a *Yes?* but only managed a sound like some creature that had been wounded and was trying to rise.

From the other side of the door he heard Doc Sparks call out, "Time for the funeral."

"So soon?" Sebastian said.

"Without embalming? You bet."

"Give me five minutes."

He checked the hour on his pocket watch. It was not yet six. He quickly washed in cold water from the jug on the stand, and put on his cleanest shirt. The transcribed papers with their unread pages lay at his bedside. He cast them a longing glance before shrugging into his coat and heading downstairs.

Muffled bangs, creaks, and running water told him that others in the rooming house were now beginning to stir. Doc Sparks was waiting for him in the lobby. He seemed fresh and cheerful, as if he'd been up and around for hours.

"Don't worry," he told Sebastian, "You'll be back in time for breakfast," and ushered him out to his waiting truck.

The funeral grounds were a little way outside town, in a marked-out meadow with a few scattered trees. There were two stone gateposts with some fancy ironwork gates, standing alone with no fence of any kind. Beyond the gateposts was an avenue of fine, plain, monuments in stone. A vault or two, a couple of angels.

In the farthest corner, where the land dropped away, were the more common graves. Some of these had painted wooden markers, many were mounds of earth with no marker at all. Beyond them, where the ground turned wild, was a Potter's Field for the nameless dead.

There was a chill in the morning, and dew on the ground. Jonas Flynn's hearse was already there, with the Reverend Partridge already present. The Reverend was off to his sister's for a visit and would be gone for four days, squeezing this interment into the hour before his train. Were it not for this handy gap in the railroad schedule, the deceased might have gone into the ground without benediction, and missed out on a chance at heaven.

Sebastian served as a pallbearer for the short distance between the hearse and the hole. He shared the burden with Doc Sparks, the County Attorney, and Jonas Flynn himself. From here onward the close-up smell of clean, planed pine would always remind him of this day. Ahead of them the Reverend waited, alongside a handsome woman in mourning who proved to be Mrs Flynn. Her calm presence lifted the occasion, and gave it an unexpectedly emotional feel.

Could one speak of a bare-bones funeral? The modest box was lowered into the ground, with the Reverend reciting his words without any need to look at the book in his hand. He rattled though them quickly; not a speech, more a song. Then he looked to Sebastian.

Sebastian stepped forward. He took no pleasure in public speaking at the best of times, and he'd never spoken at a funeral before. His only comparable experience had been in courtrooms, giving evidence.

He said, "I won't tell you that I knew William James well. I only met him on two occasions in this life, and both of those times he was in one jail or another. I was sent here to take him back to face justice, but now he's facing Judgment instead. There's no bright side, here, but maybe he's got the best of the deal. Only God can know what's in a man's heart, and decide his true reward. The rest of us can only do our best to work it out."

At least in this case there was no cross-examination to face.

He threw in the first dirt. Mrs Flynn dropped in a small posy of flowers. Sebastian felt his heart move for the stranger under the bare wooden lid. Then the gravedigger pitched in the first good shovelful, and the box began to disappear from the sight of the living.

Walking back to the truck with Doc Sparks, Sebastian was disinclined to speak. But Doc Sparks said, "So is this Kit Strong fellow in the area? Is that what this is all about?"

"What do you know of Kit Strong?"

"Only what William James wrote in those pages. And that you've been asking around about a tall man with a limp who travels with a young 'un. I may not be bright, Mister Becker, but I'm not so stupid that I can't join up the two things."

"There was bad blood between them," Sebastian said. "But what would bring either of them to your doorstep, I just don't know. William James wouldn't head for this town without a reason. Kit Strong came over to join the Seavers Wild West Show, and James knew that. But the show doesn't have a date within thirty miles of here."

The drive back to the rooming house was less than a mile, most of it on a well-graded dirt road. After being dropped back at the Continental, Sebastian said to the owner, "Can I get some breakfast in my room? Coffee, eggs, toast."

"Bacon?"

"Always bacon," Sebastian said, and went on upstairs.

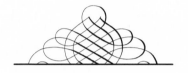

The Testament of William James (2)

22

I FOUND IT DIFFICULT TO SPEAK TO MELODY AS SHE GREW OUT OF her childhood. They were the years that coincided with her new life on the road, and in that time I think she became closer to her aunts than she ever was to me. Though she seemed cordial enough with everyone else, around me she'd often be quiet and withdrawn. Had Florence and Lottie ever been so difficult for our own father to fathom or comprehend at the same age? Though I'd little in the way of memories or evidence, I decided that they probably were. And so I went on, having found my excuse not to deal with the problem.

Kit Strong gave me a different set of concerns. On our first night in every new gaff, when we'd wrapped up the act and were settling in, he'd spruce up and head off into the nearest town and be gone for hours. I tried to take no interest. He was a grown man, and his free time was his own. But more than once I stayed awake and saw him return, a dark shape in moonlight, sloping into the camp like a wolf on the prowl. Sometimes he'd be staggering a little, though I never knew him to smell of drink.

Jack had theories about Strong's purpose in these disappearances, most of them involving women, all of them immoral.

I had other, different theories of my own.

On our summer round of fairs and show grounds, Kit Strong would sleep in a tent by the wagons. His possessions were few. He lived out of a cabin trunk that stood on its end and opened up like a book. A chest of drawers to one side, wardrobe to the other.

During one of his late-night absences I entered the tent along with Jancsek. Strong kept his trunk padlocked, but that was no obstacle to Cousin Jimmy. When he'd sprung the lock for me, I sent him away.

I'm not proud to say that I searched through another man's private effects. I did, however, feel justified by what I found.

Before Strong's return later that night, I called a family meeting. By then Melody was sleeping, so we gathered in Jack and Lottie's caravan.

When all were assembled I said, "I haven't discussed this with Strong yet, but I've made my decision. We'll work through the bookings we have, but as soon as it's feasible I plan to let him go."

There were blank faces all around. Lottie said, "For what reason?"

"I can't say."

Florence said, "After all the money you spent putting his name on the posters?"

"I know," I said. "But it has to be done."

Jack weighed in then. "I can't say I much like the man," he said, "but why?"

"There are reasons," I said. "Let's leave it at that."

Lottie protested, "The show was going under. Taking him on was the best decision you ever made."

"Then have some confidence in me now," I said, and refused to be drawn further. There was some back-and-forth and everyone made their bewilderment plain, but I didn't change my stance.

Florence said, "Have you told Melody?"

"I will," I said. "In due course."

I left them there, none of them happy. Lottie had said that hiring Strong was the best decision I ever made. I wondered if, in their minds, it was the only good one. You may think I should have shared more of what I knew. Though it would have made no difference in the end.

What I'd found in my rummage through Strong's cabin trunk was a folding leather case lined in red velvet, containing a syringe with silver-plated parts and two spare needles. It also contained two empty phials. My suspicions had been confirmed. Our star turn was an addict.

I was in no doubt that his late-night excursions were part of a constant search for supply. Voyages into a living underworld of which I knew nothing.

Despite the urge to act, I had to be careful. Every night my loved ones were exposed to his guns, whips, and knives. All was for show but the dangers we dealt in were mortal, and real. I knew nothing of addiction but as long as his hand remained steady, and his aim true, I would do nothing to upset the situation.

Our first winter engagement that year was at the Grand in Byker, just outside Newcastle. Not the most desirable booking but until we could break into the circuits, typical of the kind we would continue to play. Getting rid of Strong would be a setback to our progress, I couldn't deny it. But the path he was following had only one destination.

For a while he'd seemed like our answer. I would find us another.

Before we put the wagons into storage and boarded a train for the North, Strong asked if I would gather the company. I wondered at first if he'd learned of my intentions and was planning a confrontation. But that morning, by the railway arches in Bethnal Green, he and Melody demonstrated their proposed improvement to the act finale.

In the climax of the act with Lottie as target girl, he'd thrown a double row of knives and sported a trick blindfold for an extra air of danger. The new version involved knives, tomahawks, and something extra.

First he soaked a blanket, which he hung over the board. I stood with my knuckles to my lips, trying to seem more thoughtful than apprehensive. Melody then stood with her arms by her sides as he lined up and took aim. The knives slammed into the wet board, three to the right, three to the left, clear of her body by a wide margin. Then four hatchets, closer to her outline, into the space between.

All of this was but a prelude to the final stroke. Kit Strong picked up two large, long-handled war axes, one in each hand. Each must have weighed at least a couple of pounds. He dipped them in lamp oil, and Lottie then stepped in with a taper and set light to them. The flames burned long and bright as he lifted and threw first the right, then the left. They flew around thirty feet with a half-spin and slammed into the target board a few inches to either side of Melody's head.

Almost immediately she stepped out from between the flames and struck the Egyptian goddess pose, hands raised, palms up, an irresistible cue to applause. The company clapped. Jack stepped in with a bucket and doused the flames.

They all turned to me. I realized then that I was the only one here with no foreknowledge of what we'd just seen.

I proceeded with care.

I said to Strong, "When did you work on this?"

"In spare moments," Strong said. "With Lottie at first. But then it was clear that the routine called for a much smaller target girl."

Lottie chipped in with, "I don't mind."

My approval was awaited by all. I felt I had little choice.

Kit Strong said, "It's your call to make, William."

It was a powerful finish. No other Western act had a finale like it. Perhaps the Shufflebottoms with their Indian Torture routine, but they didn't have flames. If only it had been Lottie, and not Melody. But even as I had the thought, I was realizing how ungenerous and partial that was. Did I value my sister any less than my child?

I said, "A week's trial. No slips."

It went down well on our first night in Byker, as you can probably imagine. The Geordies howled and demanded an encore. Kit Strong relit the war hatchets and juggled them before the run-on and bow. It happened the next night, and the night after.

Midway through the engagement, on the Thursday, Florence brought me a message. Melody was unable to appear. Lottie was to stand in and we'd to revert to the old version of the act. Some of the crowd had come a second time to see our Girl of the Golden West face the flaming axes. They'd have to be disappointed.

As it happened, we didn't get that far.

I didn't see Strong until our call, minutes before we went on. As we waited out the last moments of the turn ahead of ours—Lily Arthur, Dainty Comedienne and Dancer—I looked at him in across the wings. He seemed angry and on edge, and I began to feel apprehensive.

He entered to cheers from the second-timers, his arms raised. Something was wrong. This was not the Kit Strong of our act. This was the Kit Strong of the wrestling ring, full of swagger and bravado.

In the bullwhip section, where we all cleared back to give him room, he went off-book. "A volunteer!" he cried. "A volunteer from the audience. Any lovely lady with a taste for danger!"

This was not in our theater script. It was part of his sideshow routine. He'd somehow confused the two. I watched helplessly as a Byker lass from the third row, urged on by her friends and offering them only token resistance, tripped up the steps by the orchestra pit and onto the stage. Down in the pit, I could see consternation on the conductor's face. He mouthed something to his musicians that the audience couldn't see. The band was a five-piece, not the most harmonious, but with experience of the unexpected. They extemporized their way through a repeated phrase, as their conductor watched the action above and stood ready with a signal to get them out of it.

Treating his volunteer with an exaggerated Western courtesy that had her both simpering and sparkling, Strong set her up with a playing card in each hand. He asked her name. She said Maisie. He said, Maisie, that was my dear old mother's name. I can see we're going to get along. She giggled and he had her hold the playing cards high above her shoulders, and then a little higher, with the effect that her chest was straining against her blouse. The crowd loved that.

I could do nothing. He retreated to the bullwhip's length, crouched a little, and made the leather snake back and forth across the stage in preparation for a strike. The Byker girl screwed up her eyes in terror and delight.

Lottie, thinking quickly, stepped in behind the local girl and steadied her arm. This was how we did it in the fairground. Unless your volunteer's a stooge, you always want to have them under tight control.

The first crack of the whip snapped the first of the cards in two, and drew from Maisie a shriek that entertained the audience at least as much as the trick. They whooped and cheered. Strong ignored them and repeated his build-up, focusing his attention on the remaining card.

The second whipcrack drew a scream of a different character, and I knew in an instant that the trick had gone wrong.

The conductor knew it too and signaled the band into the so-called 'disaster march', I drew my six-guns and strode in from the wings, firing blanks two-handed into the air and shouting out *Good night, good night everybody*, to draw the audience's attention as the curtain came down on Kit Strong and his gasping victim. Everyone out front could sense that something was wrong, but with confusion and distraction we kept them from knowing exactly what.

I crossed the stage behind the curtain. Strong was suddenly nowhere to be seen. Our troupe had gathered around Maisie and in less than a minute the management had joined us. The young woman was now weeping in disbelief. Her arm bore a four-inch slice from wrist to elbow that would need hospital attention. There was some very hasty negotiation and compensation as she was moved to a quieter place, while the curtain went up on London comedian Alfred Lester in his celebrated sketch, *The Restaurant Episode*.

As the show continued, I went looking for Kit Strong. I caught up with him at the stage door. He was pushing his way out.

"Strong!" I shouted. "You're a menace. What are you playing at?"

"Ask your daughter," he said, and went on into the night.

Without telling anyone that I'd left, I went back to our digs at the Talbot Hotel and banged on Melody's door. She shared a room with Florence, who I'd left tending to our victim.

Melody opened the door. She was suspicious and red around the eyes, as if she'd been crying, but I couldn't say that she seemed unwell.

I said, "What happened tonight? Between you and Strong."

"Nothing," she said.

"Then explain his behavior. He nearly killed a paying customer." Perhaps I exaggerated a little. But it was only a little.

Melody said, "It's not his fault."

I was about to speak, then I stopped. I pushed her back into the room and then stepped in after her.

"What do you mean, not his fault? If not his, then whose?"

"It's mine," she said. "I threw away his medicine."

Two things would later strike me about our exchange. Firstly, the chilling intimacy that was implied here between Kit Strong and my daughter. And second, that this was the first time I'd ever had anything resembling an adult conversation with her.

"Good God, Melody," was all I could manage to say.

"I wanted him to stop," she said. "I thought I'd be helping."

"If I thought that would help, I'd have deprived him myself. The man handles weapons for a living, Melody. An impalement artist who drinks is bad enough. One who depends on the needle…if he's not his own master, he's a menace to all."

"He's not one of those people. He really does need it. I understand that now."

"What am I to do with you?"

Her upset began to break through again. "I don't care," she said.

I left her there and had a mind to go out and walk the streets looking for Strong, but knew I'd be wasting my time. Byker merged into Newcastle, and Newcastle was vast. I had the idea of returning to the Grand and speaking to the stage door keeper. We performers were always in a new place, always passing through. The stage door keeper was often our unofficial concierge, our confidante, our source of information. Perhaps Strong had sought his advice, or asked for directions.

He had not. The doorkeeper had seen him head toward the river, but that was all he could say. Lottie, Jack and Florence had left the building in the meantime, but the House Manager soon got wind of my presence and found me before I could leave.

He said, "Clear your props. I'm taking you off the bill."

"Please don't," I said.

"Give me one good reason."

"Kit Strong won't perform. He's been taken ill."

"The man was drunk. He injured a patron."

"He doesn't drink. I've never known him touch a drop. Look, the damage is done and the woman's been compensated. And we both know how some mishaps can drive business if they're handled right."

Believe it or not, I talked him around. And although I felt a little soiled by the arguments I was using, I managed to salvage the week for us.

There was still the question of what was to be done about Strong. When I got back to the Talbot, he still hadn't returned. After climbing the stairs I paused by Melody's door and heard voices in low and earnest conversation on the other side. Both voices were female. There was nothing more I could achieve tonight. I went on to my own room, undressed, and slept.

I was told the next day that Strong had shown up at around four in the morning, banging on the door and rousing the landlord. I'd slept right through it all. After breakfast I went to his attic room and, when there was no response to my knock, I entered without invitation.

He was there. On the bed, fully clothed, above the covers. Not so much passed out, as in a stupor.

I spoke his name. His eyes were open, but he didn't see me. He didn't see anything. His clothes were soaked in sweat and his breathing was noisy and shallow, like a dying dog's. He claimed a medical need but this looked like the fruits of an addict's indulgence, plain and simple. I stood looking down on him for a while; whatever his motives, I could not understand such weakness. To be deceived into bliss, while rotting from without.

His cabin trunk stood open by the bed. A dozen or so letters were scattered on the floor, along with the ribbon that had secured them. I'd seen the cache when I'd searched his trunk, and left it alone. Now I picked up one, and then another. All were addressed to Colonel William Cody. They'd been returned unopened to a poste restante address in London.

The dates on the postmarks went back some years. One of the envelopes had almost come unsealed. With no conscience, and in full view of its author, I read what he'd set down.

> *Bill Cody you faithless lying excuse for a friend. While I lay rotting you were living it high. Well let me tell you that there is justice to be done and I mean to exact from you what I am owed. I have read your excuses and they do not impress me one bit, and you calling an end to it means nothing. Charlie Miller and Marve Beardsley got the glory and a ticket home and I got nothing. Despite the detts you have left me with I will face you, "Buffalo" Bill, you limb of Satan...*

Clearly Kit Strong held Buffalo Bill responsible for all his misfortune. I looked down. Now he seemed to be staring straight at me. But they were the glass bead eyes of a taxidermied animal, empty of awareness and incapable of reaction.

I put the letter back and left him to sleep it off.

He missed lunch, and emerged at some time in the mid-afternoon. I found him in the sitting room, looking out of the big bay window, eating an apple.

Without looking around he said, "English apples remind me of California peaches. When they're sweet they ain't ripe, and when they're ripe they ain't sweet."

If that meant anything, it went over my head. I said, "Where were you last night?"

"Hiding in my shame."

I'd seen little sign of any contrition from him, then or now. I said, "The money I gave to that young woman comes out of your pay."

"Seems fair."

"And I'm fining you double that."

"Seems less fair. But whatever you say."

"Do you care about anything in this life?"

"I find this life goes better if I don't."

"You act like a man but you're a slave to your weakness, Kit Strong. Set our differences aside. What can I do to help you?"

"Fair pay and three squares a day are all I ever ask."

"You have those. Give me one good reason not to break your contract and dismiss you here and now."

"You dismiss me, I'll survive. You won't. You know it. The others know it. All of them are depending on you."

"That's no argument."

"Tell it to them."

"We shall part ways, you and I, Kit Strong, you can be sure of that. Until the day comes, can you swear to me there'll be no repeat of last night?"

"I'll swear to nothing," he said. "Tell your daughter to stick to performing and not interfere in my affairs, and we'll be fine."

I had nothing more to add. And nothing that I'd said seemed to have had any actual effect. As I was leaving, I paused in the doorway and said, "Please stay out of Melody's company when you're off the stage."

He raised his hand and waved it above his head, still without looking around. I had to take that, and the crunch of his apple, for agreement.

That evening Melody was back in the act, while Strong remained in his attic room under orders to sit it out. He was taking my instructions and giving me no argument. As for the show that night...some had heard of the bullwhip incident and wanted to express their disapproval from the stalls, while many had heard nothing and were simply unimpressed by our reduced routine. Either way we weren't popular, but enough people had paid to come and boo and harangue us for the management to be happy at the extra ticket sales. All in all, it was not a pleasant experience.

Late in the evening, one of the call boys was sent up with a message from the stage door.

He said, "Mister James, sir, there's someone waiting who wants to meet the American."

I said, "His admirers will have to be disappointed."

"Sir?"

"Tell them, the compliments of The Authentic William James, but Mr Strong is not at the theater tonight."

With all of us walking back to the digs together after the show, I remembered our last night's conversation and attempted to build some further rapport with my daughter. Slowing to separate us from the others by a few yards, I said, "Did you finish the book Florence gave you?"

"I don't like books," she said.

"Melody," I said, "you mustn't neglect your lessons. They're few enough and you need your letters."

"Not to rope and shoot, I don't."

"I've hopes for better for you."

"A circus girl can always land a millionaire," she said. "But it won't be books that help her do it."

I could guess where that sentiment had come from, and it wasn't from Florence or Lottie.

The onstage incident had one more offstage consequence. Those callers at the stage door had not been admirers, but the brother of Maisie and two of his friends. Without us knowing it, they followed the company back to the digs that night and waited for Strong to emerge alone. They cornered him only yards from the hotel.

A mighty scrap ensued in which Strong prevailed, breaking the jaw of one and the arm of another. When the police arrived, the third was lying on the pavement and couldn't be roused.

I was called out to the police station on Headlam Street, a tall dark building with tiny narrow windows and a clock tower like a prison's. When I arrived, it was to find Strong holding court in the ward room with about half a dozen officers, their helmets off, buttons undone. Strong was drinking their tea and entertaining them with his stories.

After a conversation with the duty Inspector, I was able to get Strong released into my custody. As we walked back to the hotel, I noticed that his limp was a little more noticeable than usual.

He seemed amused by something. I asked him what.

"You vouched for my character," he said.

"I was raised to believe that every man deserves a second chance."

"Spoken like a British cowboy," he said.

23

SEBASTIAN GOT A CALL TO HEAD OVER TO THE *BULLETIN* BUILD-
ing, where his photographs would be waiting. When he got there, Frank
Lucas lifted the counter flap and beckoned him to come on through. The
printing press stood idle, the compositor's table unattended. On the other
side of the press was another door, which led into a former scullery. Its tiny
windows and heavy stone drainboard had made it perfect for a darkroom.
For now the blackout panels were down from the windows and there was
daylight to see by.

A set of postmortem images had been laid out on the drying table. These
were the pictures that Sebastian had requested.

"What do you think?" Frank Lucas said.

Sebastian said, "You're the photographer?"

"It used to be my hobby, but now it's the future," Lucas said. "All the big
city papers run pictures with stories now. I'm aiming to get halftone into the
Bulletin by next year."

He'd photographed the corpse from two angles. One showed
three-quarters of the coffin, the body clearly contained inside it. The
second, closer shot was a head and shoulders only, making the subject
much easier to identify. Though, with all due deference to the undertaker's
handiwork, no less blatantly dead. Flynn had packed out the cheeks as
requested, though the difference made was insignificant.

"Nice and sharp," Sebastian said.

"You can get 'em as sharp as you like when your subject doesn't move," Frank Lucas said.

When Sebastian had approved the images, Lucas gathered up the prints. Together they walked over to the courthouse, where Lucas had seen Jonas Flynn heading about half an hour before. Sebastian wanted the coroner's signed endorsement on the back of each picture, to verify and validate them as evidence. They would close the case on William James for good.

As they crossed the street, past a county employee shoveling copious mule-team dung onto a cart, Frank Lucas suddenly said, "Kit Strong."

"What about him?"

"I asked around. Dick Kennedy thought he recognized the name, kind of. There was a family of Strangs in the valley from about eighteen-hundred. Miners and mountain men."

"And now?"

"Eliza Davies Strang was the last of the line. She passed around ten years ago. She had a son named Christopher. Strang, Strong. He could have changed it for show purposes."

It sounded feasible. "But you say she passed," Sebastian said.

"There's a house and some land. No value in it, but it's his to inherit."

"You're saying this is Kit Strong's home town?"

"I'm saying it could be."

It was a possible explanation for William James' presence here. On the heels of a long-absent son, heading back to claim his birthright.

"Can we take a look?" Sebastian said.

"Whenever you want."

Flynn had a lawyer in with him, so they waited in the Sheriff's department, which was a high room with some etched glass and fancy woodwork and two desks, one for the Sheriff and the other for Doc Sparks. The Sheriff wasn't present, but Doc Sparks was.

He said, "How are you getting on with the life story? I reckon with a little tidying-up and a little more fighting and romance, Frank here could print it up and have a big seller."

"I'll have to consider that," Frank Lucas said.

"I read the one by Calamity Jane. I bet you that made her some money."

"That was ghosted, Doc. Someone else wrote it for her."

"So much the better. You'd be one up on Calamity Jane. Holy heck, I'm liking this idea more and more."

"The reading's been kind of a struggle, Doc," Sebastian said. "I think your typist used the oldest carbon."

"Don't complain," Doc Sparks said. "We don't usually make second copies. In this case it was just for you. It needs a proper ending, though."

"Well," Sebastian said, "I'd say we're all working on that."

The Testament of William James (3)

24

WE HAD A SERIES OF DATES, WORKING OUR WAY DOWN THE country until we reached the south coast. The last of those bookings wasn't the biggest, but to me it was the most important. I'd written to all of the syndicates, but the only positive response had come from the Barrasford circuit with an Easter week engagement at the Pavilion. Tom Barrasford had known my father. The circuit that he'd built was strong in the north, where Wild West shows played best, but at the height of his success he'd moved his base to Brighton and opened variety theaters in Paris and Brussels.

Many believed that he'd overreached himself. The Continental houses lost money, and he'd had to sell. Now his sons ran the business and those days of glory were past, but I had to be realistic. The mighty Moss Empires wouldn't even look at us, nor would the Syndicate Halls. This date was an 'in', as they say, and not something to be scorned.

Having warned Kit Strong about having too close an association with my daughter, I had to find a way to communicate the same message to Melody. I raised the subject on the train out of Hull. Strong had opted to travel on a later service, saying he had local business to complete. The others had all gone to the buffet car, leaving the two of us alone in the compartment.

"We only talk," she protested.

"What about?"

"He asked about my mother."

"What did you tell him?"

"That I can hardly remember her. What else could I have said?"

I tried to steer away from that subject. I told her that certain decencies needed to be observed. That if ever she were to find herself alone in a room with Strong, she was to make sure a door stayed open. But she wasn't to be deterred from talk of her mother.

She said, "I heard Aunt Florence say she ran away."

"Aunt Florence was thinking of someone else," I said.

I thought I might counter Kit Strong's influence if I spent more time with her myself. During our week at the Royal in Lincoln I took her to see the cathedral, pointing out the features I could spot to engage a child's attention. She followed me round with an air of someone not quite able to understand why we were doing this, but too polite to say so.

She drew many a smile from others as we went, for I can tell you, my daughter was a pretty little thing, though all she did was scowl at the stone-work and stained glass I showed her. Even the famous imp, carved into one of the column bosses by some forgotten mason, failed to raise her spirits.

As we stood before the tomb of Katherine Swynford, one-time mistress and later wife of John of Gaunt, she suddenly said, "Where's my mother's grave?"

"Why do you want to know?" I said.

"I've never seen it. Will you take me?"

"Some day."

"There's no grave," she said. "You're lying to me."

"Who's been feeding you these ideas?" I said. "I'm your father. I don't lie. I'm the one you should listen to."

She said, "You lied and you're lying again." Her voice had risen in volume and I tried to silence her, but she went on, "She didn't die. She ran away. From you."

"You're too young to understand."

"Where is she?"

This was too much. I regret to say that something within me snapped.

"Gone!" I shouted, right there in the holy chancel with my voice rocketing from stone to stone all the way up to the ears of God himself. "Of her own free will and no, she had the chance and didn't take you with her!

I came home and found you, two years old and alone in the house. You were crying and you'd been there all day. *That's* how much she cared for us both!"

"You don't care about anyone!" Melody screamed back at me. "Lottie's baby died inside her and you just nagged her to work!"

And with that she turned and ran the full length of the building, past shocked visitors and clergy, leaving me to follow, red-faced and at a barely more respectful pace.

The company continued its tour. There were no immediate repercussions from our cathedral shouting match, due to a paralysing embarrassment on both sides. Afterwards we tended to avoid each other and, when we couldn't, we both acted as if the exchange had never happened. I didn't raise the matter with Lottie—couldn't begin to find the words—so I can't tell you if Melody's assertion about her loss of an unborn was true. Though I think I knew, in my heart, that it must be. I remember Lottie's indisposition, I remember her upset. I remember my own irritation at the length of time it took her to resume her duties—under my pressure she stirred herself to return in less than two weeks, I now recall.

I suppose I should beg her forgiveness. Though in the light of all that has happened since, it would make a very small drop in a very large ocean.

We finally reached the Pavilion Theater in Easter week. After mill towns and factory crowds here was an elegant seaside resort, and a better class of booking.

In retrospect, I was deceiving myself.

I can see now that I was rejecting what I should have embraced. There is such a thing as the wrong kind of pride. As a child I'd witnessed Buffalo Bill playing to the gentry, then watched as my father toured us around the meanest gaffs and fairgrounds in the land. Never mind that we were clean, we were loved, and we never starved. I saw only our social inferiority. Since taking over the business I had sought the approval of managers, clerks and shopgirls, ignoring the worship of all those grubby little boys with their pennies in their fists. Yet theirs was a love more fierce, more loyal, and wholly sincere. Perhaps the fields and fairgrounds of the north were a British Wild West show's true habitat, those urchins and apprentices our natural constituency. They'd been good enough for The One and Only Bronco Billy James.

My father had understood them because, in his heart, he was one of them. In thinking I was reaching for more, I condemned us to fall.

Band call was on the Monday. I delivered the parts early.

By now our act was well-run, tight, and dramatic, retooled as a playlet for the variety theater and as far from a fairground sideshow routine as it was possible for a Wild West act to be. Having failed to engage a playwright—they all expected money—I'd joined up our routines into a kind of story. We played well together onstage, though most of us were barely speaking off it. The entire troupe would enter to music, me with a pistol in each hand firing off three blanks to wake up the house. We'd form a circle and Strong would step to the fore, spinning his rope, with Melody joining him for the skips. Then came Jack with his drunk act, pretending to swig from a whiskey bottle while pushing Strong aside. Jack had learned to juggle knives, prop ones with no point or edge, after which I'd come in as the town Marshal and scare him off with a scowl and my intimidating show of pistol-spinning. During Florence and Lottie's sharpshooting display Melody, as a mischievous young Indian squaw, would sneak into 'camp' and pick up a .22 rifle; Strong would move forward at the far side of the stage, pretending not to notice her as he stood there filling a clay pipe that she'd break in his hand. Then a second pipe, then a brace of them in his fist, then he'd produce his bullwhip and take the rifle from her hands with it, intimidating her with a whipcracking display that ended with him wrapping her body and pulling her over to stand against the target board for the knives and flaming tomahawks. Melody would act terror, 'learn her lesson', and offer him back his wallet as the final gag. Then the troupe all returned for the bow, all singing the final chorus. The chorus was important; it told the audience when to clap, and ensured that we left the stage to a decent hand.

I now come to the night when it all went wrong.

Live ammunition and fire involve certain safety precautions. Cousin Jimmy was in charge of the siting of impact boards, the lamp oil, the sand and water buckets, and with keeping the firing lines clear of theater employees during the act. He also serviced our firearms and kept them secure. I was then responsible for checking all his work. If anything should go wrong the fault would be mine, and mine alone.

Let me say this. You, Mr Becker, have seen the disaster that was wrought on that gilded palace out over the sea, resulting in the loss of so many of the innocent souls within it. All are on my conscience. I accept the responsibility. But let me now tell you how it happened.

Lottie came to me. It was after the call and about ten minutes before curtain up.

She said, "Cousin Jimmy says he can't find Melody."

"Is she in costume yet?"

"No one's seen her."

"But she's in the building?"

"We walked in together."

The audience was being seated, but it was too soon to worry. We had time. Ours was the fourth spot on the bill, first half, right after vent act Coram and Jerry. That was The Great Coram; Jerry Fisher was the name of his doll. He played in front of the tabs, giving us twelve minutes to set up behind.

It was when comedy duo Piero and Anita went up that we began to search in earnest. Jack threw a coat over his costume and ran back to the digs, while the girls looked in the dancers' dressing rooms. I was the one who found her. She was with Kit Strong. Strong would later claim that he'd been searching like the rest of us, and had only just discovered her in the scene dock with a couple of the stagehands. I felt sure that all four of them had been back there together for some time.

The scene dock ran behind the stage, separated from the auditorium by a solid wall. It was a workshop and storage for tabs and properties and the theater's rubbish; it had a skylight roof the full height of the building, with a long drop for a paint frame and scene painters' bridge. It was here that the theater's cloths were produced. The dock would rarely be used during an evening performance, so when I heard inappropriate laughter I was moved to investigate.

The stagehands ran off at my approach. Amongst the paint cans and turpentine rags they'd made a kind of nest or den where, like coal heavers aping polite society, they could smoke their pipes and swig cheap rum while lounging on stage furniture. Melody was sitting on a buttoned sofa that wouldn't have looked out of place in Versailles. She was bent forward, head down, her long hair hanging. Kit Strong was beside her with a hand on her back, between her shoulders, the way we encourage the unwell.

Melody looked up and saw me.

"Hello Daddy," she said, and then dropped her head again and vomited on the floor between her feet.

I was dismayed. I looked at Strong.

"What have you done?" I said.

"I did nothing," Kit Strong said, rising to his feet and moving away from her.

"She's intoxicated. Don't try to deny it."

Strong merely shrugged. I'm no bruiser, but before becoming a clerk I'd known a rough schooling on the fairground circuit. Without pause or prior consideration, I struck Kit Strong with all the force I could muster.

My blow turned his head a little, not much more. He grinned as he recovered his balance, and said, "Is that your best? I'm sure you can do better."

I struck him again and did no better. Worse, if anything—something crunched in my first and I felt pain.

"That's more like it," Strong said.

I pushed him aside to get to her. He made no resistance. I took her by the shoulders and tried to raise her to her feet.

As I was doing this Kit Strong said, "You need look no further. This is a situation of her own making. Curiosity's her natural condition, William. Imagine how frustrating that must be, in a family where everyone lies."

I said to Strong, "She's not fit to go on. Are you?"

He showed me his steady hand. Nothing here seemed to be of any concern to him.

"You're not even bothered."

"I've seen worse."

I said, "You're an animal."

"You were warned," he said.

"After tonight," I said, "you're gone. I give up. You're a lost soul. Cody was right to abandon you."

He was silent and I sensed, in that moment, that I had gone perhaps a step too far.

Then he said, "Fine by me."

Melody could barely stand; she wouldn't be standing at all were it not for my support and steadying hand. Which she then turned on and bit, hard enough to make me cry out and pull loose. Without my support, she stag-gered. Then she giggled. I had to shake her to make her stop.

I didn't want anyone to see her like this. Collecting cousin Jimmy on the way, I got her to an empty cloakroom where she immediately curled up on an empty bench and went to sleep. I left Jimmy to watch over her and went look-ing for my sisters, who were still searching the rooms where the ladies changed.

When I'd called them out I explained the state in which I'd discovered Melody and said, "Lottie, I can't let her play."

Florence said, "What are we going to do? You can't pull the act."

"One of you will have to stand in for her."

"I will," Lottie said.

Dear Lottie. The most put-upon, the least complaining of us all. She knew how much depended on this engagement and that if we couldn't make a success of it, our future all together was bleak, Though not as bleak as our future apart, given her husband's prospects as a provider. Outside the act Jack had no trade, which I always found ironic.

Jack had joined us as we were talking. He broke in then and said, "No!"

"It's a Barrasford house, Jack," Lottie said, turning to him. "If we lose this date we can kiss the entire circuit goodbye."

"No tomahawks, then," Jack said.

"Yes tomahawks, Jack!" Lottie said. "With no Melody and no specialty we might just as well go home now. I didn't come this far to give up at the last hurdle!"

"But Kit Strong says he can only use Melody!" he protested.

"Oh, Jack," Lottie said. "He can use anyone. He just *wanted* Melody."

It was true. With everyone lined up against me I'd acquiesced to that far too easily, for what had seemed like sane reasons at the time. Now I would have to carry the full weight of it on my shoulders. I left the others to get into makeup and looked in on cousin Jimmy, still watching over Melody.

He looked up at me and said, "That isn't gin I smell."

"The stagehands were smoking opium," I said. "Opium or hash. I don't have the experience to say which."

"William!"

"I know. No one is ever to hear of this."

"I've known opium eaters starve to death while they dream of heaven."

I looked down on my sleeping daughter. Jimmy had covered her with an old coat. Her sleep was troubled, her breathing noisy. I said, "How many other ways did I open for him to despoil this family?"

"She's only a child," Jimmy said. "Don't speak of her so."

"I have to," I said. "I'm responsible for this."

Our call came. Coram was now onstage. I went looking for Kit Strong and found him in Coram's dressing room. To my horror, he was injecting himself. He'd dropped his trousers and was pushing the needle into a vein amongst the scars on his damaged leg. All this under the gaze of the loose heads from Coram's spare dummies.

"Good God, man," was all I could find it in myself to say.

"If it troubles you so," Kit Strong said, "look away."

"I no longer care what you do to yourself. But do you intend to behave?"

The dosage spent, he drew out the needle. There was no blood. It was as if he'd injected a dead thing, like a dissector's knife cutting into something that had been hung up and dried for too long. Unscrewing the needle from the syringe, he said, "Where's Melody?"

"Sleeping off the poison you gave her," I said.

"For what it's worth, I didn't give her anything."

"You were there. You let her get into that situation."

"Am I her father now?"

"For her sake I won't bring the law on you. But you will leave."

With the syringe pieces back in his kit, he snapped the case shut. "I'm owed money," he said.

"You'll get what you're due."

"And don't try to tell me I haven't been worth it to you."

Kit Strong rose to his feet. As he was bucking his belt he said, "We shall get through this last evening, William James. Then let us go our separate ways. We won't need to shake hands."

"Good," I said.

Coram was onstage. I hurried off to get myself ready. Twelve minutes now and a second house later would see us to the end of this nightmare. I'd find another thrower who could handle the tomahawks. I'd give him a name and a legend as exotic as Strong's. None of it needed to be true. The new man had only to fill the niche that the real thing had created.

With Lottie standing in for Melody, this would be a slightly shortened version of the act. I sent one of the call boys with a message for the bandmaster and took my place in the wings.

Coram's vent act played to its finale. Then the band launched into *At That Bully Wooly Wild West Show* and the tabs went up. I slapped on a grin and off we went.

I did my spiel, Strong did his rope tricks solo. For a man just dosed, he showed little joy. I've heard it said that extreme pain and morphine can simply cancel out. That the injured can absorb almost fatal doses and find only a relief that falls well short of bliss. Whatever the cause, Strong was in a poor mood. He executed his spins and loops in a mechanical fashion, and turned his back on the applause when they were done.

After the sharpshooting, Florence left the stage. Now, instead of Melody sneaking on as her squaw character, Lottie stayed behind to shoot the clay pipes from Kit Strong's hand.

I don't know if she was aiming close on purpose. She'd be the first to admit that she was never as good a shot as Florence. I don't know if it was her bullet, or a flying shard of broken clay that nicked his fist. I know that when it happened he didn't flinch.

But he'd felt it. He turned toward her, reaching behind him for where the bullwhip hung coiled on his belt. At this point Lottie was supposed to change her grip and hold the rifle crosswise, one hand on the stock and the other holding the barrel, presenting it so that the whip's fall could wrap around the middle of the weapon and yank it from her hands.

Strong was too fast for her. She had no time to make the move. With no regard for her safety, he laid the whip across her arm and plucked the weapon from her grasp. I saw blood fly. The gun sailed high across the stage; he reached up and caught it with one hand before lashing out a second time with the bullwhip.

He slashed at Lottie with a crack that split her cowgirl dress from shoulder to hip. Over the playing of the band I could hear the audience gasp.

Jack and I had both set out for him at the same time, from opposite wings. But he saw us coming, and held us back by cracking to left and right as he moved to where Jack's drunk-act bottle lay. It was a glass whiskey bottle, half-filled with cold tea and plugged with a cork.

Strong dropped the whip, picked up the bottle, and slung it underarm to sail out from the stage and high into the auditorium, right over the stalls. As it flew he brought the rifle to his shoulder and took aim on the falling projectile.

Two rapid shots from the .22. The first one missed but the second one shattered the bottle and showered the audience with fake spirit and broken glass. People were screaming. Strong was manifestly out of control. Jack had reached him and was drawing back to throw a punch; Strong brought up the rifle stock under his chin and laid him out cold on the deck, then swung it around at me. I managed to protect my head, but took the force of it on my arm.

It's been overshadowed by the reporting of the fire, but what followed was a near-riot. People walking out, demanding refunds. The stage manager brought down the tabs and the second comedian was sent out front to calm and divert the audience.

In the chaos behind the tabs, I could hear the house manager calling out, "Where's William James?"

"Here," I called back, and the house manager pushed his way through to me.

"Get your company out of my theater," he said.

"Strong's dismissed," I said.

"Do whatever you like. No second house. You're off the bill."

Jack, from the floor, said, "All of us?" and the manager shook his head at Jack's naïveté. "Yes, all of you," he said. "Now go."

I was helping Jack to his feet. I said to Florence, "Get Lottie to the digs. Call for a doctor if she needs one."

Jack was looking around. "Where's Strong?"

"I don't know," I said, "but throw his things into the street. If he wants to argue, he can talk to me."

I went to the cloakroom to fetch Melody. She wasn't there. Cousin Jimmy was on the floor, dazed and struggling to orient himself, clutching a bloodied nose.

I said, "Where is she?"

"She was awake. We were talking. I don't know what hit me."

"I do," I said.

• • •

THE WRITTEN account ended there.

Sebastian turned the papers over, looked around, even checked the floor. But the typed narrative had ended in the middle of the page. With the manuscript in his hand, Sebastian went looking for Doc Sparks.

"Is this all there is?" he said.

"All there is we could read," Doc Sparks said. "Last three pages were nothing but blood and brains."

"So there is more."

"There was."

"Don't tell me you burned them."

"Not me. You buried them this morning."

Sebastian was lost for a question.

Doc Sparks said, "You told Jonas that the face was too thin. He'd no more cotton wadding so he used your ruined paper instead."

He explained further. Those last few pages had been stuck to the corpse's face. Blood from the head wound had soaked into the cheap paper, making the ink run and rendering the words illegible. With the photographer on his way over, the undertaker had used the paper in a last-minute facial reconfiguration.

Nothing had been lost, Sparks insisted. The words were already gone. But Sebastian knew from his Pinkerton days that there were washes and processes that could be tried on ruined paper. In some cases, they could make lost writing decipherable again.

But not, alas, when the pages in question were stuffed into a corpse's mouth and buried six feet deep in the Pennsylvania clay.

25

"WHEN YOU SAY THE PROPERTY HAS NO VALUE..." SEBASTIAN
began.

"Probably less than the unpaid taxes," Frank Lucas said. "You still think
William James came out here looking for Kit Strong?"

"I'm sure of it."

"What kind of bad blood sends a man halfway around the world?"

"Strong has his daughter."

"Now you say so. You don't give much away."

"I'm mindful of your profession."

"You're also riding in my car."

The first mile or so out of town had been along a graded road with county
markers along the way, but then they'd left it for a dirt trail across fields that
soon began to climb. When they entered the woods, the trail became a track
and the ride became more of an adventure than Sebastian had bargained
for. Lucas seemed undaunted by ruts or rocks, steering the Hudson around
them when he could, riding over them with the roadster's big spoked wheels
when he'd no other choice. He'd told Sebastian that he'd bought the vehicle
on a trip to Virginia, from a planter who said his new bride didn't care for
its open-air seating and sporty lines. It had been a steal. He'd found out why
when it broke down twice on the drive home.

Sebastian hung onto the bucket seat as if it were a mustang's saddle. He could hear the gasoline sloshing around in the tank at their backs, feel every tree root they bounced over through the seat of his pants. Far from fearing for his prized possession, Lucas seemed to be having the time of his life.

His defeat came in the form of a fallen oak, right across the trail with its live roots up in the air and its dead branches merged into the undergrowth. A piece had been sawn out of its middle, wide enough for a man or a mule to walk through. But not, however, wide enough for a Hudson 'Twenty' to pass. Lucas set the roadster's brake, removed the crank handle, and they walked the last half-mile to the Strang homestead.

"Someone's been here," Frank Lucas said as the trail opened into a clearing, where a one-story cabin stood with chicken sheds and an empty sty attached.

Was this the Kit Strong ancestral family home? The lower half was of logs, the top half of boards. The yard was filthy, the shack falling down. There was no smoke coming from the stone chimney, but some wood in the yard looked clean and recently-split. Sebastian's eye was drawn to a pair of work gloves on the chopping block, one atop the other, so old and so worn that they kept the shape of living hands.

They paused for a moment, but heard only woodland sounds in the still air. Sebastian called out, "Hello?"

Nothing.

So then he left Frank Lucas and ventured around to the far side of the building, where there was a breathtaking view of the vast wooded valley beyond this hill.

There was also a washing line. On it hung a petticoat and some patched-up children's clothes.

"Sebastian," he heard Frank Lucas call. "You need to come here."

"Why?"

"Just come."

He went back around to the clearing. Frank Lucas was standing where Sebastian had left him, only now his hands were raised. In one of them was the Hudson's crank handle. About fifteen feet from the newsman stood a man with a muzzle-loading squirrel gun pointed straight at his head.

With as much respect for the loaded weapon as he had for the stranger, Sebastian said, "Good morning, sir."

The man had a queer eye. Sebastian couldn't tell if he was looking his way, or still sighted on Lucas. He was short, no bigger than five feet six, yet still his work pants failed to reach his boots. His cheeks were sunken and his exposed forearms mostly bone, like willowbean poles. A flannel shirt, a shapeless hat, and that was their squatter.

The man said, "I got every right to be here. No one's using the place."

"I'm sure that's true," Sebastian said. "Do you know the landowner?"

"Are you a lawyer?"

"No, but I've suffered worse insults."

Lucas, who at the business end of the rifle was probably feeling that banter might not be appropriate to the moment, broke in with, "We're not lawyers and we've no interest in the land. Just trying to find the owner."

"And my friend will be grateful if you'll lower the squirrel gun," Sebastian added.

"I don't believe I will," the squatter said.

"Then how about you aim it at him instead of me," Frank Lucas suggested.

The squatter said, "It's my land now. Last man who wouldn't leave, he tried to tell me he owned the place. I parted his hair for him. That changed his mind fast enough. Woman who lived here died long ago. I claimed it, I work it. If he's the one who sent you, I can give you more of the same."

Lucas said, "When was this?" and Sebastian added, "Was he a tall man? Stringy-looking and moved with a limp? Did he have a girl with him?"

The squatter screwed up his face into a puzzled squint, which, combined with his lazy eye, gave his face a look like pips in a squashed fruit.

He said, "That was a girl?"

Sebastian looked at Lucas. Lucas looked at him.

Sebastian said, "What did this other man say?"

"He bad-mouthed my home. Called it only fit for a no-good hardscrabble hick like me and that's when I let him have it."

"You wing him?"

"Nope."

"Too bad."

"Put it near enough that he'd feel it pass, though. Prob'ly needed some clean drawers when he got back into town. The kid with him didn't want to walk too close when they left."

Sebastian said, "We're going to leave you now. I don't think we'll need to come back."

"See you don't."

He didn't relax or lower the weapon. Moving slowly and giving the armed man a wide berth, Sebastian circled around to join Frank Lucas. Then the two of them began to back off together. As the distance increased, Lucas lowered his arms. He shifted the crank handle from one hand to other and shook out the kinks from his wrist.

He said, "You think Strong's likely to hang around and enforce his claim?"

"Now you've seen the place, would you?" Sebastian said.

At a safe distance, they turned and began to descend the hill. Throughout the exchange there had been no movement or any sign of the squatter's family, despite the evidence of the washing on the line. They'd stayed frozen, hidden, like small mammals with a hawk passing over.

So that was Kit Strong's unclaimed heritage. Who could say what had stood here in his memory? A palace? A plantation? But the reality was a derelict cabin on an unproductive hill. No one would look at the squatter and envy his life. No doubt he loved his family and provided for them as best he could. But the reality was a diet of vermin and dirty water.

Only one thing was clear. Bred from a dirt-poor stock of miners and mountain men, Kit Strong was no more a born cowboy than any Manchester publican or Liverpool clerk.

As they reached the waiting Hudson, its long hood and fenders now spotted with birdlime from the branches above, Frank Lucas said, "I suppose we should tell Doc Sparks. Strong was here, and he has a suspect now."

"Seems only right," Sebastian said.

• • •

But Doc Sparks was ahead of them. Strong's dates didn't match up with the murder. He'd already left town when William James got in. He and his so-called nephew had gone to catch up with the Seavers Young Buffalo tour in Mahanoy City.

Sebastian said, "Where's their next date?"

"Doesn't matter," Doc Sparks said. "He won't be with them now. He was on a week's tryout and got fired two days in."

"So he could have come back."

"Not to kill William James, he couldn't. He got into a bar fight and spent the night in the Mahanoy City jail. Can't say whether the bar fight led to the dismissal, or was a consequence of it. Either way, he's alibied."

"So what happens now?"

"My boss has dropped the gambler theory. William James wasn't in the saloon that night. That was a New Jersey man named Powell, travelling salesman. He took his winnings and checked out the next morning."

Frank Lucas said, "Any other suspects, Doc?"

"It's a hotel murder," Doc Sparks said. "Stubborn as they get. The only thing we can say for certain is that for William James, it's the end of the road." He looked at Sebastian then. "But that's all you came for, isn't it? To serve up William James for His Majesty, dead or alive? You've got your picture and most of his confession. So you're done. Go in peace, Mister Becker, and have a safe journey home."

He offered his hand, and Sebastian took it. Even more of a crusher than their first, the handshake had a finality to it.

Leaving the office, he and Frank Lucas walked out of the courthouse to the waiting Hudson. Two local boys had climbed onto the running board and a third was sitting at the wheel, swinging it back and forth.

After he'd chased them off, Lucas said, "Run you back to your hotel?"

"Thanks," Sebastian said, "but I can see it from here."

"Suit yourself," Lucas said. "You know we're just a couple of hours from Mahanoy City."

"Meaning what?"

"Strong may have an alibi. But does she?"

"Melody James? Why would she need one?"

"They seem to be travelling as a pair. Wouldn't be the first time an older man turned a girl against her father. I'll admit it's a stretch, but do you think she could handle a gun?"

Now, there was a question.

Sebastian said, "Let's stick with known facts, Mister Lucas. Thank you for the ride."

Philadelphia

26

SEBASTIAN TOOK A MOMENT TO LOOK UP AT THE WINDOWS OF the Pinkerton Detective Agency before entering the building. A solid building, six stories high with a stone façade like a fancy bank. He had mixed feelings about this return. Philadelphia was much as he'd left it; a city of American Renaissance style built upon Revolutionary foundations. Back then, he and Elisabeth had lived in a nice row house off a pleasant Quaker square, just a short walk and streetcar ride from the old Chestnut Street office. His job as assistant superintendent had paid well. It was a time of sunshine in the brick yard and flowers on the table, weekends with ice cream and listening to Sousa in the park.

Then injury had taken him out of service for a while, long enough for his desk to be given to someone else. On his return he'd been reassigned. In Pinkerton terminology he became a secret operative. To the rest of the world, a labor spy.

Those had been less happy times, with months spent away from Elisabeth and Robert. He lived under a false name, in constant personal danger, sympathizing with those he deceived, disturbed by the actions of the masters he served. After he'd given evidence in court and seen his name made public, it had been an easy decision to pack their belongings and take a steamer to London.

He entered the building, and ascended the central stairway. A young man, descending, tipped his boater as they passed.

Inside the unfamiliar foyer, a familiar face. Superintendents and department heads might come and go, but Oakes the bookkeeper seemed to be a permanent fixture.

"Mister Becker," he said. "So happy to see you again."

"And you, Mister Oakes. Are you well?"

"My doctor says I have gout. But I don't know. I think it's something more serious."

"Gout's pretty serious."

Oakes seemed startled.

"Is it?" he said.

Sorry that he'd spoken, Sebastian clapped him on the shoulder and went looking for his appointment.

There were four departments to each of the Pinkerton regional offices; clerical, criminal, operating, and executive. Each had its own staff. In Sebastian's day Oakes had been the bookkeeper in clerical, but was now chief clerk reporting directly to the branch superintendent. Sebastian was met by Jonathan Newell, an assistant superintendent from the executive department.

"We expected you a week ago," Newell said. He was good-looking with a broad, unlined forehead, and hair as yet untouched by gray.

It had been almost nine days since Sebastian's boat had docked in New York. To explain his late appearance at the office, he said, "I was sidetracked by a lead."

"Did it come to anything?"

"Not in the end."

Sebastian lied without conscience. The notarized mortuary photograph was safe in his luggage, along with the faint transcript of the fugitive's last letter. Until Sebastian produced and delivered them, the shade of William James remained technically alive and abroad. The fate of Melody James was of no interest to his masters. So the deception seemed excusable.

Newell said, "The cashier's holding a float for you. You're to call in or cable this office in the event you need more."

"How long will that take to come through?"

"It will depend on your people in London."

Sebastian signed some papers and was handed a slender envelope of five-dollar bills. The *per diem* granted by His Majesty's Government was not generous. Then he went through to another room, signed a ledger, and collected the back pay they'd been holding for him.

Newell had been standing back and waiting through all the administrative procedures. He said, "We ran down an itinerary for the Seavers Wild West show."

"Thanks," Sebastian said, "but that's no use to me now."

"I thought your subject was following the tour."

"He was chasing a performer who's now quit the company. I've had to make another plan."

"Anything else you need?"

"I can use a pistol if you've one to spare. Something I can slip in a pocket. Bull Dog or similar."

"I dare say we can do that for you."

Newell took him to the stores and signed out one of the agency's stock of weapons. They shook hands, and Sebastian started across the floor on his way to the exit. Though they'd changed buildings, he recognized most of the furniture. Some of the old fittings were at odds with the modern operation. Where once there had been a single office telephone, now there was a switchboard at the counter and a handset on every desk.

"Mister Becker!"

It was Oakes, bringing him a note. Sebastian looked at the envelope. It bore a date from earlier in the week.

"Thank you, Mister Oakes," he said. "You look after yourself."

"You too, sir. There aren't so many of us left."

He was relieved to get out of the building, for no reason he could easily explain. He had once belonged; now he did not. More to the point, he didn't want to be drawn too much on his plans. Kit Strong was still out there. A man he had never met, accompanied by a young girl he had never seen. But a man of near-perfect evil, who had taken the child of his enemy for his doxy, now free to do with her as he wished without penalty or rebuke.

He paused on the street, and read the note. Then he stowed it in his pocket and moved on. From the Pinkerton office it was a short walk to the Keystone Hotel, just one block from City Hall on the corner of 16th and Market.

The Keystone was central, and it was cheap. Around the time of the Civil War it had been a row of ten houses. The hotel had been created by judicious use of a sledgehammer on the connecting walls, and the addition of a sign. The establishment ran the length of a city block, with three floors of rooms above a row of street-level stores. A canopy arcade at the front bore the hotel's name while sheltering the entrance to the Market Street subway.

Sebastian paid in advance and carried his own bag up to his room. The décor was plain, the bed soft in the middle, and all was as clean as it was fair to expect for the price. He took off his coat and then sat on the bed. First he checked and loaded the agency pistol. It was an American-made Bull Dog copy, a small handgun with a large caliber. Then he opened up his pocket knife and used the tip of the blade to unpick some of the stitches in his coat's lining. After subtracting some spending money, he carefully pinned the rest of his cash inside the lining where no pickpocket, mugger or sneak thief could reach it.

He put on his money coat. He stuck the gun in his pocket. He stood before the mirror. He smoothed his hair with his fingers, straightened out the curls in his collar.

There he was. It would have to do.

With a last glance over the note handed to him by Oakes, Sebastian set out to meet his late wife's estranged father.

• • •

RAYMOND CALLOWHILL had threatened to cut off his eldest daughter if she were to go ahead and marry 'that impecunious immigrant'. Elisabeth had considered herself disenfranchised, and gone ahead. Sebastian had met him on only two occasions before there had been any talk of a wedding, and never since. He was in no doubt that Callowhill would hold him responsible for Elisabeth's death, and for her dying in circumstances so far from those she deserved. But Sebastian felt no fear. The grief and guilt he felt were absolutes, and nothing Callowhill might say could ever add to them.

After the forced sale of the mansion on North 16th to settle his debts, Callowhill had moved to a Chestnut Hill address. It was to there that Sebastian travelled to meet him now.

The house was set back from the lane, barely glimpsed through trees. The driveway had a curve, the better to conceal the property. It was described as a cottage, though no agricultural laborer had ever lived in such splendor. Callowhill no doubt regarded it as a comedown. The family could not be linked by blood or marriage to those first Callowhills who'd married into the Penns, despite the best efforts of some very flexible and well-rewarded historians, but it had never hurt to let people think otherwise.

Sebastian rang the electric doorbell. A maid opened the door. He gave his name, and showed her the note. "Mister Callowhill should be expecting me," he said.

She invited him into a hallway that felt more spacious, and was much better furnished, than his entire Southwark home.

"Mister Callowhill is in the library," she said. "Please wait here."

But he didn't have to wait, because Raymond Callowhill came out just as Sebastian was thinking, *the cottage has a library*. His Southwark apartments had a mantelpiece that doubled as a bookshelf.

"Mister Callowhill," Sebastian said.

"Let's get this done," Callowhill said, and with a jerk of his head indicated for Sebastian to follow him back in.

Sebastian followed.

The library shelves had rows of books that matched. Their fine bindings were handsome and appeared untouched. There was a large desk and a leather buttoned chair. There was also a floor-standing globe, the kind that rich people hid drinks inside. As far as Sebastian could tell, Callowhill mainly used this room for reading his newspaper.

Sebastian couldn't help it. He said, "For a man who lost his fortune, you seem to live pretty well."

"Fortunes come and go," Callowhill said. "But a person's standards ought to stay the same, or what's it all for?"

Sebastian made a non-committal noise.

"You seem unimpressed by the idea. So what standard of living did you provide for my daughters, Mister Becker?"

"I didn't come here to spar with you, Mister Callowhill."

"So say your piece and let's get this over with."

Callowhill didn't invite him to sit, nor did he sit himself. He wasn't a big man, but in manner he was a forceful one. Money gave him confidence. Money was a measure of a man's worth. For what was money, but the hard-won mana of a warrior in the human jungle? He was entitled to look down on Sebastian. He had paid for the privilege.

Sebastian said, "I want to tell you how Elisabeth died."

"I know my girl is dead," Callowhill said. "You can spare me the details."

But it wasn't in Sebastian's plan to spare him anything. Despite their rift, Callowhill was Elisabeth's father. And Sebastian thought that he'd glimpsed something haunted behind the bravado. Callowhill had grown old, and his pride might not be the seamless armor it once was.

"You should know that Elisabeth served as a clerk to the Receiving Officer at a children's charity hospital. It was honorable work, and not without its risks. A cut from a dirty blade began the blood infection that took her life. The blade was wielded by a maudlin and drunken parent. The irony was that her assailant was able to claim insanity, and be spared the rope."

Callowhill interrupted him. "I saw your letter," he said.

Sebastian had written to him at the time of the funeral. "You saw it," he said. "But did you read it?"

"Enough of it to cause me the pain you intended."

"That was never my intention and you know it. You didn't reply."

"I chose not to."

"You still won't forgive?"

"My door was always open to her. But defying a father's wishes and turning her back on all this for a man of no talent, family, or prospects? What do you think?"

Sebastian was thinking how in this city of brotherly love, so much depended on exactly whose brother you were.

But he said, "I think you may have been right."

"What?" Callowhill hadn't been expecting agreement.

"I believe that time has proved you right," Sebastian explained. "She deserved better. More of a life than I could ever have given her. And when I look at how it ended, how do you expect me to feel? I loved her. Enough to say that for her sake and not mine, I can only wish she'd never met me."

"Rather too late to think of that now," Callowhill said.

"I know."

"There's a higher power that judges us. That boy was her punishment."

"You mean your grandson."

"I mean that tragic simpleton you sired on her."

"That tragic simpleton is a respected academic at the British Museum."

This was unexpected. "The British Museum?" Callowhill was a snob, who believed that God was as big a snob as he, and therein lay his weakness. Elevate someone he looked down upon, and all his certainties came into question.

An advantage of the Becker family's move to London had been their access to a specialized education for Robert. It was a matter of giving him the social poise to match his particular genius, something that no regular school had ever understood. Every weekday, Frances had taken him across town to a private day college in South Hampstead while Elisabeth found employment locally, to help cover the cost of the teaching and travel. If Sebastian exaggerated a little now, it was unintended. He would keep his temper.

"He's no simpleton," Sebastian said. "He's one of the most complex and intelligent young men you could ever meet. When I saw him last, he was in the company of Lords and Knights of the realm."

Sebastian neglected to mention that he was taking the coats of those Lords and Knights and throwing them in a pile.

It seemed that Callowhill's preconceptions could only handle one challenge at a time, and so he changed the subject.

"And how's my Frances?" he said.

"She tells me she's happy," Sebastian said. "I think she's the kind of person who finds a way to happiness wherever she is. It's within her. As only the truly kind can know."

"Which I am not."

"I'm not here to attack your character, Mister Callowhill. You are who you are."

"Oh, Frances." He shook his head. "She was always my lonely little one."

"You actually miss her?"

"Don't misjudge me. I've missed them both."

"I have a proposal for you."

"Which is?"

"Take her back. She never betrayed you. She tried to be the peacemaker and you cut her off for that. Now Elisabeth's dead and Robert's grown, and she has no reason to stay with me."

"So now you want to unload her."

"Unload her? I'd give anything not to see her go, but I've nothing to give. You, on the other hand...I've looked into your affairs, Mister Callowhill."

"Have you, indeed."

"It's what I do for a living. I know that one of your investments flourished. Not enough to rebuild your fortune. But enough to restore your comfort." He looked around him. "This is closer to what Frances deserves. No life that I can offer will ever match it."

Callowhill walked around behind his desk, and straightened a couple of papers.

"Very noble, Becker," he said, "but you're far too late."

"I don't understand."

"I've been in touch with my daughter. We'll see how she responds with your influence removed." Callowhill looked up. "I know you've always thought me a monster, Becker. I am not."

"I never thought you a monster. But the stance you held for most of twenty years speaks of a heart that's much harder than mine. And I have to warn you, Raymond." Callowhill stiffened at the familiarity. "Frances has a mind of her own, and she's no child to be controlled."

"You won't impede her?"

"I dread the very thought of her leaving. But it's for the best. She's young enough yet to marry. She thinks that part of life has passed her by, but she's wrong. Any man would be lucky to have her."

"I have one in mind."

"She'll make her own choice."

"Better than her sister's. I'll at least make sure of that."

"Then there's nothing more to be said."

Callowhill called for the maid to show him out. He didn't accompany Sebastian to the door. But as he was about to step outside, Sebastian heard his voice again.

"The British Museum?"

Sebastian looked back. Callowhill was standing in the doorway to his library of unread volumes.

"Natural History," Sebastian said. "A promising future."

"Philadelphia has a fine museum. The Academy of Natural Sciences."

"Take your victories one at a time, Raymond. Leave me that much."

And with that he stepped out into daylight, and a return to the chase.

27

Mahanoy City was not unfamiliar to him. It was a low-rise town of mean wooden houses and solid brick stores in eastern Pennsylvania. It sat in a wide shallow valley, surrounded by acres of scarred land, beyond which spread a seeming infinity of lush greenery. This was hard coal mining country, where Pinkerton operatives had once infiltrated the workforce with the aim of breaking a clandestine organization of Irish origin, the infamous Molly Maguires. The operation had led to a trial and six hangings, and its legitimacy was disputed to this day. Memories were long. It was a region to be entered with care.

The Seavers show—or, to give its full title, *Young Buffalo Wild West & V.C. Seavers Hippodrome & Col. Fred Cummins' Far East*, a name enough to fill up a handbill on its own—had played one date here on the way to Allentown. For every Colonel Cody, Pawnee Bill or 101 Ranch there were dozens of these open-air 'mud' shows, playing the camps and smaller towns and moving on overnight. On this particular night, one of their number had been left behind. It wasn't clear whether Kit Strong had picked a fight with the local anthracite miners, or if they'd picked one with him.

However it had begun, by all accounts it had been spectacular to see. Entertaining for a while, but quick to turn nasty. Strong gave better than he got. When someone lost an eye, he had to be overpowered.

They took him to be a drunk, though no one had seen him with liquor. Local feelings were running high so the Sheriff drove him four miles to Shenandoah to be locked up in a building that served as town hall, police headquarters, fire station, and jailhouse. He didn't sleep all night. He overturned his bunk, shook the bars, and made such a racket that no one else within earshot slept either. The next day he began vomiting. He doubled up with stomach cramps. The Sheriff brought in the County Physician. One look at Strong's veins and scars quickly established the nature of the problem.

Within half an hour Strong was quiet, lucid, and upright. Not contrite, but that would be too much to ask. He had a visitor, a boy who'd walked all the way from Mahanoy City and slept in a shop doorway the previous night. While the County Attorney deliberated over whether to bring Strong to trial or kick him over the county line, the 'boy' ran errands, brought coffee, and provided Strong with a copy of *Billboard* magazine that he'd brought from their last venue.

Sebastian learned from witnesses that Strong read every word of the magazine, and then sent the boy out with a message. Meanwhile the County Attorney was establishing that the man who'd lost an eye was also the one who'd begun the fight. On the assurance that Strong had employment lined up and would not remain and be a burden on the county, the Attorney took the decision to release him without charge. Strong and the boy were last seen on the south side of town near the Pennsylvania Railroad. They were following the tracks out toward the west, and it was thought that they may have intended to jump on a freight once they were beyond the sight of the yard marshal.

To the retired firefighter who served as watchman and janitor, Sebastian said, "This magazine. Do you know what happened to it?"

"Threw it out," the oldster said.

"Any chance it might still be around?"

"No one's gonna stop you lookin."

Sebastian used a stick to poke through a mass of peelings, paper and compost that had been piled to rot down on untended land behind the fire house. He used the same stick to carry what was left of the magazine to a spot with better air. Crouching in the open, he carefully turned the pages.

Afterwards he used the same stick to return the magazine to the trash heap, and went in search of a telephone from which he could make a long distance call.

• • •

IT WAS a gamble. But according to the trade papers the *Tompkins Real Wild West and Frontier Exhibition* was the only touring show of its kind whose route brought the company within a reachable distance. According to their advertising, Mabel Hackney Tompkins, equestrienne and co-owner of the show, had spent several years as a featured rider with *Buffalo Bill's Wild West*. Sebastian was willing to bet that he'd find her old co-performer Kit Strong newly-added to the acts.

He reached Canton in time for the evening performance. It was a logging town of sawmills and lumber yards, of tanneries and farm supplies. The advance man had done his job well and there was paper on every street, handbills and posters promising a mixed program of Wild West and circus acts. Sebastian didn't need to seek directions. The light was fading, businesses were closing up, and it seemed that most of the townspeople were heading toward the showground.

The arena had been pitched on the outskirts of town, in a field alongside Towanda Creek. Many of these open-air shows did their best business at the matinees, but this one was drawing good numbers for the evening. Sebastian stood in line at the ticket wagon and then followed the crowd inside.

It wasn't a capacity house, but it was close. There was plank seating for eight hundred or more in elevated rows on three sides of the arena. A canvas sidewall encircled the arena behind them, while the central performing area was open to the sky. The show had no electricity but was lit by incandescent limes, heated to brilliance by carbide gas from standing pipes. Sebastian took a place on the end of a row, behind a black-clad Minister and his family. From here he had a good view and was close to the exit.

Carl Mitchell's eight-piece Cowboy Band was joined by its final member as the musicians took their places. Sebastian recognized their second trombonist as the man who'd sold him his ticket just a few minutes before. They struck up a fanfare, all brass and drums, and it began.

Charles H Tompkins rode out as if fired from a cannon. He pulled his mount to a stop before the cheering crowd, and greeted all with a sweep of his broad-brimmed hat. Behind him came a parade of the cowboys, Cossacks, and Indians who'd be providing the entertainment. There was special applause for Mabel Hackney and Vardius the Dancing Horse. Most of the crowd seemed to know her from earlier visits. Some called her name. Others called out to the horse.

Sebastian was paying less attention to the headliners than to the characters making up the rest of the company. He'd become convinced that he'd recognize Kit Strong on sight, so powerful was the image that had formed in his mind. But he'd never actually seen the man. The Kit Strong of his imagination was not so much a person as a dark force, all bitter energy with a distinctive signature but no single form.

He looked in the parade for a man accompanied by a boy, or perhaps a girl in a squaw's costume if they'd chosen to abandon Melody's disguise. He saw two, maybe three possible candidates for Strong, none for a Melody.

Perhaps they simply weren't in the parade. It was a well-rehearsed routine. If they *had* joined the show, they could only have been with it for a matter of days.

Tompkins put on a good production. An expert rider of forty-and-something years, he could rope and shoot and do the talk. When not spinning a line or shooting targets out of the air, he acted as master of ceremonies for the various acts. These were mostly Western routines, along with a trained dog act, a family of acrobats and a four-pony drill providing the circus element. With Tompkins giving his rope tricks and a burly bearded Russian throwing axes into a barn door, there seemed little room on the bill for any of Kit Strong's specialities.

After a dozen acts and set-pieces, Sebastian's spirits were beginning to fall. By now he reckoned that every performing member of the company had made an appearance in one form or another, in their own right or in a tableau or in support of another speciality. The rope-dancer played an endangered pioneer and was menaced by Indians. The Indians managed the trick riders' horses. Everyone changed hats, switched costumes, took a spell in war paint, and none were the people he sought. Sebastian left his seat and moved toward the exit. But instead of leaving through the marquee, he ducked out of sight when no usher was looking.

A gap in the sidewall canvas let him through into the so-called 'back yard' where all the company's bandwagons and private tents were marshalled.

After the arena, the back yard was a dark and secret place. Part circus lot, part cowboy camp. Banjo flares lit up the artists' communal changing tent, but elsewhere it was all shadows and kerosene lanterns.

Sebastian took a moment for his eyes to adjust. Behind him on the other side of the sidewall, the show went on. It was going well. Every now and again a sudden roar would go up, but he'd no way of knowing the cause. All he could see looking back was the dark edge of the stands with the arena's radiance spilling up into the sky, where midges danced in the limelight.

There was little rest time for a show on the road. Each day meant a new stand, which meant an overnight tear-down and move for the heavy equipment. Actors and performing stock would follow along the morning after. Most would have spent the night on the lot, apart from the headliners who were accommodated in local boarding houses. On arrival in the next place, there'd be a town parade while the seats and canvas were going up, with the parade ending at the showground. Sideshows and a diving dog act would keep followers from drifting away before the matinee. Always moving on, ten miles every day, six or seven days a week.

"Hey there you," he heard a voice say. "No public allowed here."

Sebastian turned. He saw a boy of about fifteen or sixteen, wiry as they came, in shirtsleeves and waistcoat and a cap.

Sebastian said, "What's your name?"

"Never mind my name. You can't be here."

"Yes I can," Sebastian said. "I need your name."

The boy, suddenly less certain, said, "It's Denny. Dennis."

"This is just a routine check, Denny Dennis. No one's in any trouble. I'm looking for one of your performers. A man named Kit Strong?"

The boy shook his head.

"Don't know him," he said. He'd now taken Sebastian for a cop, as Sebastian had intended. Local police always came nosing around travelling shows and circuses. Looking over the workforce for runaways and parole violators, mingling with the crowds to watch for pickpockets.

"May have joined you this week. Trick roper and impalement artist. Ends the act with tomahawks."

"We got no use for one of those. We're covered for ropers and knife throwers."

"Okay," Sebastian said. "Thanks."

Even if the boy knew something, he wouldn't give up one of his kind so easily. Carnies and show folk, as he'd observed before, were a clan apart.

But as Sebastian was turning to go, the boy said, "The boss took on a new man for the sledge gang in the last town."

Sebastian stopped. "What did he look like?"

"Tall thin streak of leather and bile, but he can swing a hammer in time. I think the gaffer took pity because of the kid."

"Kid?" Now he was interested. "What kid?"

"Travelling with his son. Twelve, thirteen? Thereabouts."

"Where can I find them?"

"Can't say for sure. Try down the row, right by the horses."

Nice. Back during his undercover labor days, Sebastian had slept for several weeks in a loft over stables. He had a vivid memory of ammonia headaches caused by the rising stench from urine-soaked straw.

He said, "Out of interest. You people never confide in strangers. So why tell me this?"

The boy made a face. "Him and the kid. Something's not right, there. Don't ask me what."

Weaving his way through flat-bed drays and painted baggage wagons, Sebastian moved away from the music and noise in search of the quieter end of the lot.

A sledge gang? If Kit Strong's skills weren't needed, then pounding stakes and raising canvas might have been his only option.

Sebastian found the horses. These weren't show ponies but the company's draft animals, big-boned and docile. He estimated that there were thirty, perhaps forty of them. They were tethered on a picket line, out in the open with their feed and water on the ground before them.

Down the row, right by the horses, the kid had said. Here the men who'd be breaking down the show and hauling it through the night could grab their couple of hours of relative peace. Sebastian slid his hand into his coat pocket and checked the pistol, working by touch. With luck he might not have to draw it, although that was a lot of luck to be hoping for.

He took a lantern from a post. In the first tent he looked into he saw six bunks, uppers and lowers, with sleeping bodies in four of them. A few moments' study suggested that none was a youth. Too gray, too large, or too bearded. He lowered the flap with a much care as he'd raised it.

In the next tent, he found a group of men playing cards with a home-made faro board on an upturned bucket. Another sprawled on a bunk, reading a dime magazine. All looked up.

"Excuse me," Sebastian said, and withdrew.

He took a more cautious peek into the next. Another six-man tent, this one empty. Or so he nearly believed. He almost missed the figure on the low paillasse bunk, until it moved.

"Pardon me, sir," Sebastian said in a quiet voice, but he didn't leave. He stayed as he was, and watched for a while. It may have been the feeble kerosene light, or some sense of Sebastian's continued presence. But the figure stirred, and made a sound.

Sebastian slipped the Bull Dog out of his pocket, and held it ready in his hand.

He decided to chance something.

"Melody?" he said.

Was that a reaction? Did he imagine it? He moved closer, letting the tent flap fall shut behind him.

"Melody James?" he said.

She rolled over and looked up.

28

IT WAS A CHILD'S FACE, DARK-HAIRED AND PALE, STRUGGLING TO
focus on him. Her hair had been cropped like a boy's, but he wasn't fooled.
He moved to the bed and dropped to one knee.

"Melody," he whispered. "Wake up."

She was looking at him, struggling to focus, trying to remember whether
she was supposed to know him.

"What?" she said.

"Where's Kit Strong? I know he's here."

"In the show," she said. Then she turned away again and pulled the blanket over her face.

He set the lantern down, and reached out to shake her by the shoulder.
"He isn't in the show," Sebastian said. "I know that."

She wouldn't emerge. "I don't know," she said, her voice muffled by
the wool.

"Melody," he said, shaking her again. "Stay awake. It's important."

This time she ripped back the cover and spun on him like a snapping dog.
"*What?*" she said, the spell of sleep properly broken now.

He said, "I want you to come with me. Do you understand?"

After that quick burst of anger, her energy ebbed again. He was able to
look on Melody James for the first time. She was young-looking, even for

fourteen. Hers was an oval face with large brown eyes that were heavy-lidded from sleep, dark-ringed from exhaustion.

If he could spirit her away, he'd settle for that. No need to face Kit Strong, no need to fight or argue, no issues to untangle. If only he could get her fully awake and cooperating before Strong's return.

A wooden crate served as a washstand for the tent's usual occupants. Alongside the crate stood a bucket of water and a ladle. Sebastian scooped up some of the water and sniffed it first, to be sure it wasn't waste.

It was stale but clean. He sat Melody James upright and splashed some of the water onto her face. She winced and protested, but showed signs of revival.

Sebastian saw the needle bruises on her arm at the same time she saw his gun. Both of them were suddenly more alert than before.

Sebastian said, "I have to get you away from here." He stowed the revolver back in his pocket. "Take my hands," he said, holding out his own.

He pulled her to her feet. "Can you stand without help?"

She was not steady, but she could stand. She'd been sleeping fully dressed. Her coat was her pillow and her shoes were at the end of the bunk, along with a shapeless cap like the one worn by the boy outside.

She said, "Who are you?"

"I knew your father," Sebastian said.

She was confused.

"I knew him in England," Sebastian said. "They sent me here to find him."

"You found me."

"I know. And now I'm taking you home. We need to leave this place. You can never be safe here. Do you understand?"

She nodded.

"What did Kit Strong do? What poison did he give you?" Sebastian turned her arm to show the marks, so she wouldn't waste time on denials. "Is this morphine?"

Melody shrugged. It was hard to say whether she didn't know, or simply didn't care. He felt a surge of fury that he struggled to contain.

"He's given you morphine. Hasn't he? To keep you subdued when he isn't around."

Issues be damned. Kit Strong would pay. But Sebastian's first priority was to get Melody as far away from his influence as possible.

"I'm thirsty," Melody said, so he took the ladle and brought her more of the water. As soon as his back was turned, she sat down again. He gave her the ladle and she drank heavily.

"Don't make yourself sick," he warned.

To no avail. She drank most of a pint and then, with a sudden hiccup, brought most of it splashing back onto the ground between her feet. Sebastian wiped her chin with his handkerchief, and she looked at him helplessly.

"Come on, Melody," he said.

He got her back on her feet. She took his arm.

"I'm a boy now," she said.

"I know."

"So no one else gets to touch me. Though some of them still try."

The way that she said it was so matter-of-fact, and so unconcernedly knowing, that it sent a chill down Sebastian's spine.

• • •

"WAIT," SEBASTIAN said. "We can't go this way. We need to turn back."

He could see moonlight on water. They couldn't simply walk out into the night. The arena had been pitched in such a way that a bend in the creek effectively formed a moat around the camp. Melody was leaning heavily on his arm as they turned around, as if a yearning for sleep continued to drag her down. He'd put the blanket around her shoulders, as a gesture toward disguise. He knew that he couldn't take her cooperation for granted. In her euphoric state, she'd probably be amenable to any instruction. When that wore off, the situation might be very different.

As they followed the line of tent lanterns toward the arena, Sebastian kept a lookout for Kit Strong. Kit Strong, or any other person who might challenge them. Shadowy figures crossed their path, but none paid them any attention.

How long now, until the end of the show? He was thinking that they might be able to leave the ground unnoticed, moving under the cover of the departing crowd. Melody's step was growing steadier, her dependence on him less.

All would be well, if he could only get this child home.

His aim had been return through the gap in the sidewall, but their way was blocked by a skittish troupe of arena horses awaiting their cue to perform. The animals knew how the music went, they knew their time was coming, and they were giving their cowboy riders a hard time keeping them in line. Over on the other side of the canvas wall, the Shooting Savages were enacting a stagecoach raid with war cries and rifle blanks.

"This way," Melody said, and tugged on Sebastian's arm. She wove a little as she steered them away from the horsemen and under the seating.

Sebastian found himself in a hidden world. It was no more than a plank's width away from the light and life of the arena, but separated from it utterly. Down here amongst the secret machinery it was permanent night, but for the zebra stripes of brilliance from gaps in the bleachers above.

She guided them forward, picking a way through the jacks and stringers that supported the seating. By this means they could make their way down the entire length of the arena, passing under the audience without meeting a soul or being seen. It was like being under a great, grumbling beast, shifting and creaking and generally making itself heard.

And then, as if the thought she had been struggling to form had suddenly coalesced, she said, "How can you take me home? I don't have one."

"There's Florence. There's Lottie and Jack."

"They don't care about me."

"That's not true."

"Nobody cares. I'm a James. Everyone hates us now. That's why we have to hide."

He almost didn't see the seated figure ahead of them. The stripes of light from the bleachers were breaking up its outline, making it hard to distinguish. But then it moved and became the shape of a man. He was sitting on a stool with two buckets before him. A seat man, one of the lowest jobs in the show. There'd be one each side of the arena. The buckets contained sand and water for dousing small fires before they could become big ones. The seat man also collected any property that fell through the gaps above.

As the figure rose, Melody moved into action. In an instant she was no longer leaning on Sebastian, but reaching in and deftly taking the revolver from his coat. She was too fast. He had no warning, and no chance to stop her.

She said, "Kit! Who's this? Do you know him?"

29

ANY OPPORTUNITY TO ANSWER WAS SMOTHERED BY AN ERUP-
tion of noise from above as, out in the arena, the cowboy rescuers rode in
to take on the Shooting Savages. With a whistling and a whooping and a
popping of blanks, the unseen cowboys forced a pause in the conversation as
the seat man moved forward into the light.

When she could be heard, Melody said, "He's trying to kidnap me."

And Kit Strong said, "Is he, now."

Sebastian felt the muzzle of his own gun being pressed against the side of
his head. He heard the cocking of the hammer through the bones of his skull.

As Melody James held the gun to his temple, Kit Strong stood before
him. Not as tall as Sebastian had pictured. But rangy, his skin drawn tight,
his eyes two points of glitter in two dark pits of shadow. And in an instant
the doubts rolled back and the certainties slammed together. This was the
man. This had always been the man. Now he could imagine no other.

"Melody," Sebastian said, his gaze locked on Strong's. "Think about
what you're doing."

"She can use that pistol," Kit Strong said. "And she will. Be in no doubt."

"I'm not. Given that you've made her your slave."

"Is that what you think?"

"I'm seeing the evidence."

Without taking his eyes from Sebastian, Kit Strong said, "Are you my slave, Melody?"

The pressure withdrew, and Sebastian risked a turn of his head to look at her. She was moving back now, out of his reach so that he couldn't swipe at the gun and get inside her guard. Her expression was intense, her eyes unnaturally bright. Sebastian realized that the latter part of her dependence on him had been an act. Everything from the moment they'd emerged from the tent, a pretense.

He'd woken her up, and she'd brought him right here.

The child said to Strong, "What do you want to do with him?"

"Well," Strong said, "he's spoiled our situation. Here's another show we can't stay with."

Melody said, "What's your name?"

"Sebastian."

"Who knows you're here, Sebastian?"

The truth was, no one. But that was far too dangerous an admission to make. So he said, "The Pinkerton office in Philadelphia."

"Liar," Melody said. But he could tell that she wasn't sure.

Addressing Kit Strong, Sebastian said, "I'll make you a deal. Let me take Melody back. You disappear. No one will come looking for you."

"Here's my counter-offer," Strong said.

The punch was sudden, hard, and massively forceful. He didn't see it coming. It was like a rock to Sebastian's cheekbone, exploding his world. He wouldn't have believed that bare human knuckles could land with such impact. He wasn't even aware that he'd fallen. But here he was. He lay there looking straight up at the bleachers.

Strong loomed over him. He held out his hand toward Melody and she placed Sebastian's pistol in it without needing to be told. Strong cocked the hammer and then waited for some covering gunfire from the arena. When it came he discharged the revolver into the ground right by Sebastian's head, so close that the cold dirt splattered on his face. Strong fired again, and again, first one side and then the other, the big slugs ripping into the dirt until Melody restrained him with a hand on his arm. Not out of sympathy for Sebastian, but because the masking gunfire out in the arena had ceased.

Strong said, "See if he's got any money."

He kept the gun on Sebastian while Melody crouched and went through his pockets. The Bull Dog had a five-chambered cylinder, two shots remaining. Out in the arena, the crowd roared and stamped as the show's big finale came to its end. Grit and dust were shaken from the bleachers to fall like soft rain, while the light from above became like rays through smoke.

Melody found his cash. Not the bulk of it—that was safely hidden in his coat lining. But she found his travelling money. In another pocket she found his Chancery credentials, but discarded those.

Then she stopped. She'd found the cabinet photograph. The one used by the mortician to reconstruct the dead man's face. The one that Sebastian had been carrying since the day that he'd first heard the name of William James.

"What's that?" Strong said.

She turned it around to show him.

"Rip it up," Strong said.

Sebastian, up on his elbows now, saw her hesitate.

Strong was looking at her, pointedly. For a moment Sebastian thought that she might protest. But then she tore up the card and threw the pieces down into Sebastian's face, in a gesture that seemed to suggest a touch of petulance. They fluttered in the air and fell all around, none actually reaching him.

"Good girl," Strong said.

Above them, with the show over, people were on the move and the bleachers were clearing. The sidewall canvas at the back of the stand began to buckle. Without even waiting for the arena to empty, the teardown crew was already pulling up stakes.

When Kit Strong glanced back and saw this, he said, "Time to go."

While his attention was elsewhere, Sebastian took the opportunity to try to rise.

"Not you," Strong said, and kicked him in the head.

All went dark.

30

Over the next few hours he drifted in and out of consciousness, almost surfacing but never quite. He was aware of people moving around him, of someone pulling up an eyelid. He could remember thinking that he'd return in his own time. He could remember the anxiety that came with the prospect of revival. The world was a painful place. Down in the depths, he felt safe.

When he finally broke through to full awareness it was daylight.

He was in a tent like the ones from the night before, and alone. He was cold. This tent had been opened to the air at one end, and had been stripped of everything bar the cot he was lying on.

Feeling cold wasn't the worst of it. More of him than his head was hurting. He must have suffered a kicking while unconscious. Which he supposed was a blessing, of a kind.

But only the most perverse kind.

He wondered if he could stand.

He could, but the effort made him retch. He'd have thrown up, had his stomach not been empty. He lowered himself back down and waited to see what would happen.

He was seeing double. One side of his face was swollen. He could barely move his neck when he tried. A tooth felt loose, but all his teeth were still there. Just checking them with his tongue cost him an effort. He sat on the edge of the borrowed cot and for a while he could do nothing, nothing at all.

He decided that if he moved slowly and deliberately, like those Chinese he'd seen exercising by the railroad that one time, then maybe he could balance pain with the need for action. He had to move. He was vulnerable here. He tried it. He felt like a thousand-year-old man as he started out by patting himself down and checking his pockets.

He didn't expect to find his pistol, and he didn't. Someone had picked up his Chancery credentials and tucked them into an inside pocket. Along with them he found some free passes for the Wild West show, good for next year.

He rose again, and this time he stayed up. The double vision had begun to settle, so he moved to the open side of the tent and looked out.

Where the arena had stood was now a great empty field with some litter blowing around. Just a few baggage wagons and animals remained. Everything else had been loaded up and taken onward to the next stand.

"Hey there," he heard a voice call out.

He tried to turn his head, then turned his entire upper body instead. A man was waving to him from by one of the wagons. The wagon was painted red and gold, with decorative scrolls. The man had paused in the work of stowing horse tack into an open sidebox.

As soon as Sebastian stepped out of the tent, two men appeared and began pulling it down. So he kept walking. His gait felt like the motion of a square-wheeled cart on a bumpy road.

Wearing boots, a brown stable coat and a Derby hat, the man who'd called to him was winding reins around his fist and smiling pleasantly from behind a wide, dense mustache. The mustache had waxed ends, tapering to fine points.

"How's my patient today?" he asked as Sebastian drew near.

"Who found me?" Sebastian said. To his own ears, his whisper sounded like a threat. But the man was unfazed.

"The boys found you lying there when we started the teardown," he said. "I checked you for broken bones and I don't think I found any."

"Are you the company doctor?"

"Horse doctor. What happened, son? You get robbed? You must have been robbed. You don't strike me as the kind of man who gets into fights for fun."

"It wasn't fun," Sebastian agreed.

"You live local?"

"I'm from out of town. Do you know where Kit Strong went?"

"Kit who?"

Of course the man wouldn't know. Strong had been with the company for less than a week. And he'd been a seat man, down there in the dark, picking up small change and waiting to douse anything that smoldered. A long way down from the headliner he'd once been, for sure.

"Doesn't matter," Sebastian said. "Thanks for the looking-after."

"You're welcome. Give you a ride into town?"

"Appreciated," Sebastian said.

"Just a minute." The horse doctor opened up a compartment in his wagon box and took out a small bottle. He checked the label, gave it a shake, and then held it out to Sebastian. "This should help."

Sebastian took the bottle from him.

"Do I swallow it or rub it on?" he said.

"Take a sip every hour," the horse doctor said. "And if you feel the urge to gallop, resist."

31

It took him most of a day on the railroad to get himself back to Philadelphia. On the longest part of the ride, he slept in his seat and the conductor woke him just ahead of his stop. Whatever was in the horse doctor's bottle, it tasted like chalk and dulled his various aches. Between Harrisburg and Lancaster he borrowed another passenger's discarded newspaper and searched it for news of any political tensions at home, but all the European news that he could find was piece on the Kaiser's dismal taste in theater.

Late in the evening, he arrived back at the Keystone. He gave his room number to the night clerk, only to be told, "Mrs Becker has your key."

"Excuse me?"

"Your wife arrived a couple of hours ago. She had me move her luggage into your room. I assume that was okay?"

"I guess so," he said.

There was a message or two, but nothing that wouldn't wait. He climbed the stairs to the second floor and knocked on his own door. Nothing happened for a moment. No sound from within. Then it opened.

He said, "Frances?"

"Oh. Sebastian." She stood in the open doorway looking startled. Her hair was tousled, some of her buttons undone. She said, "My boat got in this morning. I didn't mean to fall asleep. I lay on the bed and closed my eyes for two minutes."

"The clerk said…"

"Did he confuse you? I'd no way to pay for a second room so I told him I was your wife. Don't be alarmed, it was the simplest answer." She stepped back to let him into the room. As he passed her she got a closer look at him and said, "Sebastian! What happened to your face?"

He tried to wave down her concern. "I caught up with Kit Strong last night," he said. "This is how he greets his admirers."

"Have you seen a doctor?"

"Kind of."

"Tell me what happened."

So he sat on the bed and gave her the story of his past two weeks, of the ground covered, the people seen, the trails found and lost. Of squatters with squirrel guns and 'Hey Rube' fisticuffs, of dead bodies and bloodied pages and Melody James.

As he was telling the tale of their encounter under the bleachers, he was interrupted by an odd sound that he thought at first was the hotel's plumbing, before realizing that it was actually a growl from Frances' stomach. She clapped a hand to her mouth. She was embarrassed and apologetic.

"I haven't eaten since the boat," she explained. "My father sent me a ticket but no money."

He finished the story as she tidied her hair and buttoned her dress. It was late, but there was a night café at the end of the block. He looked around at her open bags, the rumpled counterpane.

He didn't need to ask why Frances had come to his hotel, instead of going straight to her father's house. One does not enter a lion's cave, he thought, without first pausing to establish the mood and stance of the lion.

She straightened the counterpane before they went down.

On the stairs she told of the arrangements that she'd made for Robert before leaving. She'd ensured that his rent and laundry were paid for in advance. His landlady had the details and addresses to reach either of them if it should be necessary. There was little to worry about; the widow doted on Robert.

The night café was quiet. They took a booth and looked over the hand-written menu. Sebastian had no appetite. He picked at his pancakes when they came, while Frances shoveled down her meatloaf and gravy.

He said, "I don't think your joining me was part of your father's plan. In his mind, I'm the man who led both his daughters astray."

"I should be grateful he didn't have me kidnapped, then."

"When will you see him?"

"Soon. I suppose. Now I'm here I find I'm…"

"Excited?"

"Nervous. He was never an easy man. And it's been so long without even a letter."

Sebastian said, "I saw him two days ago."

She looked up from the pie list. "How did that go?"

"I said my piece. He said his. We actually found some things to agree on."

"I won't go back to him," she said.

"Then why are you here?"

"He's my father. And the ticket was free. But if he thinks he can turn back the clock and have everything as it was, that just can't be. I'm a grown woman now. I have a life of my own."

"You should at least hear what he has to say."

"You sound like you'd want me to go."

"I want—" he began, but Frances interrupted him.

"Don't say what's best for me," she said. "You don't know what that is."

"I've seen his house. It's not your old mansion, but nor is it the Borough."

"It could be a castle on a mountain with leopards in the garden. I still wouldn't care. I'll hear him out. It's the decent thing to do. But I'm here to visit my home town again, and to be with you."

She sensed his hesitation in framing a reply.

She said, "Are my bags in the way? We can ask for a bigger room."

"It's not that."

"Then what?"

"There's no couch," he said. "Just the one bed."

"We can bundle if you want," Frances said, "but I've had time to think about this." She glanced around, to be sure that their waitress wasn't near. "Hear me out," she said. "I have a proposal."

"You do?"

"I know how things were between you and Elisabeth. The pressure of her work and our financial circumstances. How she lost her interest in physical love."

Sebastian blinked. This was not going in any direction that he'd expected. "You discussed such things?" he said.

"As sisters do. You're blushing. There's no need for it."

"It's not exactly within my control."

"Sometimes I'd have to bite my tongue when she spoke of it," Frances said. "God bless her soul, but I don't think she was aware of how insensitive she could be. Never stopping to think that she might be dismissing one of life's gifts in the presence of someone who could only long for what she had."

Sebastian was lost for words. All he could say was, "I'm so sorry, Frances."

"I don't mean in any specific thoughts toward you," she said quickly. "That would have been wrong."

"I'm sure."

"She never loved you less. But Elisabeth is gone now. We mourn her but we are where we are. I don't seek to take her place. But we're both alone now, Sebastian. If you feel need of a companion to share your bed, you should know that I am willing."

"Frances…" he began, and again she interrupted.

"I know what's required," she said. "I have no experience but I do have pamphlets. Don't answer me now. Wait and be sure. I have."

"You should hear what your father has to say before you commit to anything that may involve me."

"It won't make any difference."

"It might."

"Why? Is he a changed man?"

"That may be putting it a little too strongly."

He paid for their food at the counter, and they walked the short distance to the hotel entrance.

Sebastian was not so much shocked by Frances' proposal, as taken aback by the way in which she'd explained it. Clearly she'd thought it all through, and considered it to make perfect sense.

He had no idea how to respond. He'd imagined that the relative orbits of their lives were fixed, and could not change. Of one thing he was certain; he felt that Frances could do better. As he'd explained to her father, his fear was that for Frances to continue her life with him would be her second-best option, and a poor reward for her years of sacrifice.

He could only wonder what Callowhill might make of this latest conversation.

He found the stairs more of a struggle than before. Back at the room, he gave Frances the William James transcript to read while he made his way to the bathroom down the hall. The spotted mirror gave him his first good look his injuries, and it was a shock. He did the best he could with soap and a sponge before returning to the room.

Frances had changed into a nightgown and was sitting on the bed, knees drawn up and a pillow behind her, reading the William James pages. She looked up at the involuntary sound he made as he turned to close the door.

"Sebastian," she said. "What is it?"

"I seem to have been kicked around rather more than I thought," he said. "Let me see."

His shirt was untucked, and he hoisted it up to expose one side from hip to ribcage. He heard her draw breath. Blood had pooled under the skin, turning most of the area a vivid range of sunset colors.

"There's more," he said, "but that's the worst of it."

Frances was visibly shocked. She said, "Can I do anything?"

"The horse doctor's bottle kept the pain away. I thought I was fine. But now it's wearing off."

She swung her legs off the bed and went to the nightstand for the medicine. She read the label on the bottle and then held it up to the light.

"It's almost empty," she said.

Feeling suddenly much weaker than he had at any other time since the cowboy camp that morning, he said, "Can you help me to lie down?"

She took his arm and helped lower him onto the bed. She uncapped the bottle and placed it in his hand. He emptied it down his throat in one, then sank back and sighed.

Frances lay down beside him, on her side with her face close to his so that she could watch his breathing. She placed her hand on his shoulder, the better to sense his condition.

She said, "This evil man. The police will get him. Yes?"

"He'll be out of the state by now."

"The U.S. Marshals, then."

"It's complicated."

"You can't let him get away with this."

The bed was soft, the pillow softer. Sebastian felt a sense of euphoria starting from his core and spreading outward, like the melt around hot coal dropped onto a deep-frozen pond. Did they treat horses with morphine? Was this how it felt? For some reason his inclination to judge the addicted was suddenly less severe.

He said, "I could just report the death of William James and go home."

"You could," she said. "But then, what hope for Melody?"

"Buffalo Bill," he heard himself say.

"What?"

"He blames Buffalo Bill for everything. That's where he'll head for. Cody."

"You're not making any sense."

"I know."

"Sleep, now."

"Colonel William Cody. Cody, Wyoming."

"Shhh."

32

WALKING UP THE CURVING PATHWAY TO HER FATHER'S PLACE, Frances saw the trees part to reveal a rambling Queen Anne structure in the style of a rich child's dollhouse. The lawn was manicured, the paintwork fresh. If this was penury, it should be borne by all.

She remembered Chestnut Hill as a place for parties and weekends. It was largely the creation of the city's merchants and captains of industry. They'd bought up its land for their estates and hired fashionable architects to design the thirty-roomed cottages they put on them. Cottages of every imaginable character; fairytale structures in Victorian gingerbread, in Carpenter Gothic, in faux-medieval granite or Romanesque stone. Hideous, most of them. Tasteless to a point that tested human courtesy.

Picturesque eclectic, the guidebooks said. To spend the summers here was quite the thing. To make a year-round home, sitting out the winter so far from center city and its Season, not so much.

Though he surely had servants, it was Callowhill himself who opened the door at her ring. An older Callowhill, she saw, his once-graying hair almost completely white, and less of it; his shoulders a little stooped, the skin a little looser on his bones. But unmistakably the man as she remembered him.

"Frances," he said. "Thank you for making the journey. Please. Come in." He took a step back into the hallway with a gesture of welcome, and she was already thrown.

As she entered, he said, "You seem surprised."

"Why would I be?"

"Perhaps by an invitation where you expected an instruction?"

"Your words, Father. Not mine."

There was, indeed, a maid, and she was waiting to take Frances' coat and hat. Callowhill then ushered his daughter toward the back of the house, through one room and another and into a conservatory that overlooked a walled garden. It was a bright and cheerful garden, which made for a bright and cheerful room.

He said, "Are your bags in the cab?"

"They're at the hotel. I walked here."

"Which hotel? I'll send over."

"It doesn't matter," she said, and Callowhill must have sensed some hint of evasion in her tone.

"Not the Keystone?" he said. "With Becker? That's no fit place for a Callowhill."

"It suits me well enough. And I don't recall agreeing to move in with you."

"Oh, Frances. Must we begin like this?"

"I'm sorry," she conceded. "That was rude."

"Look around you. Do I need all this space to myself? This can be your home, if you want it. For as long as you want it and with no conditions. I know you're loyal to Becker, but what use has he for a housekeeper when he's already in a hotel?"

She sensed a turn onto more dangerous ground, and so she didn't take it.

Instead she said, "Sebastian left town again this morning. He has business in the West."

"All the more reason."

"Thank you for the steamer ticket. And I'm glad to find you well. But if you've brought me here to stand with my head bowed while you forgive me, that won't happen."

"I know that. Have you considered that I may be the one who feels the need for contrition?"

This surprised her. "No," was all she could say. "I have not."

"Is that so remarkable?"

"Forgive me, but it is."

"What exactly did Becker tell you about our meeting?"

"Only that you found some things to agree on."

"He regrets marrying Elisabeth," he said.

"He does not."

"Only because their life together ended as it did," he said, and added, "I won't claim I predicted such a tragedy. But I so feared something like it. Can you at least understand that?"

She moved to the conservatory windows and looked out into the walled garden. A garden? It was almost a private park. A brick path wound through it, crossing a footbridge over a reed pond to disappear into a stand of cypress. Just below the house the summer beds were turning to autumn shades, bright colors giving way to cool lavenders and blues.

She said, "Do you remember when I was your go-between?"

"And I made you choose a side."

"It was unfair of you. Nevertheless, I chose."

"And now the world has turned and everything's changed. I can't undo the past. But let me offer you back the life you deserve."

"Before it's too late?"

"Your words, Frances. Not mine."

At this point Callowhill moved to the doorway and caught the eye of the maid, who appeared to have been waiting outside the room for this signal.

As the servant was moving off, Callowhill turned back to his daughter and said, "Do you have money?"

"Some," Frances said.

"But it's Becker's money? It must be. At least let your own father support you while you're here. Do it for Becker if not for me."

There, he had her. Sebastian had peeled off a substantial part of his Pinkerton back pay for her keep in Philadelphia. She hadn't wanted to take it, but what could she do? He'd brushed aside her objectives, saying that she was helping him by taking some of the weight out of his coat.

She said, "If I stay, and if I tell you everything I remember of Elisabeth and our lives away from you…then will I get a ticket home if I want one? The passage you paid for was only one-way."

"You're offering me a deal?"

"You rebuilt your fortune. You must know something of business."

At that point, the maid returned with a silver tray. Callowhill said, "I spread the word that you were coming back to Philadelphia. Your friends remember you."

Frances looked at the tray, and saw that it bore a small number of notelets and *cartes de visite*.

"One's from Freddie Belmont," Callowhill said. "You must remember Freddie."

"I heard he was married."

"The girl was frail, poor thing. Two children being raised by an Aunt. Reply or don't, it's up to you. I'll have the Keystone bring over your bags."

Cody, Wyoming

33

AFTER FOUR DAYS OF TRAVEL, SEBASTIAN ARRIVED AT CODY'S railroad depot. Four days on the move and only one of those nights spent in a bed, and that in a sleeping car shared with a party of Mormons who seemed to believe that conversations meant for private ears somehow created no disturbance to anyone else. When their God didn't tell them to shut up and go to sleep, Sebastian stepped in.

Discomfort had shortened his patience. He wasn't yet healed from the beating he'd taken, though he was much improved. The bruising was still black and yellow but his swellings had reduced. The loosened tooth hadn't fallen out, and the double vision had steadied. His ribs continued to hurt, and the dent in his dignity would be a hard one to knock out. But he lived, and he could move, and if anything could have increased his determination to prize Melody James from the grip of Kit Strong and see the man get his comeuppance, this was it. Previously, they'd been figures in another man's story. Now, in the most vivid and violent of ways, they had entered his own.

He'd been disarmed. That was a problem, though he'd no intention of facing Strong again in private if he could help it. He would call in the law when he could be certain of the outcome.

"Cody!" the conductor was calling out over the sound of train brakes and venting steam as he passed down each carriage. "Cody, Wyoming! End of the line!"

Cody's rail depot stood north of town on the wrong side of the river. It consisted of a two-story brick building, a water tower, and an uninterrupted view of the wide-open prairie. This was the Big Horn Basin tourist route up into Yellowstone Park, and the depot's low wooden platform was stacked high with the luggage and hunting trophies of homeward bound passengers.

Cody had named the town after himself, and its main hotel after his daughter. Sebastian had heard the Irma's boast that it was 'the most modern hotel in the Rockies'. He'd also heard of the Irma's reputation for inedible food and insanitary accommodation and didn't plan to stay there, but he accepted a ride in the waiting guest wagon.

The road into town took them over a second-hand bridge, bought from a railroad company and re-sited over the Shoshone. A whiff of brimstone enveloped the open car as they passed over the river. The Shoshone was fed by hot sulfur springs which had earned it the name of The Stinking Water, conferred upon it by the Crow tribe.

Tom Kane was late for their appointment. Sebastian waited in the Standard Restaurant with strong coffee to keep him awake. Most of the others present appeared to be laborers in the oil drilling trade, and when Kane arrived he immediately spotted Sebastian as the only stranger in the place.

He was a big, quiet man, and he didn't apologize for his lateness.

Sebastian introduced himself and then got straight to it.

He said, "If a person came looking for a meet with Colonel Cody, where would he most likely show up?"

Kane said, "That's a very roundabout way of asking, if you don't mind me saying so."

"I'm not actually looking for the Colonel. I'm looking for someone who's looking."

"Are you connected to the motion picture people?"

Though he didn't know what Kane was taking about, Sebastian sensed a ready-made alibi and said, "You've seen right through me."

"It's no big secret. Since they announced it on the front page of the Enterprise." Kane turned and called over his shoulder. "Grace?"

He had the waitress bring over the town's newspaper.

The headline read COLONEL CODY FORMS BIG MOVING PICTURE COM-
PANY: JOINS DENVER CAPITALISTS IN ORGANIZING LARGE FILM PRODUCING
OUTFIT. MEMORABLE BATTLE IS TO BE REPRODUCED.

Tom Kane waited as Sebastian read. A quick skim of the story told of
a partnership formed by two newspaper publishers and the Colonel to create a series of historically accurate motion pictures of 'national importance'.
*Colonel Cody has secured permission from the Secretary of Interior to take any
pictures he may desire on the Pine Ridge Indian Agency and will also be given
the use of the Indians.*

Sebastian read aloud, *"He has said that he would take his outfit to the T E
Ranch and there would obtain several winter pictures in the mountains."* He looked
up. "The T E Ranch?"

"That's his place," Tom Kane said. "Anyone looking for the Colonel
would most likely head for there. You go southwest of town and take the
South Fork road."

• • •

AT KANE'S recommendation Sebastian hired a car and driver from the
Holm Transportation Company. They were in the business of arranging
excursions for big game hunters down the creeks and canyons, and could
surely help Sebastian to run down one errant Colonel who never seemed
to stay in any one place for more than a couple of days. The town that he'd
helped to found had his name and likeness everywhere, if not his presence,
but it was struggling to thrive. The Irma Hotel was the only impressive structure on its main street, which otherwise was one long, wide and empty dirt
thoroughfare of low wooden buildings and telegraph poles. Of the fewer
than fifty buildings standing when the Irma had gone up, ten were saloons.
In three directions there were distant mountains; between the town and the
mountains, nothing.

This, despite the fact that Colonel Cody had invested heavily in its development. As well as building houses and a hotel he was lobbying for new roads
and a dam to irrigate the basin. He kept an office and suite of rooms in the
Irma for his personal use. It was said that he planned to retire to one of his
new Wyoming homes, should the day ever come when he could afford to. It
seemed that Cody was as adept at losing a fortune as he was at making one.

The South Fork road was a wagon road at best, and took more than an hour to navigate. As they approached the ranch buildings, a rider came out to meet them. Such was the landscape that those at the house had probably been able to see and hear the car's approach over the last half mile. The rider was clean-shaven, well-spoken, and polite. Sebastian took him for some kind of ranch manager or foreman.

The driver slowed the car to a stop before a white picket fence, and the foreman reined in his mount on the other side of it.

"May I help you, sir," the rider called.

From his passenger seat, Sebastian called back, "My name is Sebastian Becker and I'm hoping you may."

"If it's an interview you're looking for, you missed the Colonel by half a day. He's gone into the Black Hills with the motion picture people."

"I'm not looking for the Colonel. I'm on the trail of a man named Kit Strong."

The rider was silent for a moment, and Sebastian couldn't read him at all.

"Are you," the rider said.

"I'm not the law."

"Wouldn't worry if you were."

"Did he show up here?"

The rider considered a moment longer, then came to a decision.

"Come on in," he said.

He turned his horse to the gate and, without dismounting, reached down to unhook it and open the way for the vehicle to enter. Once it was through he secured the gate behind them, and then came around in front to lead the way. The General Headquarters of the ranch was a long, low building with a flagpole before it. They followed the rider past this to some freshly painted white log cabins that served as cookhouse and bunkhouses.

Sebastian's driver was sent to the kitchen for some coffee, while Sebastian was taken into the ranch office.

The foreman introduced himself as Clark Henderson. "So what's the story?" he said.

"Kit Strong once worked for the Colonel, a long time ago," Sebastian said. "He went to Europe with the Wild West company in '04. He was injured in a riding accident and they left him behind."

"It's not like the Colonel to abandon the wounded."

"Strong was busted up quite badly. There was no question of him travelling back with the show. As I understand it, there was money for his hospital time and travel but it ran out. Ever since then he's borne a grudge against the world in general and Colonel Cody in particular."

"For more than ten years?"

"He's one of those guys."

"Well," Henderson said, "I can't say where he is but I can tell you he was here."

"Was he alone?"

"Had a boy with him. Said it was a boy, anyway. Looked more niece than nephew to me. You can only get away with that trick for so long and once you get past a certain point, a gal's a gal however you dress her. They showed up at the gate like you did, but not so polite. So that's as far as they got."

"What happened?"

"The Colonel came out and had us all stand back while they talked. Told us this Kit Strong was an old friend, but it didn't have the look of a friendly conversation. I don't know what was said, but now you've told me what you told me I can guess. He must have been telling Strong the pot was empty and the money was all gone. The Colonel sent to the house for some travelling cash and Strong threw it in his face and walked away. The kid picked it up."

"Was that the end of it?"

"I'm not giving away any secrets if I tell you the Colonel was bankrupted last year. Everyone touches him for money and what he doesn't give away, he puts into one scheme or another that never pays off."

He went on to explain how Cody had been struggling financially for some time, and had launched a tour in partnership with fellow showman and sometime rival Pawnee Bill. The bank had called in Cody's debts and closed the show in Denver, leaving all the performers and workers unpaid. Cody had taken a loan and paid all their salaries in in full. The motion picture deal represented his plan for getting back on his feet.

"The man's made fortunes and he'll die without a bean," Henderson said. "Gotta love him for that. So what's your beef with Strong? You can't be chasing him for money. Is it something about the kid?"

Sebastian said, "Something like that."

"She yours?"

"No."

"Then I can say this. She struck me as kind of…I don't know. Older than her years and a little bit wild. Like one of those feral kittens you get in a barn. They look cute 'til you pick 'em up and then the claws come out."

"He's made her that way," Sebastian said. "They're going to be hard to pull apart."

"Gonna tell me how you got the split lip?"

"I caught up with them once already. I plan to be more careful next time. Did they give you any idea of where they were headed next?"

"Well," Henderson said with some amusement, "the grand exit didn't come to much when the boss called them back and insisted they eat before storming off."

"He did?"

"That's the Colonel. They sat in the tent with the motion picture folk. Then I believe they got a ride on one of the trucks heading back to California."

"California."

"That's where all the picture people are setting up now. Plenty of work for show cowboys out there. Or so they say."

Los Angeles, September 1913

34

HER NAME WAS MARGARET, AND SHE'D LIED TO GET THE JOB.

Not that her employer had seemed to care. He hadn't asked about her typewriting speed (minimal, hunting for every letter) or her stenography (nonexistent after less than a week of secretarial school). The card on the drugstore board had called for an office clerk, not a secretary, and she was the only applicant to show up, so she was in. These were hungry times for everyone, but in this case Margaret had an advantage. She'd seen the card go up on the board. When she left the drugstore, the card went with her.

It was a lucky find. Her age had been much easier to fake than any actual skills. Margaret House was fifteen years old. Both of her parents were dead, and she'd a younger brother to support. They lived rent-free in a room over her aunt's garage but while her Aunt Tillie was pleasant enough to their faces, Margaret had overheard her talking to a neighbor. By the phrase "that girl" alone, she knew their welcome was wearing thin.

Like every other young, pretty, dark-eyed girl in town, Margaret had tried for motion pictures. She'd dragged Chandler along to the same casting calls in the hope they might need a boy. In happier times back in Colorado Springs she'd taken singing lessons, and while a voice was no asset in 'the movies', she'd gained a certain confidence. She'd learned the difference between real performing and mere playing for attention, the difference between 'look at me' and 'look at this', and she'd show them what she could do, if the chance ever came. They'd had no luck to date, but she would persist.

For now, here was a job. A few dollars a week, for probably not many weeks. Her employer was a producer, he said, though she'd quickly come to doubt it. All he had to his name was a bare rented office and a box ad in the local press. The name was false, she reckoned. He wrote no letters, received no mail, and had no visitors other than the cowboys who responded to his advertisement.

Her job was to sit out front, and to turn them away.

It wasn't quite as simple as that, but it wasn't far from it. Those who made it through a short list of questions would be allowed into the inner office. Invariably they'd be out again within the minute. All references and resumés were discarded unread; she emptied them from her employer's wastebasket at the end of each day. Margaret was aware that he kept a pistol under the desk and within reach as she sent each person in.

She hadn't been busy for several days, but on the morning of the ad there had been a line out into the hall. He'd also had handbills printed, and hired boys to hand them out during morning calls at the various studio gates. In they came. Cowboys in chaps, Easterners in suits with stage experience, young men in borrowed costumes, old men in borrowed costumes, and at least two board-certifiable lunatics disrupting the morning's business at different times. Why did show business attract them so? But attract them it did.

That afternoon, a couple dozen more of the same. Not so many since.

This one didn't look anything like the others.

He stood in the doorway. He was holding one of the handbills.

He said, "You're hiring cowboys?"

"Mister Jones is looking for a specialist act," she said. He didn't look anything like a cowboy. Or sound like one, either. "Do you have any skills?"

"Roping. Riding, that kind of thing?"

"Trick roping yes. No riding involved. He needs someone who can throw knives and axes."

"Axes?"

"Tommyhawks. At a living target. I know you actors. Don't just say you can do it if you can't."

The visitor twitched a smile, bemused by such tough talk from one so young. "I wouldn't dare," he said. "Lead me to him."

"Just a moment," Margaret said, rising. "What name?"

"Becker," he said. "Sebastian Becker. I've a feeling he may know it."

"Wait here, please, Mister Becker."

She knocked, and went through to the inner office without waiting for a reply. Her employer looked up from his newspaper as she announced the visitor.

"Becker?" her boss said, and laid down the paper.

Margaret said, "He's no cowboy, I'm sure."

He pulled open the desk drawer and laid his hand ready on the revolver within. She tried not to stare at his hands, something that it was always hard for her to avoid.

"Send him in," he said. "And you can go to lunch."

"It's only eleven."

"Take your time."

She returned to the outer office. "He'll see you," she said to the visitor, and reached for her coat. On her way out she could hear the first words exchanged as the two men faced each other.

"Mister Becker," her employer said.

"William James," said their visitor.

35

SEBASTIAN SAID, "YOU CAN CLOSE THE DRAWER. I'M JUST HERE to talk."

The man behind the desk hesitated for a moment, trying to gauge Sebastian's intentions. Then he raised his open hand and leaned back in his chair. William James didn't have the look of a fugitive, or of a desperate man. He wore a decent suit of heavy cloth, and a laundered shirt with a starched collar. He'd let his mustache and sideburns grow, but his cheeks were shaved clean and his hair was decently, if not recently, barbered. Only the eyes gave him away; they had the sharp and guarded look of a forest creature that might, at any instant, fall under a predator's shadow.

He said, "How did you find me?"

"You papered the town with your handbills," Sebastian said, moving around the desk to reach for the pistol; whereupon William James slid the drawer shut, putting the weapon out of play for both of them. "If there was ever a more obvious ploy to flush out Kit Strong, I can't imagine what it would be."

"How are you even here?" William James said. "It was all over. I gave you a body, I gave you the story. You were supposed to pack up and go home."

"Are you forgetting I'm a detective by trade?"

"And I'm a showman. Misdirection's mine. Where did I go wrong?"

"It was a convincing setup," Sebastian conceded. "Apart from the absence of burn scars on the hands. And the boards in the room creaked, so no one could have crept in close enough to make a contact shot. And you left his shoes off. Shoes are the hardest things to get on when you're dressing a corpse."

"I didn't kill him."

"If I believed you did, we wouldn't be having this conversation. You saw an opportunity and took it, and now there's a family somewhere not knowing whether to hope or grieve. Was it the New Jersey man? Travelling salesman?"

"His name was Regis Powell and he was neither."

Sebastian drew over the office's second chair, and sat himself down. "Explain?" he said.

"Regis was a cardsharper and bunco operator," William James said. "I met him on the boat coming over. We were men of similar skills in a similar quandary so we teamed up at the card table and played as strangers to raise some cash. Between us we could clean out a game without anyone catching on. I'd no money or legal access to any. I'm a moral man, but…"

"Stealing from gamblers is hardly real theft."

"Needs must, Mister Becker."

"So how did he end up in your room and your clothes with his brains blown out?"

"That night when he didn't show up for the evening's split, I went looking and found him dead in the alley by the hotel. Someone had coshed him and taken the pot. I couldn't do anything for him. But we were of a size and type—he could help me break the trail."

"You knew I was coming?"

"I did. I'd tipped the clerk to let me know if anyone enquired after me. Once you'd telephoned, I knew it was only a matter of time before you showed up." He looked Sebastian in the eyes, more in the way of a challenge than an appeal. "So what now?" he said.

"I'm the only one who knows you're still alive," Sebastian said.

"What did you tell London?"

"Nothing either way. But I do have a convincing photograph of your corpse."

"Can you persuade them I'm dead?"

"That would depend."

"You must believe in my innocence. Or you'd have turned up here with the law behind you."

"Innocent or guilty, I've no idea. I still don't know what happened on the night of the fire."

"I left you a full account."

"Without an ending," Sebastian said. "The undertaker used the final pages to stuff out your cheeks before he sewed up your lips."

The idea might have horrified another man. But William James had travelled too far, and seen too much, to be anything other than amused by this specter of his own mortality.

"Poor Regis," he said. "Not only buried under another man's name, but with another man's words in his mouth."

One thing still bothered Sebastian. The man that he'd buried bore a post-mortem gunshot wound sustained at the desk where Sebastian had found him. It had obliterated the fatal injury and distorted the features enough for the subsequent deception. Yet no one in the building had reported hearing a shot.

He said, "How did you manage to fire off a gun in a crowded hotel without everyone knowing?"

"Waited for sunup," William James said. "When the storekeepers down below pulled out their awnings, the clash of metal was enough to cover the sound. Then I was off to the station in Powell's clothes and eyeglasses. Dropped his key at the empty front desk on my way out."

He stood up.

"We should go," he said. "Either Kit Strong hasn't seen my advertisement, or like you he's seen through it. In which case I'm risking discovery for no advantage. Who else knows you're in town, Mister Becker?"

"No one," Sebastian said. "And to the best of my knowledge, no one is following my movements."

"Do you have a plan?"

"I imagine it's the same as yours. To get a vulnerable child out of Kit Strong's control and return her to safety."

"I have rooms close by," William James said. "Shall we go there and talk further?"

Sebastian made no move as William James opened the desk drawer, took out the firearm, and slipped it into his coat pocket. There was a sense of each man testing out the trust of the other, a sense that they were reaching an understanding—a delicate one that would not survive if spoken of too soon.

In the outer office, William James stopped to write a note to his absent clerk. He placed it in an envelope along with some folded bills.

"Very generous," Sebastian observed.

"She's an orphan," William James said. "Supporting her brother. She can't be more than fifteen but you should have seen how she dealt with some of the wild types who came through that door."

"Did you hire her because she reminded you of your daughter?"

"Not in any particular," William James said.

He wrote Margaret's name on the envelope and left it sticking out from under the blotter. He gave a last look around the office, which was otherwise bare of any trace of occupation. A running man, who'd learned to move on and leave no mark. Then they went out, with William James closing the door behind them, and took the building's cage elevator down to street level.

• • •

BETWEEN THE Ferguson Building and the Third Street tunnel, a funicular railway climbed the short but steep incline to the Bunker Hill district. The ride was a nickel a head. After disembarking at the upper station they crossed the relative quiet of Olive Street to the Argyle Hotel.

From here there was a view out across the city's growing downtown of office blocks and grand hotels. The Argyle was an apartment rooming house, and not one of the best. It was a four-story wooden building, the uppermost an attic floor, the lowest half-sunk into the hillside so that it was part-basement. The entrance was to the side. As a residence it was the choice of struggling artists and music teachers. It seemed run-down when compared to the Bunker Hill mansions springing up all around.

William James had taken a small suite of rooms on the second floor. The hotel's European Plan was a dollar fifty a day and included no meals. The building manager or some member of his family would run out to a local restaurant in return for tips. It wasn't luxury, but as the fruits of card-sharping went it wasn't so bad. Sebastian had spent the previous night in a five-to-a-room hostel with three prospectors and a drunk.

Some of the Argyle's rooms had a panoramic view of the city below. This one did not. William James said, "I can send a boy for coffee."

"I don't need any," Sebastian said.

His host took off his jacket and slung it over the back of a chair. "So what more do you want to know?" he said.

"I know about the first-house debacle that got the company dismissed," Sebastian said. "I read how you sent everyone back to the digs, ordered a doctor for Lottie, and told Jack to throw Kit Strong's possessions into the street."

"Nothing beyond that?"

"No."

"Jack took me literally," William James began.

36

"You can imagine his anger after the onstage assault on his wife. While the doctor was tending to Lottie in a back room of our digs, Jack pushed Kit Strong's cabin trunk out of an upstairs window and it fell fifteen feet or more. Burst open when it hit the pavement and most of Strong's worldly goods ended up in the gutter. When he came back, he was greeted by the sight of a crowd picking over his belongings and passing his Cody letters from hand to hand, with the choicest passages being read aloud. Anything of value was long gone."

Sebastian said, "How did he respond?"

"I wasn't there to see. I imagine not well. I was searching everywhere for Melody. I even went to the railway station because I was convinced that it was his intention to make off with her that very night. On my return I was told that Strong had tried to collect his properties backstage but the manager had barred him from the theater. I'm not sure how much he cared about retrieving his axes and trick ropes, but securing his morphine supply was another matter.

"By this time the second house was under way. I went out to the pavilion and presented myself at the stage door. The doorkeeper confirmed that Kit Strong was barred from the house, but he'd had no specific instructions about other members of the company. He'd allowed Melody to enter and pick up Strong's effects. Unless she'd left by some other exit, she was still inside.

"He let me in and I went to our dressing rooms, but other acts had already bagged the space. Coram told me that our goods and chattels had been stacked in the farthest backstage corner of the building, out of everyone's way. I went looking for them—looking for Melody. All was now dark. I could hear laughter from the house. I have to say that it gave me a surprising and poignant feeling of loss. I'd embraced the performing life reluctantly, but now I would miss it. Though for the moment I had more important concerns.

"I went and stood in the wings. I could see our baskets and trunks on the far side of the stage. But with the stage in full use, I couldn't walk over. When you build your theater on a pier, backstage space is limited. During a performance, the crossing was by a fly bridge overhead.

"At that moment, I saw a shadow move. I suspected it to be Melody. I didn't wait, but moved to the flybridge ladder and started to climb. The bridge was high up in the fly tower but it was sturdy and well-anchored, with safety rails for the nervous. Below me as I passed over, Frank Elliston's sketch company were in the midst of their *Three and a Fool* routine. Some 'dainty irresistible comedienne' would be up next, and then the acrobats.

"Once across the bridge, from up there among the ropes and lanterns, I could see her properly. Melody was a silhouette against a lurid backwash of stage lighting. Or so I thought in those first few moments. Then I realized that the glow came not from the stage, but from something else. It was the smoldering wicker of our property baskets. For a moment I couldn't believe it. She'd set one of them alight and was standing there, watching it burn.

"My heart took a diving fall. Not just to see her taking out her resentment on the family's few props and possessions, but at the potential for an act of petty vandalism to blossom into disaster. A theater fire is a terrible thing to imagine, and I doubt that she'd even imagined it. I'd once seen a show tent fire in which no one was hurt, and that was bad enough. And yet I called no warning; a panic can be just as dangerous, and many a small blaze is stamped out backstage. There were sand buckets and beaters close to hand in every part of the house. I needed to raise the alarm without alerting the audience.

"As I reached the end of the bridge but before I could start to descend, the first of the lamp oil bottles exploded. This was the paraffin mixture for Strong's flaming tomahawks. There was a bright flash and a terrible burst of flame. I saw Melody move, and that's the last time I saw her. A second, even brighter explosion came after the first, and it blew out the sides of the basket.

"Elliston's company knew immediately that something was wrong but, troupers all, they carried on. There was a scuttling of invisible bodies backstage as the theater's crew began to respond.

"For a moment nothing more happened, and then all at once the canvas below me took fire.

"Imagine touching a match to muslin curtain and seeing the fire sweep from floor to ceiling in a second or less. The speed of it surprised me but that was down to the burning oil and wicker, flung hot and wide. I had to scramble back along the flybridge to avoid being engulfed. It really did move that fast. Flames were already spreading the entire width of the backcloth in a wave of raw heat. Ropes were beginning to burn. I was now less concerned with tackling the fire, more focused on thoughts of reaching my daughter and getting her to safety. But she'd fled, and I didn't know to where.

"I saw the safety curtain begin to descend, and then jam. I saw stagehands running to beat out the flames. They say the band played 'God Save the King', but I never heard it. Just the audience rising and surging for the exits in a great rumble, men fighting their way over women and children.

"As I was making another attempt to reach the ladder, the heavens fell. There was a banshee-like whistling sound that quickly grew in volume and ended with an almighty crash from the stage, as a bar carrying several hundredweight of electric lighting thundered down from the grid and exploded on the boards in a shower of hot glass and metal. The ropes holding it had burned through. Someone below me was looking up, and pointing. They'd seen me on the bridge but I couldn't hear what they were saying.

"There was screaming from the auditorium, and further crashes as loose poles and chains followed in the lanterns' wake. Had anyone been caught or crushed underneath? From where I stood, I could not tell. Nor could I see any way to get down.

"I moved from one end of the bridge to the other, looking for a safe way to descend, finding none. The tabs caught and billowed in the heat, conveying new fire from one place to another. At some point the rubbish and paint materials in the scene dock went up. Someone opened the freight door and a rush of explosive wind turned fire into furnace. Unable to descend, I made for the roof.

"The higher I climbed, the more blistering the heat. Open stairways led from gallery to gallery until I reached the roof vents. In the event of a backstage fire, they were meant to draw smoke and flames away from the auditorium in a chimney effect. But that depended on a working safety curtain, not one that was snagged in the halfway position.

"When I reached the gallery under the skylights, I found them shut. The heat was now so intense that I swear I could smell the flesh of my hands cooking as I struggled to open one.

"I was all but blown out onto the roof by the upsurge of hot air as the skylight burst open. My clothes were scorched and when I spread my arms there was smoke rising from all parts of my body. I must have seemed like a human firebrand.

"Despite the building's ornate appearance from the ground, the pavilion roof was a flat one behind a facade of cement, plaster and wood. The minarets and towers were one-sided, and only for show. They did, however, offer footholds and other features for a determined climber in fear of his life. Down on the pier I could see the gathering crowd of the escaped, the would-be rescuers, and the inevitable sightseers. I was desperate to know if Melody was among them. If she was not, I would re-enter the building at ground level and find her.

"The façade was an Aladdin's palace of balconies and galleries. I slipped and fell some of the way, clambered down the rest, all in full view of the crowd. I was quickly identified. Word spread of the first-house incident, and of our company's dismissal by the management. Of how I'd entered the building only minutes before the first cry of 'fire'. By the time I reached the deck I'd been accused, tried, judged, and sentenced. The crowd tried to lay hands on me, but the police got there first."

Sebastian said, "And this is the reason why you sat in the cells and offered no defense?"

"How could I?" William James said. "In order to walk free, my only option would have been to expose and condemn my own child."

37

THE LOS ANGELES COUNTY COURTHOUSE STOOD ON BROADWAY and Temple, two wings and a clock tower of red sandstone castle built on a garden rise. On the show side were sloping grass banks and gleaming white steps. On the business side, a turning circle with a few palms and a view of the Women's Christian Temperance Union building across the way.

This was the sight that greeted small-time actor and part-time dope dealer Claude Walton as he emerged from the courthouse, squinting in the unfamiliar sunlight and grateful for the open air, not least because he'd now been wearing the same clothes for the past four days. Most of that time had been spent sitting or lying on a hard mattress in a jail cell, with the occasional change of scene to the inside of a courtroom. This took place whenever some judge or other official felt the urge to bring him out and take a look at him. His bail had been set at five hundred dollars pending an arraignment before Police Judge George H Richardson. Claude's number was in the contact books of many people who could afford the five hundred, not one of whom would dare risk their reputation by laying it down for him.

Claude was thirty-four years old, with farmboy good looks and thick dark hair. In person he was handsome. On camera, not so much. Right now he was tired, shaken, and scared for his uncertain future. He'd fallen into the trap of thinking that 'friend to the stars' meant those stars were his friends. One whiff of trouble and the sound of slamming doors echoed all through the hills.

He was barely a dozen strides from the courthouse steps when he was aware of two strangers falling in on either side of him.

"Who are you?" he said.

"Your benefactors," one said.

"We just stood your bail," the other added.

"I don't know you," Claude said. "Where's the catch?"

"You have to earn it," the first man said.

"I don't like the sound of this."

"Of course you don't. It's honest work."

• • •

THE PLAN was Sebastian's. They knew that Kit Strong had come to Hollywood on the prospect of show cowboy work and that wherever he might go, the need to source a regular supply of morphine always went with him. As a long-term addict, his intake would be significant. Recent changes in antinarcotic law made it impossible to buy the drug openly. Locate the supplier, and they could locate the man. For that they needed an insider to the illegal trade, and the week's crime pages of the *Los Angeles Herald* had given them Claude.

Every movie set had its man with connections. Sometimes it was an obliging studio doctor, often a bit-part actor given work as a personal favor to some star whose supplier he was. There was a player on the Sennett lot whose line, "Hangover? I can help you with that," had been the start of many a wrecked constitution and a crashed career.

Four days ago, according to the *Herald*'s crime desk, Claude Walton had taken a taxicab to the home of a prominent actor on Summit Drive, unaware that he was being followed by three detectives in an unmarked police automobile. They arrested him 'trying to sell his wares' in the actor's home, and seized from his person morphine with an estimated value of eight hundred dollars. Walton was taken to the city jail and booked on a charge of violating California state poison law. Police declined to name the actor, declaring him an innocent in the entire affair.

This was Hollywood, after all.

Claude was apprehensive. Though Sebastian affected an easy demeanor, William James could barely hide his contempt. As the three of them crossed the street, Sebastian held him back a little.

"Let me do the talking," he said.

"The man's a cockroach."

"I don't disagree. But you're too invested. I can hide it."

They entered the Pacific Electric streetcar station, where the Palm Garden and Buffet offered an inexpensive lunch counter. They took a booth. William James sat beside the doper, effectively trapping him against the wall. Sebastian sat opposite. William James put on a smile, but even Sebastian could sense his latent fury.

Sebastian said, "Did they feed you in jail?"

"Only on slop," Walton said.

Sebastian called the waitress over. "Bring him breakfast."

William James found some reason to look away. Though he'd only met the man not ten minutes before, several weeks' worth of impotent anger was backed up in him like steam in a boiler, awaiting some outlet. And Walton peddled dope.

Keeping it amicable, Sebastian said, "I'm guessing you don't use what you peddle."

Walton showed surprise. "How would you know that?"

"Three days in a cell and your hands are steady."

"I don't even use tobacco. I've got scars on my lungs and I can't face needles. TB when I was a kid. I spent so long in treatment that the nurses used to let me follow them around and help out."

"Some apprenticeship."

"What do you want from me, Mister?"

William James spoke then. "We're looking for a man named Kit Strong," he said.

"What makes you think I'd know him?"

"You probably don't," Sebastian said. "But we already bet five hundred dollars that you can find him for us."

Walton's breakfast of eggs and pancakes arrived, with coffee for all three of them. William James pushed his away.

Walton said, "Why me?"

"He uses morphine," Sebastian said. "A lot of morphine. Been using it for years and he's got the tolerance of an ox. First it was to control pain. Now it's just to function. He came here to work in pictures. Wherever he goes, he needs a steady supply."

"He's an actor?"

"Just a cowboy. Travels with a child."

"I'll ask around."

"Keep it discreet," Sebastian said. "We don't want to tip him off."

"Okay."

Sebastian slid a handwritten card across the tabletop and said, "Here's where you reach us."

"Okay," Walton said, and dug into his breakfast. Across him to Sebastian, William James said, "He won't do it."

"Yes he will," Sebastian said. "You know why, Claude? While you were in jail, we went to your place. We took our time and found what the coppers didn't. Don't make me say more. Not here."

Claude stared at him, believing the lie, a chunk of pancake forgotten in mid-air.

Sebastian said, "You know what I'm talking about."

"I'll find him," Claude said.

"I know you will, Claude."

The two men got to their feet. Sebastian said, "Finish your breakfast."

William James added, "Then get to work."

38

PRESENTING HERSELF AT THE WANAMAKER'S BUSINESS DESK, Frances said, "My father says he's established a line of credit for me. What do I need to do?"

The department store clerk, a young woman of Gibson Girl looks and ironclad poise, smiled politely and said, "Your name?"

"Callowhill. Frances Callowhill."

She saw a change in the young woman's attitude. Nothing less than professional before, it now shifted up a gear. Unremarkable in London, the Callowhill name meant something in Philadelphia. A Callowhill had been the second wife of William Penn. Different Callowhills, but who would know? The effect on hearing the name was still there—a glazing of the eyes, a calculation behind them, a sudden adjustment of warmth and welcome.

"Of course, Mrs Callowhill," the young woman said. "Just give me a moment."

"That's Miss Callowhill."

"I do beg your pardon. Please take a seat."

A nervous employee of teen age, starched to within an inch of her life, offered to bring Frances a coffee or a refreshing drink. She declined, and looked around. This amount of attention was already making her uncomfortable. These were her good clothes but she felt shabby and ill at ease amongst the Wanamaker's shoppers, all of them well-heeled, many of them with servants following.

The young woman returned with some papers.

She said, "I need a sample of your signature for our finance department. Then any goods you care to sign for will be wrapped and delivered to your home."

And not, Frances imagined, wrapped in newspaper and delivered by a boy on a bicycle, the way they did it back in the Borough.

It was her first time in Wanamaker's, previously the Grand Depot at Thirteenth and Market. They'd expanded it in her absence. Frances had walked over from the trolley station by an underground tunnel and taken an elevator to emerge in the store's Grand Court, a soaring atrium some six stories high featuring an enormous bronze eagle and an even mightier pipe organ that played twice a day and was presently silent. This new and much more opulent store had been built around the old in stages, so that trading could continue with no interruption to business. Maine granite without, Tennessee marble and gold within, the store had opened in the summer of 1911 with the President himself performing the dedication.

She found its opulence daunting. Yet there was no reason why she should. She'd known rich and she'd known poor, and she felt inferior to no one. Rich was better, only a fool would argue otherwise. But while poverty was neither virtuous nor ennobling, the poor had to find strengths that the rich would never know.

When the paperwork was done, the younger girl led Frances up to the womenswear department. Here a handsome woman of mature years supervised the taking of Frances' measurements while samples were gathered. An assistant fetched a chair and she was obliged to sit while models paraded the chosen styles before her.

Frances endured the process with a feeling somewhere between embarrassment and alarm. So much service—to someone who'd lost the skill of ignoring the servant, it brought an acute sense of discomfort. She was more accustomed to dealing with her Lambeth dressmaker, negotiating a price for hard wear and general adaptability. Flair and frivolity rarely entered into it.

After she'd viewed the styles, other assistants brought her bolts of material to look at.

The supervisor drew out a length from one of the bolts and said, "With skin as clear and soft as yours, the brocade will look wonderful on you."

"It's lovely," Frances agreed.

"Isn't it?"

"I want to think about it."

"Of course."

The truth was that she needed to escape the pressure of all this close and constant attention, at least for a while.

She went exploring. On the third floor was the Egyptian Hall, a performance space for concerts and recitals that had been cleared of its seating for the display and sale of grand pianos. Here was the peace she'd been seeking. A handful of people browsing, and none of them close by. The instruments stood in ranks like an army, deeply polished, on expensive green rugs under Tiffany-style lighting.

Her eye was caught by a Baldwin Parlor Grand with a light mahogany case. She lingered in passing, and ran a light forefinger across the keys. Depressing them slightly, feeling their resistance, not quite enough to strike a note.

"Would madam care to play?"

She hadn't heard the floorwalker approach, and when he spoke it startled her. He wore a morning suit, with a flower in the buttonhole like a bridegroom or a dandy. She withdrew her hand quickly, as if at a reprimand.

Then she gathered herself. "Can I?" she said. "I mean—Madam would."

Without the floorwalker making any obvious sign or signal, a youth in a bellboy's uniform appeared with a piano stool and placed it for her to sit. Then both he and the salesman moved to a polite distance. At the far end of the hall, there was a family conferring over something; she had no other audience. Frances sat for a few moments with her hands folded in her lap, knowing that her playing could never match the quality of the piano, but unable to resist its invitation to dance.

She chose one of the simpler Chopin nocturnes, one that she knew quite well, slow and pleasing and with less of a chance to stumble. The first rich sound of it shocked her a little, being so used to the saloon-bar tones of Jankowski's 'bangers' in the little Southwark shop. She was hesitant at first, but then the instrument's ease of play drew her in and smoothed out her technique. The Baldwin was perfectly tuned, with effortless action. She began to relax and lose her nerves.

When it was done, she realized that the family at the far end of the hall had stopped their conversation to listen. She blushed, and took her hands from the keys.

The salesman said, "A fine American instrument. Only the Steinway Model A comes close. The case is solid mahogany."

"How much?" Frances said.

"We can offer terms…"

"How much?"

"The Baldwin model L is fifteen hundred dollars," he said. "Delivered and tuned. Miss Callowhill, is it not?"

Frances might have been awed by the price, had she not been so taken aback by his use of her name. She hadn't given it. What kind of behind-the-scenes commercial machinery did they have in operation here?

But then the piano drew her attention back. Sign for everything, her father had said. And although she wasn't seriously considering it, she entertained the idea for a brief moment in mischief and memory of her late sister. It would serve her father right.

"It's lovely," she said.

"It certainly is."

"I want to think about it."

"Of course," the salesman said.

• • •

WELL, SO far her shopping trip had been less than productive. She had neither the hang nor the habit of spending. With armloads of other people's parcels going by her, and bills of sale zipping through vacuum tubes from every sales point, Frances was finding it all somewhat overwhelming.

Feeling a little lightheaded, she now made her way up to the cafeteria on the ninth floor and was shown to a small table where she could sit alone and gather her thoughts. Yet more luxury surrounded her. This was not just a tea room, but the Grand Crystal Tea Room. It had warm dark wood columns and a ceiling of ornate plasterwork panels, and was abuzz with conversation.

There were a few men here but most of the morning's clientele were women, well-dressed women, here in their twos and threes with their hair styled and pinned and their social diaries filled with appointments like this. Had her life taken a different course, she might be one of them. She knew she shouldn't envy them. But a part of her did.

Then she heard, "Frances? Frances Callowhill?"

A woman was peering at her from another table. Plump, dark-haired, no one she recognized. She took in Frances' blank expression and said, "Imogen. Imogen Blackwell, now, but I used to be Imogen Belmont."

Imogen! Everything suddenly clicked into place and recognition came. Imogen Belmont. Frances rose, and they hugged like children. They caused a ripple of awareness to run through the room, smiles everywhere.

Imogen begged leave of her friends at the other table, and came to sit with Frances.

She said, "I heard you were back."

"It's only a visit."

"Make it a long one," her old friend said. "I heard about Elisabeth. So sad."

"I know."

"It was in the stars when she ran off with that policeman. But Lord knows, she was head over heels, and you have to envy her that. What about you? How are you?"

"I'm well."

"You look it. You haven't changed at all. Look at you! You tiny thing. Have you heard from Freddie yet?"

"I only got off the boat a few days ago."

"Don't give him excuses, he's got enough of his own. We must all get together. Do I hear you've patched things up with your father?"

"I moved into the cottage."

"Good for you. You're overdue a little paternal kindness. Freddie says he's mellowed over the years. You know they do some business together? I've no idea what. Something to do with logging and railroad ties."

Frances found that her initial unfamiliarity was quick to fade as this new Imogen overwrote her memories of the old. The thin-as-a-rail tomboy who'd once been her best friend was now a pleasant-faced and matronly young woman. It was a shock to realize how much time had passed since they'd last been together. More than a decade since they'd written, even.

She said, "Is Freddie still in Powelton?"

"He kept the brownstone and built a little villa out in East Falls. He wanted somewhere smaller for just him and the children. And, you know… without so many memories. It's nice, you should see it. In fact, you will. I'll twist his arm and organize a lunch for us."

"Don't put yourself to any trouble," Frances said.

"I can call Caroline and Annabel. And Bill! You remember Bill? He's teaching Greek at Penn. The old stammer's completely gone."

"Imogen, please," Frances said, thinking of her failure to rise to the day's challenge and upgrade her wardrobe. "I can't meet everyone looking like this."

"You look fine."

"This is all I have to wear."

"So they're your travel clothes. As if anyone will care."

"I'll care."

"Look," Imogen said, "it's not a problem. I can lend you whatever you need until your finery arrives."

Little did she know. Frances said, "I couldn't do that."

"Do it for me," Imogen said. "I've a room full of gowns that I'll never get back into. I keep looking and wishing, but after three boys it just isn't going to happen. I'd rather see good clothes on you than gathering dust on a rail. Isn't it lucky we bumped?"

"I know," Frances said. "It's strange."

"I can't get over it," Imogen said.

Frances was thinking that her friend had never been a good liar, even when she did it with the best of intentions.

She said, "Did my father tell you I'd be here today?"

"I never see your father."

Frances waited and, sure enough, after a few moments Imogen's conscience caught up with her.

She said, reluctantly, "I believe he may have mentioned something to Freddie."

Frances teased her, and they chatted some more, and then when Imogen's friends at the other table were rising to leave she quickly wrote down her address and number on a page from a tiny notepad. They embraced again. After she'd gone, the waiter brought the check and Frances signed it.

After she left the tearoom, she looked down from one of the galleries and saw that people were crowded into the Grand Court for the daily free concert. The organ recital had yet to begin. Frances remembered a sunny afternoon in Willow Grove, Sousa playing on the bandstand, in what seemed like a previous life.

Might that be her life again?

She thought about Imogen's reference to awaiting the arrival of her 'finery'. She was wearing it.

Frances couldn't face a return to womenswear. Not twice in one day. So not wishing to admit that her trip was a washout, she stopped by the millinery department and bought some gloves that she didn't want. Again, she signed, and the gloves were taken away to be wrapped in tissue, boxed, and delivered.

On her way back to the trolley, she couldn't even remember her choice.

39

IN THE CRISP AIR OF AN EARLY CALIFORNIA MORNING, SEBASTIAN Becker and William James sat low in the backseat of a Levy taxi-cab in order to keep a watch on the building across the street without making their interest obvious. Their chauffeur snoozed at the wheel. The building stood on the corner of Sunset and Gower, and was a former roadhouse that had expanded onto adjacent land to become the first purpose-built film stage in Hollywood. Where liquor sales had failed to sustain business, Al Christie comedies and Western one-reelers now paid the bills.

Apart from a roof-wide hoarding with the company name, there was little about the business to impress. On the street side was a five-roomed wooden bungalow; behind it, a former barn and corral where interior scenes were photographed in the muslin-filtered light of the California day. Cars were already lined up on the street outside for an early morning call. The Nestor Film Company turned out three subjects a week, and made the best use of its facilities by shooting its dramas in-house, its comedies on the streets, and sending out the Western unit to Griffith Park or the San Fernando Valley.

Sebastian shaded his eyes, the better to see. Between the cars and the building, a crowd of day players and hopefuls was beginning to form.

Many were in costume. Dowagers in furs, men in dinner suits who could equally serve as toffs or waiters, tramps, generals, a bishop. And cowboys. Cowboys of all ages, of all kinds.

Sebastian said, "They have to show up dressed like that?"

"Owning wardrobe is a good investment," William James said. "Showing up in costume can get you a job."

"How do people know what's needed?"

"Word of mouth. Chance. Nestor turns out a Western every week, so a Stetson and chaps make a fairly safe bet."

Their chauffeur grunted faintly in his sleep, like a dog dreaming of the chase. In the context of their conversation, it sounded like agreement.

Information from dope pusher Claude Walton had brought them here. According to Claude, he had a friend who knew a friend who'd been approached for morphine by one of the day players on the Nestor lot. The day player was looking for a regular supply, and this friend couldn't immediately come up with the quantity asked for. He'd put out word for more, and the word had reached Claude's ears.

They'd no assurance that Claude was a reliable informant. That also applied to any friend of Claude's. But the incidental details of the story made it worth their attention.

Sebastian had approached the surveillance with due diligence. Today's job for Nestor's Western unit was _Retribution_, a story with romance, guns, Indians and a silver mine. It featured screen lover and action man Wallace Reid. They'd be making scenes at the company's own Providencia Ranch, less than an hour's drive away on the far side of the Hollywood Hills.

From the back of the taxi, Sebastian could see a young assistant moving among the hopefuls. He was a boy of sixteen or seventeen, in tweed britches and a cap that almost matched, seeking out particular individuals and crossing names off a list, handing out lunch tickets, shaking his head at those seeking his attention. As he worked his way through the crowd, a passing streetcar made a brief stop and the alighting passengers swelled the numbers.

Sebastian said, "Is that who I think it is?"

William James rose in his seat. He'd brought a pocket spyglass, a tiny folding thing of brass and leather, but Sebastian wouldn't let him use it so close in case a flash of reflected sunlight gave them away.

"Oh Lord," he said.

It was Kit Strong, stepping down with the crowd from the streetcar. His hair was braided, and he wore the buckskin and beads of a screen 'Injun'. Under his arm, a long cloth bundle that had to be his tomahawks. The assistant saw him straight away, and pushed through to him.

By Strong's side came Melody James. She stood by, waiting silently as the two conversed.

They'd abandoned any attempt to pass her as a boy. She was once more costumed as a young squaw with headband and a single feather, her skin darkened with makeup. She stared at the ground as she waited, neither curious nor alert.

Sebastian said, "Steady, William."

"I'm all right," William James said. His voice was almost a whisper, but it crackled with suppressed feeling. Their sleeping chauffeur sensed its electricity and, without knowing why, began to stir from his doze.

The selection had been made. The disappointed began to drift away, some to look for work on other lots, some to walk or ride home in their incongruous outfits. Those remaining all climbed into cars and trucks which set off, one by one, for the day's location.

Sebastian leaned forward and shook their driver by the shoulder. The driver attempted that sudden show of energy affected by the newly-awake who were trying to give the impression that they hadn't been sleeping, no, not at all.

"Now?" he said.

"Now is good," Sebastian said patiently.

• • •

THEY FOLLOWED the convoy at a safe distance, out of Hollywood and into the hills, up through the Cahuenga Pass and down into the rolling valley beyond. When the studio cars turned off toward the Forest Lawn site, they overshot the turn and had their driver pull over at some shacks by a creek so they could observe and plan.

William James had made arrangements for Melody's rehabilitation, but first they had to get her away from Kit Strong. By force, if necessary. Claiming the child through any legal process was not an option. On paper her father and legal guardian was a dead man in a distant grave. And Melody would never come willingly—Sebastian had once imagined that she might, and was not about to revisit that mistake.

The Nestor ranch lay before them, a natural bowl of open land sloping gently up toward scrub-covered hills. The motion picture camp was about a quarter of a mile away. A fair number of people were at the location already, and were now being joined by the convoy from town.

With the sun behind them now, Sebastian borrowed the spyglass and studied the distant scene. He could see a gathering of tents, makeup huts, and horses. There was no distinct perimeter to the camp. Two truckloads of people and equipment were setting off for some other part of the ranch; some of those left behind were finding shade and settling to wait for their call. Others had joined a line at the cook tent.

Even with the spyglass he was unable to make out faces at this distance.

"Let's go in," Sebastian said.

Their driver guided the car back up the road to the turning, and then across the open field. The camp was beginning to settle, but there was enough going on for one more vehicle to roll up without attracting any particular attention.

They stopped at the end of a row of cars. As he and William James opened opposite doors to climb out, Sebastian said to the chauffeur, "Turn around. And keep the engine running."

"What if I get moved on?" the driver said.

"Say you were told to wait. You don't know who by."

Amongst the parked vehicles they had cover; once out, Sebastian felt exposed. They walked over to a couple of trucks where an awning and picnic benches had been set up. Sebastian had been thinking that he might have seen a figure like Melody's standing in the line, but she wasn't there. The line was for picking up box lunches from a cookhouse counter, he now saw.

They stopped, and scanned all around. William James said, "I don't know what I'll say to her."

"Save it for later," Sebastian said. "You start making speeches, she'll just call for help."

Something had caught his attention.

He nudged William James, prompting him to follow his gaze. Melody was sitting on a packing case, her back toward them, no more than a couple of dozen yards away. One of the box lunches was open on her knees and she was investigating its contents. He couldn't see her face, but there was no mistaking her by the squaw costume, the feather, and the fact that she was by far the youngest person in the company.

William James was looking all around. "I don't see Strong," he said.

Sebastian began, "Let's be sure he's not going to—" but William James had already set off toward his daughter. Sebastian started after him, but it was too late.

William James stood before Melody and spoke her name.

She looked up. For a moment it was as if the world took a pause. From behind, Sebastian saw her shoulders rise as she drew breath, and didn't wait to find out what would follow; he stepped forward and grabbed her, clamped his hand over her mouth to stifle her call, and lifted her bodily from the crate. The box lunch hit the ground and spilled. Melody kicked her legs and tried to get free, and Sebastian was off. He left William James to follow.

Though there appeared to be very little to her, she was heavier than he'd expected and she fought like a cat in a sack, biting at his hand and kicking at the air to break his grip. He heard a *Hey!* from someone but he didn't look back. He put all his efforts into getting this rebellious spitfire to their vehicle.

Somewhere along the way, William James overtook him. He got to the car first, and opened the door. Their chauffeur was sitting with his engine running, hands on the wheel, mouth hanging open. They hadn't warned him that the day's hire included the role of getaway driver in a kidnapping.

Another *Hey*, this time a *Hey, you, stop there!* from the kid assistant in the tweed britches. He was running toward them and without releasing Melody, Sebastian said, "California State Child Services. Who's your boss?"

The kid slowed, looked uncertain.

"That's Mister Robards," he said.

"Go tell him we're shutting you down."

"What?"

"Go!"

The kid hesitated for a moment. Then he fell for it. Overwhelmed by the possible urgency of the situation, he turned and ran to warn his boss. Sebastian turned back to the car and shoved Melody inside.

Melody was now clawing at her father. Sebastian jumped in after and slammed the door.

Their driver didn't hesitate or argue. Through his windshield he saw a party of tough-looking cowboys running across open ground toward them and immediately floored the gas pedal, spraying dirt and grass and shaking up everyone in the back. Over Melody's yelling he could hear the driver cursing in his own language, which was something other than English.

Melody was yelling Kit Strong's name.

"Speed up," Sebastian told the driver.

"It's only a dirt road."

"They have weapons."

"Holy Mary, Mother of God, what have you gotten me into?"

They sped up, the car bucketing around on its leaf springs as they flew over ruts and dry hollows. There would be a quarter-mile of this before they reached the good road.

William James was using all of his strength to keep his daughter pinned, and she was using all of hers to fight him. Sebastian dodged her flying fingernails and looked out of the back window. He couldn't be sure, but he thought that Kit Strong might be among their pursuers. Perhaps even the one who was waving a rifle and firing it into the air. The rifle was most likely loaded with blanks, but he couldn't be sure of that.

"Melody," William James was pleading. "Don't you know me?"

She knew him. That was the problem. Sebastian got her attention and told her, "You scream, you get a gag. You fight, you get wrapped up in a sheet and sat on. Your choice."

They didn't have a sheet, but the child didn't know that.

She grew quiet until they reached the turn, but then as the car slowed she reached across Sebastian and tried to get to the door handle. William James pulled her back, and she bit right into his fire-ravaged hand. The pain was too much for him to bear, and he let go. Melody lunged again and had the door open when Sebastian grabbed the collar of her buckskin dress and flung her back against the seat, hard.

It knocked the breath out of her. Then in a moment she seemed to shed years, and cried like the child she truly was. Still clutching his twice-wounded hand, William James tried to placate her, speaking her name, making her promises.

But Sebastian said, "Your daughter put a gun to my head. You want to say that's the devil in her, fine. But she put a gun to my head and watched as her boyfriend beat me unconscious."

He looked at Melody.

"Do we understand each other?" he said.

Melody was defiant. She sniffed back some of the tears and said, "He'll come for me."

"Maybe," Sebastian said. "Maybe not."

"He will."

"This was never about you. He cares nothing for you. It was always between him and your father."

"Kit loves me," Melody said. Though Sebastian sensed him flinching at the words, William James did not respond.

"That'll be why he's treated you so well," Sebastian said.

40

THERE WAS NO PURSUIT, OTHER THAN THE SHORT-LIVED FOOT chase down the dirt road by a handful of extras. Sebastian had wondered whether Kit Strong might commandeer a mount and have an advantage on the terrain, but according to William James he hadn't climbed onto a horse since the race accident that had stranded him in London. No production vehicles followed them out, either. The day's business was not to be diverted or jeopardized for the personal concerns of one bit part player.

Melody remained subdued for the rest of the journey. She seemed to sink into a state of depression even more harrowing for her father to observe than her earlier, more violent behavior. Sebastian watched him switch between studying his broken child and staring out of the car's window in helpless anger.

Sutherland Place was a private sanitarium, close to the center of Hollywood on a corner of Santa Monica Boulevard. William James had chosen it even before Sebastian had tracked him down. He'd taken a good piece of the money he'd made from sharping and put down a retainer to keep a bed open. The sanitarium was a complex of individual bungalows and rose gardens, advertised as a retreat for the care and treatment of nervous exhaustion. It was handy for the studios, and handy for the stars. No one came here for medical attention. All came here to 'rest'.

Nurses came out to meet the car, backed by two burly Mexicans in orderlies' uniforms. This arrangement was a precaution against Kit Strong showing up behind them. Melody offered no resistance as they took her away.

William James stayed with her. The plan now was for Sebastian to return to the Bunker Hill apartment and wait for some word. While there, he planned to write to Frances. Though what he would say to her, he wasn't yet sure.

The same cab took him the rest of the way. In downtown Los Angeles, he paid off the driver from the cash float given to him by William James and said, "There's five dollars extra for the gas and inconvenience."

"Inconvenience?" the driver said. "How about something extra for getting shot at?"

"With blanks?" Sebastian said. "I don't think so."

41

OVER BREAKFAST IN THE CONSERVATORY OF THE CHESTNUT HILL house, Raymond Callowhill said to his daughter, "I hear you ran into Imogen."

"She ran into me," Frances said. "Are you trying to pair me off by any chance, father?"

"With Imogen?"

"With Freddie."

"You can do better than Freddie," Callowhill said, lifting the napkin from over a dish and looking doubtfully at what lay underneath.

"At my age?" Frances said.

"Well, there's that," Callowhill conceded, and let the napkin fall.

After a week in her father's house Frances had adapted to her situation, though to say that she had settled would be taking it too far. She was like an uneasy guest in a fine hotel, ever mindful of the invisible charges being run up against her name. As the keeper of Sebastian's house, with Sebastian's erratic income, she'd known debt and learned to fear it. Debt gave others an advantage. Her father had never been less than genial during her stay, but she knew him of old. While not doubting his sincerity, she wondered if she was headed for a reckoning in some currency other than money.

What could he want of her? He was alone, but he'd lasted until now without her company. He spent half of each day on business, and was a member of several men's clubs in town. From hints in conversation and odd presents that she'd seen around the house, she knew of friendships with Society widows.

The possibility remained, unlikely though it seemed, that he might actually be driven by concern for a daughter's happiness. Despite their long estrangement, he would claim that he always had. Perhaps it was true. After all one could be wrong, and yet sincere.

Frances became aware of the housemaid at her shoulder. An Irish woman of around forty years, in the family's service since girlhood. Never married, dark and shy, she had the ability to move around the property in almost uncanny silence.

She said, "Please, Miss Frances."

"Annie?"

"There are two trunks sent over from the Blackwell house."

"Trunks?"

"I believe it's dresses. Where do you want them?"

"In my room, I suppose."

During this brief conversation Callowhill had taken the opportunity to open the morning's *Inquirer*. He spent the next quarter-hour at the breakfast table reading snippets of the news aloud to Frances, thereby satisfying the need for courtesy and conversation without having to give up his paper. As soon as was reasonable, Frances excused herself and went upstairs.

The empty trunks stood against the wall, their contents unpacked and spread across the bed. True to her word, Imogen had sent over a selection of dresses for all occasions. Silks, chiffons, taffetas…daywear and evening wear, even an outfit for riding. A few seasons out of date, probably, to those who cared about such things…but to Frances' eye, all new and none visibly worn. Most had been expertly packed in tissue for storage. A folded note with no envelope lay on her dressing table.

She picked it up and read, *Dear Frances, Try these for size. I'll consider it a favor if you can make use. But keep or discard, whichever you choose.*

She sat on the bed among the scattered finery and found herself close to tears, for no reason. So she sniffed hard and rubbed her eyes, and tried to think practically. She ought to try something, she supposed. If Imogen was wrong about their relative sizes and none of the clothing fit, then this was all for nothing anyway.

Out of everything she chose a plain walking suit in practical, putty-colored wool. But then at the last moment her hand strayed to a dove-gray morning gown in filmy taffeta. Dare she? Well, she was alone. No one would see.

The fit was perfect.

She stood before the guest room's full-length mirror. She was barefoot and without makeup and her hair was down, so the effect was not complete. But the sense of empowerment that came with good tailoring was not to be denied.

"You have to keep it," said a voice from the doorway, and Frances jumped a little. She turned to find Annie, who faltered as she realized that she'd spoken a private thought aloud. The housemaid's innocent stealth was the product of a lifetime of service.

"I'm sorry," the housemaid said. "I didn't mean to speak out of turn."

"Say whatever you like," Frances told her, turning her attention back to the mirror. "I take it you read the note?"

"Only in that it passed before my eyes," Annie said.

Frances turned this way, then that.

"I don't know, Annie," she said. "I just don't know."

She looked from the mirror to her old dress, now lying on the bed amongst the others. It stood out, but not in a good way. It was honest work, in hard-wearing material. But she saw the repairs, the fading color on the seams.

Annie said, "After all that you did for Miss Elisabeth. It's time to think of yourself."

"I'm not used to that," Frances said.

On the day of the lunch she picked out a tea dress in white cotton and lace. Annie styled and pinned her hair. Two days before, Frances had steeled herself for a return to Wanamaker's and had picked out accessories and several pairs of shoes. After signing her name for that first time, shopping on account became easier.

At eleven, a car arrived to collect her. It was a deep blue Pierce-Arrow limousine with whitewall tires, driven by a uniformed chauffeur who held the door and offered his arm as she hitched up her skirts and climbed in.

Freddie Belmont's 'little villa out in East Falls' was a sprawling two-storied structure in a local architect's version of a European style, calling for at least twelve staff to run it. Though it was late in the year, the day was pleasantly warm. A table had been set on the patio outside a south-facing music room, its French doors thrown open to the air.

"Bill couldn't make it," Imogen said, leading her to the patio. "Everyone else is here."

There they were, all waiting for her. Old friends, grown older. Caroline, Annabel, Freddie. For a moment, first impressions fought with memory. Then somehow they resolved, and these people ceased to be strangers.

Freddie Belmont was dressed in summer casuals, flannels with a light striped blazer and a straw boater. He was tanned, had gained a little weight, and his face bore a few lines.

He said, "Frances. Imogen told no word of a lie. You really haven't changed."

"Nor you, Freddie," she said, whereupon Freddie raised the boater to reveal a startling absence of hair. Everyone hooted with laughter, and Freddie joined in.

She had been nervous. There was no need for it. Freddie's children, a boy and a girl of five and eight years old, were brought out and introduced and then taken away by their nanny. Freddie opened a bottle of French champagne and they all welcomed her back and toasted her health, at which she blushed.

Then over a picnic lunch of oysters, cold meats, and gingerbread, they talked of remembered friends and places and of their lives to date. Her friends treated her Lambeth stories as one might any traveler's tale, with interest and a little awe. She might have been speaking of adventures in the Congo, or Peru. Frances did consider the possibility that their fascination might be no more than a pretense, and would give way to pity once she was safely out of range. But she saw nothing to make her suspect their sincerity. For the afternoon's sake, at least, she would choose to believe that their interest and affection were as they appeared.

After an hour or more, Imogen contrived some reason to disappear off to the far end of the garden with Annabel and Caroline, leaving Frances and Freddie alone together. As the table was being cleared, they moved across the patio to a couple of steamer chairs. Freddie had called for a small whiskey. Frances agreed to a cordial.

Checking to ensure that the others were out of earshot, Freddie said, "Frances, I have something to say. I'm delighted to see you again after all these years. It's been far too long. And despite the good intentions of your father and our friends, I'm no more on the hunt for a wife than you are for a husband."

Frances said, "I'm so relieved to hear you say that."

"Gets it out of the way, doesn't it?"

"It certainly does."

This amused Freddie greatly. "'It certainly does,'" he said. "How very English of you."

"What can I tell you? Live there a while, and it rubs off."

Frances glanced down the lawn to the Japanese garden, where an unnecessary bridge crossed a man-made pond to an equally useless pagoda. Imogen and the others were now on the bridge, pointing at fish.

She said, "What are they saying now, do you think?"

"Probably something about 'poor Freddie'. I've been poor Freddie for the past five years. Not to make light of my loss, but I can live without the pity. Does that make sense to you? I lost a wife, you a sister."

"For me it's been different."

"Oh?"

Frances said, "Losing Elisabeth felt like Sebastian's tragedy. Much as I shared it, he took the worst. It makes me feel guilty to think that I may have lessened my own grief by diverting it into concern for his."

"Don't feel guilty. He's a lucky man."

"Did you ever meet him?"

"Can't say I did. Saw his name in a newspaper once, around the time they were hanging those union men. What was the story? He'd been under cover?"

"He was giving evidence for the Pinkertons. He had death threats over that."

As if at a signal, the first of the afternoon's clouds moved across the sun.

Freddie said, "A whole other world. How did you stand it?"

"People deal with worse," Frances said.

"God bless 'em if they have to," Freddie said, and then, "It's not so warm any more. Shall we go inside?"

"If we must," Frances said, but it was said with a smile. Freddie stood, and offered his hand to help Frances to rise.

The gesture did not go unnoticed at the far end of the garden. And, to their shared amusement, both of them knew it.

42

For a day Sebastian suffered the discomfort of being alone in another's apartment, unable to settle, unready to leave. His letter to Frances was begun and abandoned several times over. His point was...he didn't know *what* his point was. He couldn't offer to release her, because that would imply some kind of a claim. But if she felt an attachment that he now failed to acknowledge, that would be cold to the point of cruelty.

Dear Frances. I have no right to expect...

She'd offered to share his bed, after all.

Dear Frances, the only path...

Seem to ignore or appear to presume, he couldn't win. Yet still he persisted.

That night he took a blanket from the bed, and settled himself on the apartment's couch. Many a time he'd slept in his clothes, but he drew the line at sleeping in another man's sheets.

He could leave California on the morrow. He had just enough money to cover his train fare back East, and his steamer ticket was paid for. He'd achieved his aim; Melody James was out of her abductor's hands and reunited with her father. It might not be a joyful reunion, but that was hardly Sebastian's problem. He was no one's fairy godmother, just a hired investigator working beyond his brief.

With that thought in his mind, he drifted away.

• • •

OVER BREAKFAST at a downtown automat, he reached a decision. He made up his mind to pack his bag and quit. There was nothing more he could do here. He'd go back to Philadelphia where, instead of being awkward in writing, he could meet up with Frances and feel awkward in person. William James would get a note. One he wouldn't have to agonize over. Some notes were easier than others.

But those plans were disrupted when, after breakfast, he climbed back up the hill to the Argyle and there found William James waiting.

The showman was dark-eyed and haggard from a night without sleep. But insomnia alone could not account for the wounded, haunted look in his eyes, or the despair expressed in his posture. He sprawled on the couch, looking up when Sebastian entered, not otherwise moving.

Sebastian said, "How is she?"

"That stuff is more vile than poison," William James said. "It's entered her soul. I never saw anything like it."

"But they can help her?"

"They call it a cure. I can only take their word for it." He shook his head. "She swore and screamed at me all night. I don't even know her."

"You'll get her back," Sebastian said. "Have faith."

"It'll take more than faith. Funds are running low. Can you do something for me?"

For a moment, Sebastian feared that he was about to be asked for a loan. He had his back pay, but it was mostly spoken for. While he knew he must refuse, he was afraid that he might not.

"It depends," he said.

"Stay with her while I go out and raise some cash. I don't want her to be alone."

"But she despises me."

"Not as much as she despises me. If I don't continue to pay, they'll stop the treatment. She'll die or slide back. I don't know which is worse."

"How long will this take?"

"I heard of a game in Whitley Heights," William James said. "They don't know me there. A few hours should do it."

• • •

So Sebastian's funds stayed intact, but his plans were disrupted. While William James stayed to splash his face and change his shirt, Sebastian set out to Sutherland Place.

He was expected. One of the nurses led him through the rose garden, but instead of entering one of the Spanish-style bungalows, she took him into the main building that stood some way back from the street. On the ground floor were offices and a dispensary. By the dispensary, a stairwell. She told him to watch his step, and led him down a narrow stairway to the level below ground.

There was no daylight here. A basement corridor ran the length of the building. Down each side of it were half a dozen identical numbered doors, all closed. She unlocked door number three, and stepped back to allow Sebastian to enter.

The odor hit him as he stepped over the threshold, a sour mix like the smell of an untreated wound. The room was small and windowless, with a single unshaded lightbulb hanging from a cord in the middle of the ceiling. The walls and the inside of the door were padded with a layer of unbleached cotton quilt. On the back wall there was an enamel sink, and a toilet without screens or a seat. In the corner, a mattress. It was not on a frame, but on the floor. On the mattress, squeezed up in the angle of the walls, a tiny huddled shape that he took to be Melody James.

"This is it?" he said.

"If you plan to sit with her, I'll fetch you a chair," the nurse said. Her manner was bright and pleasant, as if this were a solarium in a spa hotel rather than a padded chamber with no daylight. No cell at Bedlam was ever so grim. She disappeared, leaving the door open.

Sebastian crouched by the mattress. Unsure of what to do, or what response he might get, he spoke Melody's name.

And all he heard, from the muffled depths of her curled-up form, was, "Where's Kit?"

"He's gone," Sebastian said.

"No."

"He's no good for you, Melody. He made you like this."

She rolled over to face him then and stared up at him, her face lacking all color other than the deep red rims of her blood-shot eyes. Her hair dark and damp, her expression wild. It was the face and frame of a child but she was like a macabre doll, made for a curse out of porcelain and bile.

"I want Kit," she said.

"You want him or his needle?"

"To hell with you," she said, and rolled back over. She curled up into a tight ball and sobbed uncontrollably.

"It hurts," he heard, her voice muffled by her face pressed into the mattress.

He saw a blanket rucked up against the wall. He hesitated, and then reached forward and drew it over her. With a violent movement, she threw it off.

Sebastian didn't know what to do. The nurse brought him a chair and he sat, watching the child's bony, shivering, hunched-up form. Her only covering was a thin cotton shift, stretched tight across her back. There had been times when his young son had withdrawn in a similar way, balling up his fists and screaming if he was touched. Sebastian had learned to read the signs, and to wait them out. But that experience seemed irrelevant here.

He could be of no use, he could offer no comfort. He wondered for how long William James would be away.

In the middle of the afternoon, a white-coated man of fifty years and an authoritative manner came into the room, followed by a different nurse bearing a kidney-shaped bowl and a tray of fearsome-looking instruments and rubber tubes. The man introduced himself as Doctor Herman and, for no obvious reason, Sebastian responded with an instant feeling of dislike.

He said, "How long will this go on?"

Doctor Herman looked down at Melody. He was neither surprised at her state, nor seemed troubled by it. He said, "Several weeks, at least. Morphinism is very hard to treat. What you see are the first effects of deprivation. They're a necessary part of the process."

"Are you sure?" Sebastian said. "What process is this?"

"We use the Crebo Method on our more extreme cases. I can assure you that Melody is an extreme case. I won't deceive you, Mister…"

"Becker."

"She's in a bad way, Mister Becker. I have to ask you to leave us now."

"Why?"

"For procedures of a personal nature." In the absence of a table the nurse had set her tray across the sink, and as they were speaking had been preparing the treatments. Sebastian saw swabs, lint, an enema syringe, and several labelled medicines. He counted at least half a dozen bottles, all different sizes and in different colors of glass. In the enameled bowl, on a folded towel, lay a very large needle.

"I'll be outside," Sebastian said.

43

HE TOOK A WALK IN THE GROUNDS. ALL WAS QUIET. HE SAW little evidence of organized security; in fact, other than those two Mexican orderlies from the previous day, he saw none. Most who came to this private compound with their various forms of 'nervous exhaustion' would check in voluntarily. Those sent by a studio would have too much to lose if they walked out. And where the cases were most extreme, those patients were probably too weak to leave. Discretion was key to the service. It was quite unlike the Bethlem Hospital, with its window bars and high walls and controlled access. Here, too much visible security would be bad for business.

Would Kit Strong track Melody to this place? Would he dare to come for her? If his purpose had been to get the better of William James, then his trophy had been stolen. She might yet be saved and his work undone. Some might consider her ruined, but her father had faith.

Sebastian went back into the main building and descended to the basement. Doctor Herman was emerging from Room Three, while the nurse was tidying up after.

Herman said, "You can sit with her if you want. But she won't know you're there."

Sebastian waited for the nurse to finish, and then went in. The light was no less harsh than before, the room no less bare, but now Melody was still and the blanket was covering her. His chair had been moved back against the wall. Sebastian brought it over, and once again sat to watch the child.

Though she'd been cleaned up and her trembling had stopped, her condition seemed no better than before. Just differently distressing. Where her skin had been pale as bone, it was now gray and soapy-looking. Her eyes were only part-closed, her breathing shallow and labored. Less than half an hour ago, she'd been jittering with uncontrollable life; now she barely seemed to be clinging to it.

He slid from the chair to sit on the floor beside her. He spoke her name, but she didn't respond. He found her hand, and took it.

After a while, he rested back against the padded wall.

Some time after that, he was woken gently by a different nurse.

She'd brought a bowl of water and a cloth. She said, "Would you like to bathe her face?" But Sebastian released Melody's hand, got stiffly to his feet, and moved aside so that the nurse could get in and do the job.

Watching, he said, "How many of your patients die?"

"What a question." She meant to sound surprised, but Sebastian sensed evasion.

He said, "So it's never happened?"

"I'm not allowed to say," the nurse told him. "You'll need to ask Doctor Herman."

After a while he realized that he'd lost track of the hour. The light burned all the time, but the only alternative in this windowless below-ground space would be total, unrelieved darkness. He gave the nurse some money for food, and one of the orderlies arrived with it around thirty minutes later. The meal was some kind of hash with gravy, and a bottle of beer. The hash was cold and the beer was warm. The smell of food took a while to get through to Melody, but after a while she winced in disgust and began a weak struggle to sit up. Sebastian slid the tray away across the floor, and helped her into a sitting position.

"Do you want to eat?" he said.

"No," she said. "My legs ache."

"That's because of the morphine." He had to hold her up. She couldn't hold herself.

She said, "Whatever it was, I need more."

"I know," Sebastian said.

"I need it!"

"I know."

"Fuck you," she said, and fell asleep against his chest.

A few times, she struggled in her sleep. More than once, she clenched up with cramps and keened at the pain. When that happened, he held her until she began to relax and sleep more deeply. Time passed, and again he thought of his son. Robert had never been affectionate, had never sought comfort. But had needed it just the same.

Sebastian began to ache, but couldn't move without disturbing Melody. He tried anyway. His attempts to shift around a little and relieve the pressure caused her to stir.

He heard her say, "Mama."

"Shhh," he said, and he stroked her lank hair, damp with cold sweat. He heard *Mama* again, so quiet he almost missed it.

"It's all right," he said.

"I can't see," she said. "Mama, put the light on."

Her voice was suddenly stronger, as if her consciousness had risen from the depths and broken the surface. He shifted in place. She clutched at him.

"I can't see!" she said, though her eyes were wide open.

Was this a worsening of her condition, or a waking dream? She didn't want to let him go, but he disengaged himself for long enough to get to the door and call out for help. Then he returned and waited with her until someone appeared.

The doctor was fetched. This was a new man, not Doctor Herman, but younger. He called for a small flashlight, and shone it into the child's eyes.

Sebastian felt helpless. He was getting to witness first-hand what a cruel mistress a morphine habit could be. Kit Strong had taken a normal, healthy child and refashioned her into this dependent stick-creature of longing and pain. Poison had hollowed out and sustained her. Now that the poison had been withdrawn, she was falling apart.

How long would it be, until William James returned?

Though the beam shone directly into her eyes, first one, then the other, she claimed to see nothing. Speaking as if she wasn't even present, the younger doctor said to Sebastian, "Her eyes are undamaged. Her pupils react. She may only imagine she's blind. I've seen that before." He felt the glands in her neck, and pulled open her jaw to look at her tongue. And then he said, "I'll have to discuss this with Doctor Herman. We may need to step up the treatment."

After he'd gone, one of the nurses said to Sebastian, "You don't have to stay with her all the time."

"I'll stay anyway," Sebastian said. "Is there any word from her father?"

"No."

"This treatment," he said, "I've never seen anything like it. Can you be sure it's helping?"

"I think we can trust the doctors to know what they're doing," she said.

• • •

A WHILE later, when they were alone, Melody said, "Don't let them hurt me again."

She'd taken Sebastian by surprise. He'd thought her unconscious but the remark came out sudden, clear, and strong.

He said, "They're trying to help you."

"You haven't seen what they do."

She fumbled at the buttons of her shift. Sebastian reached out to stop her, thinking that this was the beginning of some delusional episode. But she pulled down the cotton to reveal a series of angry, unhealed puncture wounds around her breastbone.

She began to cry, and soiled herself.

The nurses came to clean her up. Sebastian was once again obliged to leave the room.

Here by the top of the stairwell was the dispensary, all brass handles and handwritten labels. Its doorway served as the counter to a narrow room with three walls of square-drawer cabinets. On shelves above the cabinets were glass carboys and traditional pharmacy jars. On the other side of the counter, a sturdy woman was separating tablets on a counting tray before funneling them into pill boxes.

Sebastian waited until he had her attention, then smiled and gave a greeting.

On hearing his accent she said, "Another Englishman?"

"I'm Doctor Becker," Sebastian said, "of Bethlem Royal Hospital in Lambeth. I'm here with my patient, she's downstairs. Doctor Herman's a busy man so can you answer something for me?"

"I can try."

"The Crebo Method. It's new to me. What does it entail?"

"I'm sure my husband will be happy to explain," she said.

Sebastian leaned on the counter and lowered his voice to a conspiratorial level.

"I'll be honest with you," he said, "I'm embarrassed by my own ignorance. I got my medical training in England. We do things differently there."

"Well," she said, "as you're a colleague…" and then she rattled off a list of drugs and treatments of which Sebastian grasped and remembered no more than two or three. The method involved injections directly into the chest.

"And they can only be given by a qualified medical doctor?"

At that, something in her eyes changed.

"My husband owns the sanitarium," she said.

Sebastian walked two blocks, and found a Western Union Telegraph and Cable office. When he returned it was to find Melody sitting upright, propped by pillows and still looking deathly. She watched him as he crossed the room and he said, "Do you see me now?"

She nodded. She was wary.

He said, "I'm Sebastian. Do you remember me?"

"Under the bleachers. I watched him hurting you."

"I'd say he's hurt you worse. How are you feeling now?"

"All my bones ache."

She'd been given a cup of water. She tried to raise it for a sip, but lacked the strength. Sebastian crouched beside her and helped, feeling her hands trembling with the effort.

"You can beat this," Sebastian said.

"What if I don't want to?"

"Then you'll die."

"Fine," she said, and turned her face away.

Sebastian set the cup aside. "You don't mean that," he said.

"You don't know me."

"You're right, I don't," he said, letting a trace of irritation into his tone. "But when a father's ready to hang for you, I imagine you must be worth something."

She looked at him. He went on, "I know you started the theater fire. But no one else does. He's still protecting you."

"Why would he do that? He hates me."

"Because he didn't tell you about your mother? That doesn't mean he hates you. He may have been in the wrong, but his intentions were good."

"He's lied to me. All my life."

"He let you think that your mother was a saint. A saint who the angels took away, when the hard truth is that she abandoned both of you to go off with someone else. How would *you* explain that to a child?"

"I'm not a child."

"You were at the time. So for your sake he committed to the lie. Try to imagine the problem that created once you were grown. How would you deal with it?"

She had no answer. She changed the subject.

She said, "Why are you here?"

"I was sent to find your father and take him home."

"So they can hang him?"

"If they do get their hands on him, there'll be a trial. But you're right, it won't be fair. They need someone to blame."

"They can blame me."

"Then everyone suffers, except the one man who deserves to."

"You mean Kit."

"How did he get you onto the morphine?"

She tilted her head back, and closed her eyes. "He began by feeding it to me. In treats and fancies, while we practiced for the act. They were my rewards for doing well. I didn't know. Then he stopped it so I'd feel bad."

"As bad as you feel now?"

She shook her head, miserably, eyes still closed. "This is worse," she said.

"What happened then?"

"The longer it went on, the worse I felt. I couldn't tell anyone else. He let me suffer and then he said, 'this can help you with that,' and he showed me the needle. He made me beg for it. All the agony went away, just like that. In the end I'd keep begging him for more."

Sebastian said, "What do you want, Melody? What do you want now?"

"I don't want this," she said.

"This was never about you. You understand that?"

"What will happen to me?"

"You'll get through this. You'll feel better than you do now. But you can never go back to Kit Strong. Because then it will just start all over again."

She was silent for a while. Then she said, "He plays games. With people. It's the only thing that seems to give him any pleasure."

"I don't call them games. I call him evil."

She looked at him then.

"I do whatever an evil man wants," she said. "What does that make me?"

• • •

SHE CONTINUED to refuse food. The sight of a bowl of oatmeal made her gag. After a couple of hours she drifted into a doze that Sebastian took for genuine sleep rather than a stupor, although it was hard to be sure. He checked the time and saw that it was late in the evening. He'd been with her for the entire day, and it seemed even longer. He wondered whether he should return to the Bunker Hill apartment and come back in the morning, or find a room in an inexpensive hotel somewhere close by, or stay at his post until William James returned.

There was always the possibility that Kit Strong might show up in the night, to take back his undefended prize. In which case, all would have been for nothing. So Sebastian went prowling, found some clean bedding in an unoccupied room, and stole pillows to provide himself with some comfort in the chair.

He was reluctant to leave her alone. He'd little experience with addicts, but his memory of the few so-called 'dope fiends' on the wards at Bethlem Royal was that they'd been treated with a staged withdrawal. Deaths were rare and always due to overdose, or to the lasting effects of dangerous cocktails suspiciously like the so-called Crebo Method. He'd recognized at least one surgical anesthetic and one deadly poison in that pharmacy list.

Melody had a restless night, twitching, cramping, and crying out in thirst. At three in the morning he had to help her to the toilet and then, after giving her ten minutes of privacy, pick her up off the floor where she was too weak to crawl back to the mattress. No nurse appeared until after seven.

It was almost nine when 'Doctor' Herman, the administrator who treated patients with no apparent medical qualification, came down.

She had to be held up for his examination. Though her eyes were sunken and her lips cracking, though she slurred her words and struggled to stay awake, he seemed satisfied with what he saw.

He said, "I think a further treatment's called for."

Sebastian said, "When she's like this?"

"No better time. You can see how we're driving the addiction from her body."

"All I see is a patient getting worse," Sebastian said.

"That's because you're not a medical man, Mister Becker."

Sebastian was about to argue but was interrupted by the arrival of a message to say that he was needed outside. He had an inkling of why, and so he left the discussion and took the stairs two at a time.

At the door to the building, a young man stood with a bicycle. He wore the telegraph boy's uniform of knee britches with shirt, necktie and a baggy cap.

On seeing Sebastian he said, "Looking for a Mister Becker?"

"That's me."

"Telegram for you."

He handed Sebastian the envelope and waited. "Any reply, sir?"

Sebastian tore open the envelope and took out the paper. "What's your name?" he said as he began to read.

"Curtis, sir."

"How old are you, Curtis?"

"Fourteen."

He'd read the message now. Six words. Six words was all it took. Sebastian lowered the paper, reached into his pocket, and said, "Here's a dollar for you. See how fast you can get a taxicab here."

"A dollar?" the boy said, probably lucky to make as much in a week from his tips.

"Another if it's waiting when I come out."

"Yes *sir*." He swung his bicycle around and launched off. By the time the seat of his pants hit the saddle, Sebastian was back inside the building and heading down the stairs.

"Stop," he called out as he reached the doorway of Melody's room. Doctor Herman and the two nurses looked up in surprise. One of the two nurses froze in the act of handing a prepared needle to Doctor Herman. The other was holding Melody down in readiness.

Herman said, "What do you mean?"

"I'm telling you to stop the treatment. You touch her again, you'll be sorry."

"I beg your pardon?"

"She's done, here. We're leaving." Sebastian moved amongst them to get to Melody, disrupting their group.

"She can't leave," Herman said. "I forbid it."

"Melody?" Sebastian said. "Do you think you can walk?"

Sebastian saw a look pass between Herman and one of the nurses. The nurse began to move toward the door and Sebastian said, "You. Stay where you are. We'll keep your bruisers out of this."

"I answer to her father," Herman said. "Not to you."

"Answer to this," Sebastian said, and thrust the cable into his hands, freeing his own to pick up the blanket and draw it around Melody's shoulders.

The cable read, *Discontinue treatment. Charlatans killing the child.* The return address was for William Stoddard, Supervising Physician, Bethlem Royal Hospital, London.

Herman said, "This is outrageous."

"There we agree," Sebastian said. "Stand back."

"I will not."

"Then I'll remove you from my path, and I promise you won't enjoy it. Though I think I will."

It was as if his very anger rendered Melody weightless. He swept her up against their protests and carried her out of the room and up the stairs. Herman tried to follow, still protesting, but the stairway was narrow and he could not pass or bar the way. Melody took hold of Sebastian's lapel and hung on.

She turned her face from the sun as they emerged into daylight.

"I wish you'd hit him," she murmured into his chest.

"So do I," Sebastian said.

44

CURTIS GOT HIS SECOND DOLLAR AND THE TAXICAB BROUGHT them all the way to the Argyle. Melody said she felt strong enough to walk into the building. But she had no shoes, so Sebastian carried her as far as the lobby. Then she managed halfway to the second floor before he had to pick her up again.

He got her a bowl of hot water and a damp cloth to bathe with, and laid out one of her father's long undershirts to replace the hospital shift. Then he went outside and sat on the porch under the window, watching the morning traffic go by until she knocked on the glass to tell him she'd finished.

She'd drained all her energy, and couldn't rise from her chair. He lifted her into the bed.

"How do you feel?" he said.

"Better."

She didn't much look it, but he took her at her word. He said, "I need to see if there's any message from your father. I'll only be a few minutes."

He went looking for the employee who described himself as the concierge, actually an unkempt man with broken teeth who lived with his family in the basement rooms. He combined the duties of janitor and building manager. Sebastian followed the sound of a hammer and found him nailing up a broken shutter.

Sebastian said to him, "Have you seen Mister James?"

"Not since yesterday," the building manager said. "I sold him my pistol."

"I need a few things from the store. Is there anyone who can go for me?"

"I'll send up the Mrs."

Sebastian returned to the rooms. Melody was still awake. Once Sebastian had closed the door she said, "Where is he?"

"I'm guessing he found an all-night game," Sebastian said. "He should be back soon."

So he'd taken a pistol. That was no doubt a precaution, but it was also a worry. A gambling den was never the safest place to be. Especially for someone who'd set out with the aim of cheating the regulars out of some fast money. William James was no novice, but he was no longer teamed with a more experienced partner.

Melody said, "He always hated anything connected to gambling. He said it was only for mugs and thieves."

"Well," Sebastian said, "we've all been on a long journey. You pick up new skills when you have to."

He hadn't even finished speaking when she spoke over him and said, "Where did my mother go?"

It seemed like a sudden switch of subject, but it must have been playing on her mind since the evening before. Sebastian said, "I never knew her. You'll have to ask him."

"I can't do that," she said.

"Why not?"

"I just can't."

There was a knock on the door. It was the building manager's wife, a woman who dressed all in black like a Greek widow and who shared her husband's stance on dental hygiene. Sebastian gave her a list of supplies and some money. Then he moved to the window and watched her head off down the street. He saw no sign of William James returning.

Melody asked for some water. For once she was able to keep it down. The coughing made her cheeks red, which perversely gave her a healthier look.

Handing over the glass and leaning back, she said, "How many people died?"

"In the fire?"

She nodded.

"No one should have died at all," Sebastian said. "But some of the fire exits were locked and the safety curtain was obstructed. That burden's on the management. People think they can break the rules when it suits them."

"How many?" Melody persisted.

"The last count I heard was around fifty."

At that, she fell silent for a while.

Then she said, "God won't ever forgive me."

"It's a poor God who wouldn't," Sebastian said. "Especially since He'd know who was really responsible."

"I'm responsible," she said.

"You were far from yourself. Kit Strong had made you his instrument. Are you his instrument still?"

"I don't know," Melody said.

"The choice is yours."

"So you say."

They sat in silence for a while. A miserable silence, on Melody's part. Sebastian was remembering that occasion under the bleachers, when she'd held a gun to his head and then watched as Kit Strong dealt out a beating. It had been one of the lowest of many low moments in his life. Yet he was unable to hold that against her now.

She said, "Will I have to go to prison?"

"As far as I know," Sebastian said, "your father's the only witness. I don't see him giving you up."

"Melody James is not worth protecting."

"William James is of a different opinion."

She said, "Whatever happens to me, promise me that he'll be safe."

"What do you mean?" Sebastian said. "Nothing's going to happen to you. You're not going to prison. And you're not going to die."

"You have to tell him I'm sorry."

"Tell him yourself. You'll see him soon enough. Unless he goes straight to the sanitarium with the money."

"Why would he do that?" she said.

"To pay those quacks for your treatment."

"It was all paid up-front. Every penny. I heard them say so."

Sebastian was about to explain it further, at which point he realized that he had no further explanation. If the bill was already paid, then it followed that William James had lied.

Melody said, "He's not out raising money. He's gone looking for Kit."

45

Sebastian said, "He knows better than that."

"Kit will kill him," Melody insisted. "You've seen what he can do. He's killed three men that I know of, and he's boasted of more." She found the strength to sit up. "Can you stop him, Mister Becker? Will you?"

She was right. That had to be her father's reason for acquiring a weapon, and for ensuring that Melody was not left without protection. Because there was a significant chance that he might not return.

Sebastian said, "I don't know where he'll be."

"We've been staying in a camp. It's like a movie town for cowboys."

"Where?"

"I heard the place called Ynez Canyon. It's on the coast." She threw back the covers and started to swing her legs out of the bed. "There's stages and a teepee camp and everything. They let us bunk there when we got to California. We had cabin number fifty-four."

"Hey," Sebastian said. "Lie back down."

"I'm coming with you."

"Not a good idea."

"But I know Kit. I know what he'll do."

"I've a fair idea myself. You don't have the strength for anything right now. If you want to help your father, finish what you started here."

She protested a little and then dropped back onto the pillows, exhausted. Her face twisted as she fought not to cry.

"Get well," Sebastian said. "Get clean. Trust me with this."

He wished that he could feel more confident. He might already be too late. In stories, the good were fated to prevail. But in life, the most righteous would always be at a disadvantage faced with an opponent unhampered by conscience or decency.

He made sure that Melody had water within reach, something to read, a chamber pot for if she needed one. Then he went down to the basement apartment and knocked on the door. The building manager's wife opened it.

He said, "I think my niece has the flu. She's taken to her bed and I have to go out. Can you look in on her?"

"What do I have to do?" the Black Widow said with some suspicion.

"Nothing," Sebastian said. "Just make sure she's okay. Give her fresh water, Maybe fetch her something if she gets hungry. I'll pay for your time, of course."

At the mention of payment, the woman grew more interested.

"How often?" she said.

"Every half-hour?"

"And fetch whatever she needs."

Sebastian saw a lingering trace of suspicion, and said, "It's nothing contagious."

"You said it's the flu."

"It's not the flu. And she's over the worst of it."

"Whatever she needs?"

"I'll reimburse whatever you spend. Plus twenty dollars."

"You're the boss."

46

THERE WAS MORE TO SANTA YNEZ THAN A COWBOY CAMP. JUST north of Santa Monica, the entire canyon from the mountains to the sea had been leased by a motion picture producer the previous year. In that short time he'd built five sound stages on the beach, moored a pirate ship in the bay, and created fake towns and villages of all nations in the hills. People called it Inceville. It now had its own reservoir, its own armory, a power house, herds of cattle to feed the workforce, and a resident tribe of Lakota Sioux. With a system as tightly organized as the studio was sprawling, Thomas Ince was able to turn out more than a dozen quality two-reelers every month. Most of these were Westerns, with their casting drawn mainly from his own picture cowboys. Players and employees who didn't live onsite could ride the Red Car line to its end, and complete their journey on a buckboard shuttle that covered the last mile up the coast.

Unlike Melody's father, Sebastian had the advantage of knowing where to go, without having to ask around and nail down the location first. With luck and a fair wind, he might even get there ahead of William James.

Estranged from the daughter he'd saved, with his past life over and his future a blank, the showman must have set out believing that he'd be facing Kit Strong with nothing to lose. Sebastian needed to catch him and make him understand that the situation was not so bleak, that with his help his daughter might yet come around. That the wise course would be to take her, walk away, and begin to heal what was broken.

Beyond that, the prospects got a little hazy. But then Sebastian had never been much of a fortune teller.

Streetcar 149 followed the railroad tracks and terminated by the switching yards for the Long Wharf, a mile-long wooden freight pier like a trestle bridge to nowhere. Trains ran along it to meet ships out at sea, while a graded road continued northward along the shore. Sebastian found the horse wagon shuttle to Santa Ynez Canyon, paid his fare, and clung on for the final leg of the ride. Ahead, the Pacific coast stretched onward in a curve to Malibu and beyond.

He didn't enter Inceville unchallenged. He was spotted by a man on horseback who rode up and said, "Can I ask your business, sir?"

There were no gates or fences but Melody had warned him of armed and mounted patrols, mostly on the lookout for patent spies from New York. "I've business with one of your cowboys," he said.

As soon as he spoke, his accent raised suspicion in the rider. Most out here couldn't tell the difference between an Englishman and an Easterner.

"I'm gonna need a little more than that," the horseman said.

"Kit Strong? He came in from Cody."

"I mean from you."

For the first time in weeks Sebastian was obliged to show his Chancery credentials before being allowed to pass.

"You're my second Englishman today," the horseman said.

The resident company was making scenes out on the sands, involving people and horses and tents down by the shore. Up here, the canyon sets were relatively empty. A solitary painter working on a French village façade pointed him in the direction of the cowboy camp.

Sebastian climbed a well-made dirt trail between scrubland hillsides that could equally pass for Tucson or Tuscany. The property ran for a good seven miles into the hills, but most of the construction was down at the beach end. Higher up, the canyon widened and it was here that the company-owned stables and corrals stood hidden from view.

He passed a row of broken down pioneer wagons, then a stack of haylage. In a ravine farther along, he found what he was looking for. It was a picturesque facsimile of a mining camp with pine cabins that doubled as bunkhouses for the workforce. There was a fake well, and a fake mineshaft that ran no more than a few feet into the hillside. Each cabin had its number painted on a moveable rock beside the door.

He stopped in the shadow of an open horse shelter, studying the lie of the land before risking an approach. He was now in no doubt that William James had reached the camp ahead of him. The smart move for a man of murderous intent would be to wait on one of the bluffs. From there, a sharp-shooter could pick off his target with ease. Kit Strong would never know what was coming.

But William James had a pistol, not a rifle, and Sebastian feared that he had something less impersonal in mind. No easy, sudden death, such as you'd give an old dog or an injured horse. More likely a confrontation.

A Western ending.

Never mind that such was the invention of dime novelists and those film scenario writers who now followed in their footsteps. It was an instant myth, made for those who lived unromantic lives in cities. Under such circumstances, a Manchester publican's son had as much claim to authenticity as any of the pearl-handled, buckskin and silver-buckle boys.

Nothing was moving out there. Sebastian spat to get rid of the dust he could taste, and then moved toward the cabins.

Cabin number fifty-four wasn't hard to find. He came up on the shady side of the buildings and risked a look in through the window. There was no sign of Kit Strong. There was, however, William James.

He was sitting on a wooden chair in the middle of the floor, facing the window. His head was down, his coat was off, and his shirt was stained with blood from a beating at least as severe as the one Sebastian had experienced.

A Kit Strong trademark, it seemed. It was a one-roomed cabin and, as far as Sebastian could establish, William James was in there alone. If he raised his head, he'd see Sebastian. But he didn't raise his head. Sebastian moved to the door. It was latched, but had no lock.

He stepped inside. On the floorboards before him, there was blood. From the splash marks it looked as if William James had been tied to the chair and beaten in place, and set upright again whenever a hard blow knocked man and chair over together.

But as he hung forward, he was breathing. His leaning body gently moving with each breath, like the motion of a calm sea. Sebastian could now see that his arms had been bound to the chair.

They were rodeo knots, simple hitches. As Sebastian knelt and worked on the first of the ropes, he said, "Where did he go?"

One arm freed, William James tried to stir. Until this moment he'd seemed not to be aware.

But a voice behind Sebastian said, "Right here."

Upon which, the sky fell in.

47

SEBASTIAN RETAINED NO MEMORY OF BEING DRAGGED ACROSS the floor and thrown against a bunk. He regained awareness to find a leather belt being pulled tight around his neck, securing him to the bedpost. He grabbed at it, but too late. As a means of trussing a prisoner, it was makeshift but quick. His hands and legs were free, but he could neither rise nor get himself loose. Only by hooking his thumbs under the leather could he keep himself from choking.

Kit Strong was standing over him and pulling on a pair of rodeo gloves, one snug finger at a time. Once they would have been soft yellow leather. Now they were as fouled as a butcher's apron.

He saw Sebastian looking up at him. "Beatings are hard on the knuckles," he explained. "Got to keep these hands nice and soft. Now William here wouldn't tell me, so maybe you will. I'll bet you know. Where's my baby?"

"Can't imagine what you mean."

"You know who I mean. My Melody. You both took her. Where is she?"

"She's not your Melody," Sebastian said. "That's over now. Why don't you give it up?"

"Don't do this to yourself," Kit Strong said. "The more you annoy me, the harder I can make it. It's gonna be pretty hard already. Right now your face is still familiar. We'll have to see what we can do about that. I remember you, Pinkerton man. Didn't I give you enough of a message last time?"

From across the room came the voice of William James.

"Clearly not," he said.

"You shut your stupid English mouth," Strong snapped back over his shoulder, before returning his attention to Sebastian.

"Waiting for an answer," he said.

"Sorry," Sebastian said. With William James in the room, he felt compelled to show some spirit. This was despite the apprehension that was crawling from the hard floor up into his gut.

In response Kit Strong pulled out a pistol and fired into the floorboards between Sebastian's legs. Sebastian flinched, but the leather collar kept him pinned. The detonation in the enclosed space was sudden and shocking, and he'd felt the wooden boards jump.

He recognized the revolver as the Pinkerton-issued Bull Dog copy that had been taken from him under the bleachers of the *Tompkins Real Wild West and Frontier Exhibition*.

"Clever," Sebastian said, with the shot still ringing in his ears.

Kit Strong signaled his indifference and said, "It's a picture town. Guns are firing off all the time. No one pays them any attention."

"Those are movie guns firing blanks. You might have trouble explaining a real dead body."

"Not for very long. Drag you up into the brush, give it a few days, and between the buzzards and coyotes there'll be nothing left to explain. So where is she?"

Sebastian said, "Who?" and Kit Strong fired again, closer this time, close enough for Sebastian to feel the flying splinters and wince.

Sebastian said, "You assume I even know."

Kit Strong hunkered down before him. "Let me explain the position to you," he said, lowering his voice and affecting a menacing sincerity. He indicated William James, behind him and across the room. "Him, I'm inclined to keep alive. His discomfort entertains me. You—it doesn't matter to me either way."

William James called out, "He needs me around to shout at and show off to. Like a little boy. You see any kind of dignity in that?"

"Button it," Kit Strong said, only half-looking back.

"I wasn't talking to you."

"I said button it! Don't make me come over there."

"Listen to him," William James went on, unfazed. "A man who's dedicated his entire working life to whining about the boss. He got nowhere with Buffalo Bill so now he makes do with me."

"Hey, both of you," Sebastian said. "Let this drop."

"Don't tell me what to do," Kit Strong said. "You're way out of your depth in this one, Pinkerton."

Sebastian saw a movement; William James was leaning right back in his chair, trying to see past Kit Strong to Sebastian. He said, "How's Melody?"

"Getting better," Sebastian said. "Doing fine. How did you get past the guards?"

"Told 'em the truth," William James said.

"Hey," Kit Strong said, moving to block their line of sight. "She's mine now. Melody and me, we're hell-bound together. And before we're done you'll tell me where she is."

He'd clearly given up any hope of extracting the information from William James. Such a display of nerve made a hard example for Sebastian to follow.

"Won't happen," he said.

"You want to fuck with the Devil?"

"Is that how you see yourself?" Sebastian said. "The Prince of Darkness? Come on."

"Hey, Kit," William James called out. "If you're the Prince of Darkness, am I the Holy Ghost?"

Kit Strong's patience snapped. He sprang to his feet and turned around, levelling the firearm at William James.

"Choose an ear," he said.

"Left," William James snapped back without hesitation or fear.

The two men faced each other across the cabin. Nothing happened for a moment.

Kit Strong seemed to realize that whatever he did now, hit or miss or back down, William James had already won the point. Strong might have the two of them at his mercy, but he wasn't in control of the situation.

Meanwhile Sebastian's attention had been captured by the sight of a second pistol, jammed into Kit Strong's waistband in the small of his back.

A cheap handgun, a so-called Suicide Special. This would be the gun that William James had bought from the building manager at the rooming house. Sebastian stretched out his hand as far as he could, but failed to reach it.

William James went on, "All this talk of the Devil. He doesn't want to face the truth. Which is that he's just a failed Carny who raped a child."

"William—" Sebastian said with a note of warning, worrying that the showman was pushing Strong too far. He was thinking that if he could slide the leather up the bunk frame just an inch or two without throttling himself, he might yet reach the second gun.

"Let him kill me," William James said.

"Then what?"

"Then I win."

Kit Strong reached behind his back and pulled the second revolver out of his waistband. Sebastian saw it plucked from his almost-grasp. He gave up and slid back to the floor. Kit Strong was crossing the room to William James.

"Here," he said. "You think you can take me on? Take it. Two sharp-shooters. We'll see who's the best."

He tossed the second gun to the man in the chair. Though one of his hands was now free, William James made no effort to catch. The gun clattered to the floor.

Kit Strong said, "Why didn't you catch it?"

"Didn't see it coming."

"Pick it up."

With an enormous effort, still tethered to the chair by one arm, William James leaned over to stretch down for the gun on the floor. It appeared that with one eye completely closed by the beating, he could barely see. His fingers scrabbled around on the dusty boards until he found it, and then scrabbled around some more until he had enough of a grip on the handle to lift it.

With the gun in his hand he rocked back into the chair, all but exhausted by the effort. The weight of the cheap pistol seemed too much for him to hold. Even with his elbow on the chair arm, he could barely keep it raised or steady.

Yet his defiance couldn't be faulted. He said, "If you know any prayers, Kit, now's the time."

Kit Strong was incredulous. "You seriously think you can win?"

"You're the one who made the challenge. Doesn't it depend on who's the best?"

"Like there's any question. I remember the day you came begging me to work for you. I warned you then how it would end."

"Still talking? I guess you're just one of those people who can't shut up when they're scared."

"Scared? You're a joke, old man. I'll even use my left hand."

"Whatever you like. Just stand where I can see you."

William James had his head tilted like a blind man's, searching to get a fix on Kit Strong with his one good eye.

"I'll be the last thing you see," Kit Strong said. "Pinkerton can count us in."

He moved around to stand between William James and the window, presenting a silhouette that even a half-blinded man couldn't miss. Here was an opportunity, but William James was sitting there with a loaded gun of dubious accuracy that he could barely lift. There seemed a dread inevitability about the outcome of the next few moments.

William James made no effort, nor did he fire. But within the same fraction of a second, the window broke and Kit Strong's throat exploded.

"Three sharpshooters," William James said.

And then, as Kit Strong dropped to his knees, "Learn to count."

Kit Strong flopped forward. When he hit the floor, he raised the dust. He was most likely dead before he fell. The bullet had cut through bone and spinal cord. Once he was on the floor there was very little blood.

There was silence in the one-roomed cabin. Then some more glass fell out of the window and broke on the floor. William James let the unused Suicide Special fall into his lap. All the breath went out of him in one enormous sigh.

The cabin door opened then. The shooter was coming in. From where he was tethered, Sebastian first saw the barrel of a rifle, trained on the face-down body of Kit Strong. It was the same kind of semi-automatic hunting rifle carried by the mounted guards. It was slowly brought into the cabin, one cautious step at a time, by Melody James.

She handled the weapon with assurance. Without looking back, she closed the door behind her. She wore an assortment of clothing that gave her the look of a hand-me-down farmboy. The hand with the rifle was steady, her tread on the boards was confident. All her attention was fixed on Kit Strong.

William James said, "Make sure he's dead."

She took a step forward and placed the gun barrel against the supine body's head, and William James said quickly, "That's not what I meant!"

So she nudged the body with her foot a couple of times. There was no response.

Sebastian realized that he was still holding his breath. Some things made sense now. William James had seen his daughter taking her firing position beyond the window. All of his goading had been a means to maneuver Kit Strong into place for the shot.

The mystery lay in her transformation. Only a few short hours ago he'd left Melody James bedridden, incontinent, prone to shakes and weeping, physically incapable and beset by emotions she'd been holding down for years. He wouldn't have judged her fit to make her own way down the stairs. Yet here she was. She laid down the rifle and moved to free her father. There was a tense silence between them. She didn't look at him, and neither spoke.

Throughout this time Sebastian was attempting, with almost no success, to free himself from the strap that bound his neck. It was a good two inches wide. Strong had cinched the belt up to the buckle and then knotted it around the timberwork of the bunk behind him.

When she'd finished with her father, Melody came across the cabin to help Sebastian. For a moment she had to pull the belt tighter in order to release it, and he almost passed out. Then as she tugged the loosened strap free, she glanced down at him.

One look into her eyes, and he knew.

The blue of her eyes was startling, all one color with tiny constricted pupils like flyspecks at the center. Though he was no doctor, he knew immediately what the explanation had to be.

Morphine had restored her. She'd sacrificed her recovery to save her father.

48

IN DEATH, KIT STRONG COULD TEST THE VALIDITY OF HIS OWN theory about buzzards and coyotes and the disposal or corpses. With Melody keeping watch down the canyon they carried his body out of the cabin and over the next rise, dragging him as far into the brush as he'd go. Sebastian had to put in most of the effort, while the battered William James did what he could to help. Back in the cabin, some handfuls of dirt and a filthy rug served to cover the bloodstains on the floorboards. The bullet holes in the timber, they ignored.

Cowboys, was the only explanation that would ever be required.

Then while William James cleaned his wounds in one of over a hundred busy dressing rooms behind the Inceville stages, Melody unloaded and returned the target rifle to the property store.

They took the horse shuttle back down to the wharf. Though he fought to disguise it, the showman's stoicism in the face of pain was tested with every rock and rut that the buckboard struck. The streetcar into town gave him a much easier ride. He and Melody sat side by side, with Sebastian opposite. After a while, Melody leaned her head on her father's shoulder. Other than that, there was no public expression from either.

A damaged pair, for sure. Though matched now, like never before.

It was late afternoon when they reached the Bunker Hill apartments. Leaving father and daughter alone to talk, Sebastian went out to begin the necessary arrangements for travel back East.

First he stopped by the basement to settle accounts with the building manager's wife. Melody had been able to persuade the woman that Sebastian had okayed the procuring of morphine as part of his instructions. It was only a couple of years since opiates had been on open sale in California. Narcotics were now covered by the state's poison laws, but some druggists continued to sell morphine and cocaine 'under the counter' to their regular customers.

"I took a risk, you know," the hotel woman told him.

"There's extra for your trouble," Sebastian said. "And listen. If anyone comes asking questions, we all have something to lose."

It was unlikely that she'd talk. Not to any official, anyway. And drugstore morphine would at least be clean.

The effect on Melody's symptoms had been swift and dramatic. It wouldn't last for more than a day or two. There was no way of knowing how Melody would cope with a long train ride and for that reason, they'd need a private compartment; At the La Grande Station ticket office he was offered a stateroom on the California Limited, departing that same evening. It was all first-class service but William James had given him a roll of bills, the winnings from an all-night game in Barstow, to cover such necessities.

That left Sebastian with one final matter to take care of. From the station he went to Bullock's department store on Broadway, where he had one of the sales supervisors put together a basic travel wardrobe that would see a young woman through a train ride and a steamer trip. Knowing nothing of sizes, he pointed out a young assistant of comparable height and build. As she went about the selection, Sebastian retired to sit amongst the rugs and ferns of the tea room where he could check the late editions of the city papers for any mention of a dead man in Santa Ynez Canyon.

For today, there was nothing. Tomorrow they'd be far away. And in a few short days he'd be meeting with Frances.

He let the newspaper fall and stared into space, until some of the women at a nearby table grew plainly uncomfortable in the belief that he was staring at them.

• • •

THE ARCHITECTURE of La Grande Station boasted gilded Moorish domes and the lush palms and gardens of a Sultan's palace. The Santa Fe

Railroad's Los Angeles terminus stood in an unlikely neighborhood of warehouses, wholesale grocers, and lumber companies. Sebastian and the Jameses arrived together in a taxicab, and left the Redcaps taking care of their bags. The California Limited departed for Chicago at 6:10pm every day, a first-leg journey of over two thousand miles. In Chicago they'd connect with the Baltimore and Ohio service to Philadelphia, where Sebastian would pick up the trunk he'd left at the Keystone Hotel and learn of Frances Callowhill's intentions.

At the bottom of his grip Sebastian had stashed a hypodermic kit and three grains of morphine that Melody knew nothing about. This was Kit Strong's supply. Sebastian had discovered it in a search of the Inceville cabin while Melody was getting rid of the murder weapon. He was hoping it wouldn't be needed.

The California Limited came with a club lounge car, air-conditioned dining, even an onboard barbershop and beautician. Their stateroom in the Pullman Palace car comprised one full section and toilet conveniences. By day the doors of the stateroom could be opened and the rooms 'thrown together'. The upholstery followed a color scheme throughout, with paneling in old oak and maple. In everything other than proportion it equalled a suite in a fine hotel.

Melody sat on one of the stateroom's wingbacks and drew up her legs, making herself so small that it was as if she was trying to disappear into the chair. William James took a plaid rug from the couch and spread it over her, and drew the stateroom's other chair in to sit close. She huddled down even more. Sebastian kept his distance. He felt he had no part in their conversation, but he could see her watching her father. At fourteen—no, fifteen, now—she might still be a child, but those eyes had several lifetimes behind them.

When the station clock sounded the hour, William James rose to his feet. "It's almost time," he said. "I need to speak to the guard."

His eyes met Sebastian's as he left the compartment, and they exchanged the slightest of nods. Melody was looking through the window, out across the depot, and didn't pick it up.

Sebastian took William James' chair. Without looking around, Melody said, "You know what I did."

"I do."

"I wasn't weak. I did it for a reason."

"I know," Sebastian said.

"I will never fall like this again," she said. "I have to be strong. I don't know what he's told you, but when we get to London I'm going to confess."

"That's not what he wants."

"I know. But it's what I have to do."

"It's a noble intention," Sebastian said, "but they may not choose to believe a confession. Have you considered that?"

"They'll have to if I swear on the Bible."

"You can swear on a stack of Bibles. It won't make any difference. The men who sent me to find your father hold the sincere belief that God works for the Empire." Somewhere outside, the guard was calling their departure. Sebastian went on, "It's not a matter of truth and justice, Melody. They want your father for other reasons. I was sent to bring back a scapegoat, for a purpose I can't even remember."

She looked at Sebastian. "You can't take him back to hang," she said. "Does he know what you're doing?"

Sebastian said, "He knows exactly what I'm doing."

The train started to move. Melody tried to rise. Sebastian put his hand on her arm.

"Listen to me, Melody," he said. "My report has gone ahead of me. It states that the man responsible for the theater fire is located, identified, and dead. It'll be backed by a coroner's certificate and an undertaker's photograph. I viewed the body and supervised the funeral myself. They have their scapegoat. As far as your father's concerned, it's over."

"You're covering for him?"

"We're the only ones who know."

"But how can he ever go home?"

"He can't," Sebastian said. "But this way, they'll stop looking."

She didn't understand. Not right away. But then she saw Sebastian's glance toward the window, and followed it.

The California Limited was rolling out at a steady walking pace. The train wouldn't pick up speed until the depot was way behind. Passing below them were family groups, friends, sweethearts, anyone who'd turned out to see a traveler on their way. There were more than a few servants, and the occasional family dog. One figure stood some way apart from the rest.

"No," she said.

There stood William James across the tracks, his hand raised in farewell.

49

THEIR FIRST STOP WOULD BE SAN BERNARDINO. SHE TALKED about leaving the train there and riding the next one back into Los Angeles, but when the time came made no effort to rise. She didn't sleep that night. She was withdrawn and uncommunicative all the way to Albuquerque, and then cried most of the way to Denver. Between Denver and Topeka, the shivering was at its worst. Between Topeka and Kansas City, she spent most of the time in the toilet. She complained that her bones were aching and she couldn't keep still. Sebastian began to understand the appeal of the deadly quack 'cures' they sold in the Hollywood hills. There was a dread helplessness in watching the symptoms play out, while doing nothing.

Somewhere around Carrolton she felt the stirrings of an appetite, so Sebastian ordered some food. He paid an extra twenty-five cents to have a steward bring it to the compartment. She managed a couple of mouthfuls, and spluttered on the third. The rest had to be scraped from the plate and discarded, but the mouthfuls stayed down. At night somewhere in Missouri, Sebastian waited until they were crossing an iron bridge over water and threw the unused hypodermic kit out of an open window.

When he returned, train staff had been along to turn down the beds and Melody was back in her chair, hugging her knees.

"I'm sorry," she said.

"What for?"

"Everything," she said. "I don't deserve any of what anyone's doing for me."

"You've been badly used," Sebastian said. "That's what you didn't deserve."

"What will he do?"

Sebastian drew down the blinds. "It's probably better we don't know," he said. "Then we can never expose him without meaning to."

Melody thought about that for a while. Then she said, "It'll be like he died. For real."

"It won't be the same," Sebastian said. "You'll be thinking of him. He'll be thinking of you. You'll always know he's out there. You won't need to let go."

She seemed to accept that. But then after she'd been thinking for a while longer, something occurred to her.

She said, "Why would you have to let go? Don't you think the dead watch over you?"

"No," Sebastian said.

• • •

BY GALESBURG, Melody reckoned she was feeling stronger. She didn't look it, but Sebastian took her at her word. Despite the fact that the continental USA had been rolling by the window in a succession of cold mountains, deep gorges, sunblasted deserts, and fertile plains, she said that she needed a change of scenery.

He understood. It involved nothing more ambitious than a walk along the long side aisle to the club car and back. She hung onto Sebastian's arm the whole way. They exchanged a pleasant greeting with every other passenger they met.

As a first trip out, it was a success. Her energy was limited, so he'd set the target low.

"Everyone's so nice," Melody said as they returned to their stateroom.

"I told them you're my niece."

She was hungry again. Genuinely hungry, now, which was encouraging. A full recovery might take weeks or months, but these days and nights would see the worst of it. From the dining car's A la Carte menu she asked for a bowl of clam broth and some vanilla ice cream.

As they waited for it to arrive, she said, "Do you have a wife at home?"

"I did once," Sebastian said.

"What happened?"

"She died. It was...it shouldn't have happened. She worked in a hospital and a man came in drunk with a knife. She was cut and the wound got infected. It was weeks later, it was a stupid awful thing. She came through all that and then died anyway."

"I'm sorry," Melody said.

"It hurts, but you don't want to forget," Sebastian tried to explain. "So you don't. Instead you kind of—I don't know. Rearrange yourself around the pain. Take it with you. It's the only way to go on."

"So you've nobody now."

"I have a grown-up son."

"No one else?"

"I have a sister-in-law," Sebastian said. "She's been loyal. But she's given up too much. It wouldn't be fair to ask anything more of her. I expect she'll be moving on."

At which point, the steward arrived with Melody's broth.

50

MOST OF THE CLOTHES IN HER READY-MADE TRAVEL WARDROBE were a reasonable fit, but of California weight. Chicago was cold. The thin wool dress that she wore for the change of trains left her pinched and shivering. But her grip on his arm was steady, and as they crossed the tracks she did not tire. Their accommodations on the Philadelphia-bound train were more standard, less lavish. Once they were under way, Sebastian took her to the observation parlor for something hot to drink.

Along with its big picture windows and thick carpeting the observation car offered rattan easy chairs, a selection of books and newspapers, even a writing desk for anyone who needed to catch up with correspondence during the journey. Over a glass of hot tea from the buffet, Sebastian said, "Can I make a suggestion?"

Holding the Russian-style glass in both hands, she looked up at him. "What?"

"When we get back to England, don't tell your family that William's alive."

"But that would be cruel. They'll want to know."

"I'm thinking of his safety. It's a hard secret to keep."

"You don't know show folk," she said.

She sat for a while looking out, not drinking, just warming her hands. The Illinois landscape was green and flat, the sky leaden.

She said, "I can't imagine going back to the act. I don't mean the life. That's all I know. But I've had it with the Wild West."

"What will you do?"

"I can rope-dance. Or fortunes. You don't need gypsy powers. You just have to read people."

"Read me," Sebastian said.

She set down the tea glass. "Give me your hand," she said.

He did as he'd been told. She took his hand in both of her own, turned it, inspected his palm. It suddenly struck him what a strange and capable child she was. Not yet sixteen, she had a set of skills about as far removed from the domestic as it was possible to get. She also had the conscience of a soldier. Only days before, she'd taken careful aim and killed a man. If such a dark deed troubled her spirit, nothing of it showed.

He wondered where such resilience would take her. Far beyond the fairground, he was sure.

She looked up into his eyes and said, with an earnestness and a certainty that was entirely convincing, "You feel others' pain. But you won't share your own. There are people who love you. They love you more than you know. But you can never bring yourself to believe that you deserve it."

There was silence in the observation car. Most seats were empty. The train rolled on. Someone folded and refolded a newspaper.

Sebastian said, "That's very impressive."

She released his hand.

"Anyone can do it," she said.

• • •

THEY REACHED Philadelphia at around four in the afternoon, and rode the subway to the Keystone Hotel. At the desk he learned what he'd suspected, that Frances had checked out shortly after he'd left. His trunk had been moved to the baggage room and the unused credit added to his account. He used some of it now to take a single room for himself and another for Melody, right alongside his own.

He said, "Is there a note or a message of any kind?"

"Nothing, sir," the clerk said.

First he installed Melody in her room. She dropped like a dead weight onto the bed and slapped her hand over her eyes. Sebastian said, "When you're rested, we'll go out and buy you a winter coat for the voyage."

"Will it be steerage again?"

"We can't afford the best. But it won't be steerage."

She didn't say anything else. She was probably asleep before he'd even closed the door.

He went into the next room, opened his grip, and set out the few things that made each new place his own. He was tired, too. Bone tired. He'd lost sight of the point where it had all begun. In the morning he'd have to find the steamer company's office and book a second passage for Melody, and at the same time mail off a more detailed report to expand on the bare-facts telegraph that he'd sent from Los Angeles. He wanted get the completed story in ahead of his arrival, not to have to stumble through it while officials barked questions designed to knock him this way and that. For some men it was more a matter of using their rank to dominate the interview, than of eliciting the facts.

On the writing desk, he laid out the documentation for a *fait accompli*. The two-part Death Certificate, with signed declarations from both physician and undertaker. The mortuary photograph, with a notarized statement on the back declaring it to be a fair and true likeness in death of the late William James. He would have liked to have provided the showman's cabinet card for a comparison, but that was gone. He'd seen Melody tear it up at Kit Strong's instruction. Those in London could always get hold of another; otherwise they'd have to be content with a clipping from the *Bulletin*, written by Frank Lucas and giving the facts of the interment, along with his own account of the body's discovery and identification.

He took a sheet of the Keystone's stationery and began to write. He'd barely completed a page when there was a knock at the door.

He opened it to find a hotel messenger boy standing in the corridor. The boy said, "Mister Becker, sir," and handed him a note.

Sebastian read it, tipped the boy, and grabbed his jacket.

"No reply," he said. "I'm coming down."

He listened for a moment at Melody's door before heading for the stairs.

There was an elegant woman at the far end of the Keystone's lobby. No one would mistake her for a guest at the hotel. Not this hotel, anyway. She wore a petrol-blue walking suit with buttoned boots, white gloves, and a matching bonnet. For a moment when she turned, he hardly recognized her.

"Sebastian," she said.

"Frances. How did you know I was back?"

"I tipped the clerk to call me the moment you checked in. Did you find her?"

"I did," he said. Never one to care much about his own appearance, he was suddenly feeling travel-soiled and frayed around the edges. He wished that he could stop the clock, so that he could run off for a clean shirt and a haircut.

"And?"

"She's sleeping. Exhausted, but herself again. I'm taking her home."

"What about Kit Strong?"

He was about to speak, then thought better of it and indicated for them to move out of the lobby and into the empty morning-room. Once in the room, with its herd of mismatched furniture and its Fire Sale paintings on the walls, he said in a lowered voice, "Kit Strong can be safely forgotten. Let's say no more than that. But what about you? I take it you reconciled with your father."

"We're back on speaking terms. Though I wouldn't exactly call it a reconciliation. He's grown old, Sebastian."

"I can't say I found him much changed when I spoke with him," Sebastian said. "But I imagine he showed a more generous spirit toward his own flesh and blood."

Almost immediately, he regretted his choice of words and wished he could take them back. Frances was looking so well, and seemed so pleased to see him. He shouldn't be trying to spoil the moment.

But if anything he said had dented her mood, she didn't show it. She said, "I doubt he can ever be warm. But I think he realizes that a little grace will sometimes serve him better."

"That's good," Sebastian said. "It's good." And then, less certainly, "Isn't it?"

"It's been a strange time," she said. "Reconnecting with the old life."

"I can imagine. But Philadelphia suits you."

"Does it?"

"More than Southwark. Look at you. I'd hardly know you."

She said, "I've received a proposal of marriage."

This was...not expected. She was waiting for him to say something and he realized that he was taking too long to say it. He struggled for a moment like a fish in air, but then he quickly recovered.

He said, "My congratulations. A whirlwind romance?"

"Hardly," she said. "I knew Freddie when we were children."

"It's no less than you deserve, Frances," he said. "You gave up so much for us. Robert will be…"

He hesitated because he wasn't entirely sure whether Robert would be delighted, heartbroken, or *how* his son would react to the news. But this time his hesitation went unnoticed, because she interrupted him.

She said, "Wait. I didn't say that I'd accepted."

He wasn't sure he understood.

"Will you?" he said.

"I don't need to be married, Sebastian. But I do need to be valued." He could see that she was serious. She said, "Remember that day at the White City?"

That day in the White City, when she'd led him straight to the James family with information she'd beguiled out of a variety of sources, from a mendacious journalist to a range of idling players. The family that half the police in London had been looking for, and had yet to find.

He said, "I do. I do remember."

"I came to life that day. I'd trade a day like that for any amount of this hand-me-down finery."

He realized how profoundly he'd been misreading her. Her fine looks and carriage had deceived him. She wasn't radiant, she was actually upset. Thinking he might find out why, he said, "Tell me about Freddie."

"Leave Freddie out of this," she said. "You don't have to match his offer, so don't let that scare you. I just want to know where my true place is. Answer honestly. I know he has money and you don't, but for God's sake don't think you'll be doing the decent thing if you drive me to him. That's not what I'm asking. Do I stay here or do we go home?"

There are people who love you. More than you know. But you can never bring yourself to believe that you deserve it.

What could he honestly say? Look at her. She belonged here. From her teen years she'd been a transplant from Philadelphia society and now here she was, back in home soil and already beginning to bloom. Contrast that with London, south of the river; the Borough, the Bethlem, the pie stand. The sum total of what he might realistically offer.

Given those circumstances, what would his honesty mean? What would be fair?

She awaited his answer.

London, May 1914

51

SUNDAYS WERE SPENT WITH ROBERT. THEY'D MEET AT HIS LODG-
ings in South Kensington. Though his son was now a man in his twenties,
Sebastian would never be able to think of him as other than a boy. He
wished that Elisabeth could be here to see the independence that Robert had
achieved; not just a job in the museum trade, where it seemed that eccentrics
flocked like starlings, but one with a regular wage and a home of his own.
It was what Elisabeth had always wanted for him yet—or so Sebastian had
suspected—a development that she'd also feared. The protective instinct of a
parent was strong, especially with a child such as theirs. Yet the job was never
really done until you let them go.

They'd fallen into a routine. Meet after Church, lunch at Gatti's, and a park
or an entertainment of some kind in the afternoon, depending on the season.
Robert attended the morning service at nearby St Stephen's with his landlady
and fellow-lodgers, though he always seemed to enjoy Gatti's rather more.

In the landlady's show parlor overlooking Queen's Gate, Sebastian said,
"What's it to be today, Robert?"

"This, father," Robert said, and showed him a piece that he'd taken from
a newspaper. Its edges were torn, but neatly, as if along a steel rule. It was an
advertisement for a programme of films at a local Picturedrome, a theater
near the station that had recently begun to put on popular Sunday perfor-
mances in defiance of the licensing authority.

The advertisement announced '*the EXCLUSIVE ENGAGEMENT of MONTANA JIM the cowboy lecturer, Direct from Montana, USA, who will Lecture to his own Film*'.

Montana Jim. A show cowboy. Sebastian had been keeping his eye on any news concerning show cowboys. The James family, as far as he could establish, was out of the Western business altogether. Any show people he'd talked to were less than forthcoming. Yet within a week of him beginning enquiries on her behalf, Melody James was taken into the care of a Norfolk ridemaster's family and vanished off into the life, almost certainly to be reunited with her aunts and Uncle Jack.

After lunch they stood in line at the Picturedrome. Once inside, Sebastian ensured that they were seated on the end of a row near an exit. Robert had a low tolerance for anything that failed to engage his interest. Grab his attention, and he was deaf and blind to all else. Bore him, and he'd certainly let you know it.

There was a three-piece orchestral overture and then a curtain-raiser of a film from Germany which involved hansom cabs, bodies in trunks, and a duel to the death. After that came the main attraction.

Montana Jim was a man of sixty-something years who kicked off his act by riding a horse down the center aisle to the stage, where to the delight of his mostly juvenile audience he strode up and down in full Western regalia, spinning his six-guns and telling tall tales of life on the prairie and adventures in the Indian wars. The six-guns fired blanks. The horse was on loan from a local dairy.

Then the lights were lowered. The projector was fired up and Montana Jim stood by the screen with a tin megaphone, giving a running commentary as his two-reel drama played. On the screen his younger self lived again, riding the prairie and fighting with Indians.

Midway through, Robert leaned over and whispered, "You know, father, for all his talk I don't believe he's the real thing."

"No?"

"His accent's all over."

"It's your day, Robert. We can do whatever you want."

"There's a new Jekyll and Hyde at Pyke's in Piccadilly."

So under cover of darkness they left their seats, exited the Picturedrome, and headed for the all-day continuous program at the Cinematograph Theater on Great Windmill Street.

Sebastian bought sixpenny tickets and they took their seats midway through a factual subject titled *Our Navy; Britain's Bulwarks.*

Official panic over the loss of Prince Max of Erbach-Schonburg in the Pavilion Theater fire had subsided, and the suggestion that a European conflict might be started by the death of a minor royal in a foreign country now seemed, in retrospect, to be somewhat improbable. Yet war was still in the air. Many thought it inevitable.

The *Our Navy* camera lingered over one warship after another, sailors stood on deck and grinned, big guns fired in silence, and the piano accompanist leaned heavily on her repertoire of patriotic songs. *Rule Britannia* raised a weary cheer from the stalls.

Next came a Chrissie White one-reeler, then the inevitable Western. This one was *The Dangling Noose*, a tale of frontier love and water rights from the Selig Polyscope Company.

When it reached the point where Indian Jim, friend and protector of the lovely Rose Watkins, was being threatened with a hanging for the theft of land option money, Sebastian unconsciously gripped the arms of his seat.

Robert was absorbed in the story, and didn't notice. But the woman seated to Sebastian's left had sensed his sudden shift in mood, and was glancing his way in the dark.

He made a deliberate effort to relax, and she returned her attention to the screen.

The lynching party of mountain men dragged the Indian to a tree. The lovely Rose broke into the explosives shed and held them all at bay with a stick of dynamite. Someone showed up, someone confessed, and somehow everything was resolved. By now Sebastian was shaking with silent laughter.

He felt a tug at his elbow.

Sebastian turned to Frances, seated by his side, her arm through his.

"What's the joke?" she said.

There on the screen, in an uncredited role as the leader of the hanging party—an irony in itself—was a face barely recognizable behind a heavy mustache.

Sebastian lowered his voice to the lowest murmur, so even his son wouldn't hear.

"That," Sebastian said, "is the one and only, the authentic William James."